THE WRITING IN THE WALLS

THE HALETHORPE CHRONICLES

ALX ANDERS

THE
WRITING
IN THE
WALLS
ALY ANDERS

Self-Published, Aly Anders Books
www.alyanders.com
a@alyanders.com

Cover Art by Aly Anders
Cover & Chapter Header Font: Joker by Perfectype
(letterserif.15l@gmail.com)
https://www.creativefabrica.com/designer/perfectype
Used under Commercial License
Print Font: Crimson Text by Sebastian Kosch
Used under OFL (Open Font License)

eBook ISBN: 979-8-991647 1-3-7
Paperback ISBN: 979-8-991647 1-4-4

First Edition

For Rylan, I hope I leave you a worthy legacy in the words I write.

For the artists who grew tired of talking to walls that wouldn't talk back.

"THE SECRET TO CREATIVITY IS KNOWING HOW TO HIDE YOUR SOURCES."

- MAYBE ALBERT EINSTEIN, MAYBE NOT

INTRODUCTION

Every masterpiece the world covets was created from the parts and pieces of an artist who sacrificed themselves to make it. Every beautiful story told, tragic or triumphant, was torn from the heart of a writer who bled it onto the pages.

To create is to hold a consuming madness at bay, a ravenous insanity that haunts when ideas run dry. It plagues the artist with doubt and defeat and allows stagnation to take root where creativity should wildly grow.

It's said that when an artist creates, a piece of themselves lives permanently in their work. Their blood, sweat, and tears bring their creation to life, giving it a voice and a message. Their art, now alive with a heartbeat, shouts its intent with a savage voice, unashamed, unruly with power, and untamed by expectations.

What is spoken of far less often is what happens when artists have shattered themselves into too many pieces, when the art has collectively taken too much. An artist with nothing more to give succumbs quickly to the encroaching madness of stagnation. For, without a voice, an artist is like a clock with no hands or a bird with no wings.

As their fall into obscurity begins, panic sets in—the terror of irrelevance, of unimportance. The platform on which their creations once shouted louder than any other begins to crumble, leaving few choices. Reinvent themselves or disappear.

But what lengths would a creator go to hide the evidence of their hollowed-out soul? What madness would they invite to help bury the empty husk after the art has taken it all? What would you do to claw yourself from the pits of insignificance to feel the fleeting rush of success?

This is, without a doubt, a cautionary tale. It unravels the threads of one woman's life as a creator and recounts her descent into a different kind of madness.

Fame found Taylor Halethorpe unexpectedly after she made a bold writing decision that propelled her to national acclaim. She was reluctantly thrust into the spotlight, and as the demands required of such artists followed, she adjusted quickly to the lavish lifestyle of fame and fortune. Indulging in the amenities and luxury it afforded her.

Years later, her career is crumbling, much like the exterior of the grotesque Halethorpe Estate. Atop a winding hill surrounded by untouched farmland and a distant graveyard, the Estate is Taylor's last remaining possession. Left to her after the passing of her mother, Vivian Halethorpe-Turner, the Estate has become a haunting reminder of what she's lost.

Faded and peeling wallpaper, exposed slats behind dusty plaster, doors that won't latch, and drafty radiators that scream at night. Little magic is left in the grand, historic walls of the disintegrating manor, but perhaps...

There is just enough.

THE EARLY YEARS

GLASS HEELS ERA

2010-2014

CHAPTER 1

A FLASH FORWARD
2013

I'm unsure if I wrote the story or if the story wrote me. But here we were in an exclusive ballroom at *The Royale* in Baltimore. The champagne flowed from bottles like a raging, bubbling river whose current had no intention of slowing despite the wafting drunkenness in the air.

The subtle *'tink'* of the glass flutes sprinkled in my ears, a sound I would forever associate with *success.*

A series of presentations, a swell of applause, and another glass statue, my name carefully engraved in the pricey paperweight. I quickly handed it over to my assistant, who'd indulged a little too freely in the endless flutes filled with Dom Pérignon.

A dimly lit party was the way to my heart. I liked living in the shadows. I felt less vulnerable. Tonight, the chandeliers created stark cuts of brightness, and I briefly imagined what type of crazy one must have been to stand under the unflattering bright beams. They showed every imperfect and oversized pore, every line and crinkle of sheer fabric. They were inescapable secret revealers I did not want to introduce myself to.

Speaking of inescapable imperfections...

I hadn't thought about my father, Edward Turner, in months, but memories always resurfaced when I was forced to remember why I wrote the book in the first place.

It started as an innocent retelling of *Cinderella*. Of course, I had the decency to wait until he was in the ground before I dared to have the audacity to publish it.

A story, a book, a novel was something Edward would have found disillusioned. It was bad enough that my growing freelance and editorial career was too untraditional for him, and if I'd shared my dream of becoming a full-time author, he'd likely have me committed.

It was crazy.

It was stupid.

And he wouldn't extend financial support if I didn't disembark on the notion of becoming a renowned writer someday.

My *Cinderella* version was a little literary play on words for how I truly felt about the dearly departed. It was an allegory for the princess mentality and how women of today's society had been groomed to search for a husband by being helpless.

Glass Heels, I called it.

It was my best work at the time, and it was *work*. My agent and I self-published it using contacts we had made in the industry, and before I knew it, I was holding a copy of the overly cartoonish cover and sixty chapters of blood, sweat, and tears. The pages still smelled like literature, no matter how unimpressed I was with my writing.

Not six months after the first units hit stores, a couple of A-list celebrities speaking out on the political climate of the United States got ahold of *Glass Heels*, and it grew into a cultural phenomenon with a cult-like following of dedicated readers.

The next thing I knew, my agent, Cassandra, or *Cass*, had lined up a publisher and multiple six-figure deals and endorsements, and I was the face of a feminist movement taking the country by storm. All because I wrote a three-hundred-and-fifty-page "fuck you" to my dead daddy.

I even won the globally renowned *Aurora Prize*, and so far, that has been the penultimate moment of my writing career. Even this event paled in comparison—an event marking the end of my national book tour. I'd be able to finally settle down and start to work on my next story, book... series—anything that wouldn't bear the fruit of endless small talk and repeatedly emasculating men in my speeches.

Tonight was a celebration of all I'd achieved in these few short years, and this time, I was *local* to my hometown. I was grateful because it allowed me time to share my roots with my fiancé, Dante Graves, a high-profile criminal defense attorney from California.

And, as a subplot to this visit home, I hadn't seen my mother, Vivian Halethorpe-Turner, in at least six months, and her excessive 'accidental' calls to check in on me were becoming too familiar of an annoyance.

I wasn't looking forward to going to the Estate, but she refused to let me move her into a nicer apartment—somewhere with some actual *amenities*. Her refusal to move is only second to her refusal to sell the decaying estate, a Halethorpe relic from the 1800s.

So, visiting *her* was visiting the Estate. They were the same, and despite how the Estate made me feel, it haunted me even when my eyes were open—my mother was all I had left. I'd have to grin and bear it for yet another visit.

I'm the last Halethorpe after my mother, and I can tell you now that I will *never* call that place my home. I'll be living in LA. It's the best place for my career. Dante and I agreed that we were meant for more than that museum.

We have been together since just after I published *Heels*. It's always been a low-pressure relationship, with the mutual understanding that, for both of us, our careers are our priorities. Someday, we'll start a family, but for now, we're *having fun.*

He satiated my desire to be a strong, independent woman who also wanted mind-blowing orgasms, and I honestly found this to be the sexiest thing about him.

I could fly to LA, have a few great nights of wild sex in a luxurious sky-rise apartment overlooking the lights of the city, and then sail off to my next appearance without being trodden by the guilt of leaving him behind.

Before I'd left the hotel this afternoon, he had a little black lace number delivered, along with two dozen roses. The card read, "A secret for you to wear and for me to keep." And now, I couldn't help but salivate just a little as I watched him work the room of high-level executives, movie producers, and writers. A heat washing over me that needed immediate cooling.

Dante was everything I wasn't—confident, effortlessly wealthy, and magnetic. With his sandy, slicked-back hair and piercing blue eyes, he commanded attention, making getting what he wanted very, very *easy.*

His fitted suits were tailored to his perfectly proportional body, and his wrist was always adorned with the finest timepiece. His cufflinks alone were worth more than some people's homes. And if you managed to get close enough, he smelled of leather, cardamom, and jasmine sambac.

He was luxury embodied.

I excused myself from the conversation I'd been paying little attention to with a quick nod. That was the universal language for "I had better things to do" in the celebrity world, and given that I wasn't born into this life, I'd mastered it quite well.

His eyes met mine, and a smile spread across his face. It was like seeing him for the first time, and every time he did that thing where only one side of his face cracked a smile, my heart thudded like it had grown a pair of papery moth wings and delicately fluttered across the room.

"Hello, stranger," he whispered into my neck as I smoothly slid beside him and wrapped my arm around his lower back. I'd invited myself into whatever conversation he was having... after all, this was my banquet, and I was the guest of honor. Most of these people were here specifically for *my* attention, and that fact alone was still inexplicably unbelievable to me.

I listened to Dante speak, complimenting his captive audience with the precision of delivering a closing argument. I nodded a few times at the nonsense conversation I had subjected myself to, and when I realized I was bored out of my mind, I casually tapped Dante's back with my fingers.

A little push in *my* direction, and he quickly diverted his conversation about investments to fetch himself another glass of the most expensive bourbon *The Royale* had on their shelves.

The smile I had worn for too long tonight felt brittle, like glass ready to shatter. I was grateful for his graceful exit, to which he pulled me along by my hand, leading me into a private bar in a separate, unoccupied room.

I had a ballroom full of high-powered people with the potential to network and grow my brand, but *really*, I wanted Dante's undivided attention, if only for a fleeting moment. Awards shows and banquets were often like this, but I did my best to make the most of them.

"You look stunning in that dress, Tay." He said, his eyes fixed on my mouth and then dragged down my body as if I was a prize he'd won, and for a split second, I wondered if that's all I was to him.

"How nice of you to notice," I smiled at him, swirling my new bourbon neat nervously.

"I can't wait to take it off of you later," he grinned, running his hand up my backside and planting a soft kiss on the nape of my neck. This was a pleasant surprise, as Dante always made it clear that most of my brand was about independence and feminism and that leaning too heavily into him *publicly* would send the wrong message to those who'd invested in me.

I didn't even wear the ring he'd proposed with on my finger; it was permanently attached to a long chain that hung under my shirt. *"Closest to my heart,"* he'd said, tying it to sentimentality, but I knew it was so that he could continue to play a role. So that we *could both* play our roles.

"Don't make threats, Dante." I kissed him instantly, tasting the tang and burn of the bourbon. As I pulled back, I playfully teased him by biting his lip. He reached for more, but I slowly sauntered away toward the exit when I recognized another familiar face.

"That's not a threat, Ms. Halethorpe. It's a promise." He grinned and followed me out of the private room. He grabbed a champagne glass off the busy waiter's tray without looking.

I shooed him away as I walked across the room toward the tiny beacon of light I'd seen from the other side.

"You two are revolting. You know that, right?" Cass said as she tapped away at the glowing screen. She hid it under the high-top table, but I could see the slight reflection in her eyes. Working at events like this was bad form, even for her.

"I'm not supposed to work tonight, but you are my easiest client. Everyone else is horseshit." Her agitation increased with the firm finger taps and grunts of frustration.

"It's my circus *and* my monkeys," she sighed deeply. Usually, she was far better at tucking her exhaustion behind the blue glow of a phone or computer, but tonight, she was without her shields.

"It's a celebration night, Cass. There's champagne, there's bourbon. There's a very blond, Viking-like man staring in your general direction," I joked as she hesitantly looked up across the room and then immediately back down at her phone.

"I bet he's a Skarsgård," I said as I made eye contact and swirled my drink again. He smiled and then looked away quickly.

"Oh my..." my heart jumped slightly. " Okay, enough." I snatched Cass's phone and tucked it into my bag.

"You can have that back later," I teased, grinning. "But now, my brilliant, capable, annoyingly gorgeous best friend—go talk to him before *I* do." I leaned in and kissed her on the cheek. Cass was my closest friend these days, given that she was my *only* friend.

In a world of glitter, champagne, and leased Maseratis, to Cassandra Lopez, I was Taylor from Halethorpe, not *Taylor Halethorpe*. I was *still* the lost writer who'd begged her for a chance a few years ago. After she'd said yes, our careers were permanently affixed to one another, and we were stuck on this train *together* as it approached warp speed.

I had friends before, but fame drives a jagged wedge between the life you once knew and the sparkling life you chase. The friends who were your equals now gaze at you from a distance. Sometimes with longing, sometimes with an inane jealousy, and *always* with regret. No matter how tightly you hold onto being 'down to earth,' the ground falls from under you.

Cass stood and nervously yanked at the bottom of her dress, pulling the tight fabric over her hips. Her long, dark, layered hair rustled, and for a fleeting moment, I smelled the warm scent of vanilla and coconut.

"I can see it in your face. You're worrying again." Cass touched my shoulder, bringing me back to life almost instantly. "You're overthinking, trust me," she said, looking at my expression as I arched an eyebrow. She grabbed her blazer from the back of the chair and flung it over her shoulder, "Take the win, Tay. You deserve it." I couldn't recall a single event, ceremony, or banquet where she hadn't told me *I deserved it.*

Someday, I'd hoped she wouldn't have to tell me, but that day hadn't come yet. She smiled at me one last time, and I watched her walk toward the highly receptive Viking. I sat at her table, letting out a sigh of relief. I looked again at all the chaos created for *me,* for a piece of art I'd written that millions *loved.*

For all that it was, *Glass Heels* used to be something I spoke of with a fiery passion. I'd poured every ounce of anger and defiance into it. But now, it was a hollow thing.

When I read passages, as I am so often required, I cringe at the combinations of words that I sloppily scrolled across papers and napkins. The voice notes I'd left while walking through malls. The crumpled receipts with blurred love notes I'd peppered my two-door coupe with. And the late nights sitting under the stars near BWI Airport, watching the planes land and scribing bits of poetry to include in the *masterpiece* I hadn't written yet.

It was a story that millions of people had mistaken for gold, not realizing it was merely gilded.

I glanced again at Cass, whose hand was now intertwined with our friend, the Viking, and her casual nod and shit-eating grin meant she was leaving. I winked at her and immediately regretted the embarrassing gesture when I saw Dante eyeing me from across the room. My face flushed with heat as I looked down at the warm champagne I'd barely touched.

As a fast-paced server strolled past, our eyes met, and he offered me a fresh glass. I took a sip, preparing for the explosive tingle of expensive champagne, but it hit with a bitterness I hadn't expected, and the disappointment felt oddly familiar.

No matter, I tipped my head back, swallowed it as I'd become accustomed to doing, and wiped my face gently with the corner of the cloth napkin, *like a lady.*

Had I fooled an entire world into believing I was more profound than I was, or was I indeed an author? The thought plagued me often, especially in moments of intense celebration of my talents. While we were still cruising on the *Glass Heels* yacht, what might happen when the wind in our sails deflated and it was time to write something else?

What if, when the time came, I had nothing left to say?

CHAPTER 2

BEFORE GLASS HEELS
2010

The tattered scraps of the various mediums I'd been forced to write on were *problematic*. Transcribing the incohesive thoughts of intoxicated nights or the jarring fragments of bullshit stained onto napkins with marker wasn't the worst of it. It was reliving the trauma that had made me so... *angry*.

I was angry for all the reasons I should have been, but I still carried the regret of not sticking up for myself more. I regret not *being* more... For not going to college, for not serving tables until 1 am to pay the tuition.

Fresh out of high school, I had imagined that I'd change the world. I'd master this craft, hone my art, and paint the world with colors and words that would drive it wild. My father denied me the financial support to do it easily, forcing me into the wild streets of Maryland at eighteen. *Writing* wasn't a career in his eyes.

That was over five years ago, and now, I can barely make it through a day without smoking a blunt and conceptualizing what the Romans must have been thinking when they, I don't know... built Rome.

"Don't fear, world..." I muttered, staring at the scrawl of pen marks on the back of a paper diner placemat. A tragically beautiful, half-finished poem danced with three games of tic-tac-toe while one barely legible game of Hangman mocked me from the margins. The clicks of the keyboard on my white laptop echoed in my barely decorated studio apartment.

A silence I'd come to adore. It was *my silence*.

Something about this moment gave me pause as I scanned the room. I wanted to catalog it in a vault of memories.

To remember the beginning of it all—the loneliness of the hustle, yes, but also the flicker of hope that motivated me, I wanted to hold on to the certainty that someday, when the story born from these fragments of genius took its shape, it would be everything I'd ever dreamed of.

Black bed sheets hung over the windows. My mattress sat bare on the living room floor, and my clothes—dirty *and* clean—cluttered every corner. No, it wasn't much at all, but it was mine.

And in a silent vow, I'd turn the doubt my father had cast on me into a determination to succeed, to be something *more* than just a mattress on the floor, and I would do it without his help.

I looked at the gold bracelet my mother had given me before I left our Estate. Before I packed everything I owned into my Honda and *escaped*. It represented a glint of hope that I'd make her proud someday. I'd let her see that sometimes, *leaving* is the best thing someone can do for themselves, especially when their dream is too big for the life they are living.

It didn't matter if the life I knew before was in a mansion with thirty rooms. My dream was too grand for that Estate, too much for Halethorpe.

This apartment was a far cry from the Halethorpe Estate, where everything felt like old luxury, with an air of haunting overindulgence. I often had a recurring dream of being trapped there with no way to escape. The walls closed in on me as I gasped violently for air. The fancy floral wallpaper was the last thing I'd see before my suffocated awakening in a room far less lavish.

But it was only a nightmare, fortunately—those you can wake up from.

I was writing professionally, *barely*. If you can call freelancing and penning garbage articles for newspapers who were converting to digital, under an anonymous name. While not fulfilling work, it afforded me this studio apartment in Glen Burnie, and it wasn't that god-forsaken Estate. It was embarrassing enough to be approaching twenty-five with a nonexistent life plan. To *ever* move back home and be under the rule of my dictator of a father was a firm "No, thank you." I said it aloud, my thoughts crossing into the real world through my whispers.

I spent most of my nights here, transferring years of feminine rage from my notes into a word-processing program. I would turn these scattered rantings into something profound, something... *great.*

***

Edward Turner finally passed away. So, now, when I tell people that my father is dead, it won't be a lie.

***

"It's called *Glass Heels*," I said, swallowing the lump of fear in my throat. My hands were shaking subtly. I'd rehearsed this conversation a million times before this moment, and my hands never shook.

"I've been working on it for two years." I sipped from my cup. "It's a Cinderella retelling without the *prince*." I smiled as I slid the printed stack of full-sized letter paper across the café table toward the woman I'd just met.

"Cinderella is overdone." I saw the glint of pity in her eyes as she glanced around for the waiter to bring the check. We had just sat down, and she was already looking for a way to say 'no.'

I knew I had to change her mind.

"Cinderella is an old tale. Of course, it's frequently revisited. But I wrote it *differently*." I replied, trying to bring her attention back to me.

"I've heard that a thousand times, Ms. Turner." She reached out and put her hand on the top of the manuscript, debating whether to pull it toward her or leave it in the neutral space of the table.

"It's *Halethorpe*. I go by Taylor Halethorpe."

"Ms. Halethorpe." She repeated my name with a smile.

Her eyes flicked to the watch on her wrist—an expensive silver Cartier—and my stomach knotted up.

I had minutes, maybe seconds before she made up her mind, and the odds weren't in my favor; I could see the "no thanks" reverberating in her designer blazer, the Coach bag hooked on her chair, and the polished black Anouk heels pointed perfectly at the tips of her toned, tanned legs.

She looked like someone who had never had to beg. And she was the woman holding my future in her hands. I was envious, in a way, of the luxury and how she wore it so flawlessly.

"Ms. Lopez," I begged, watching her facial expression detach and fly off like a hot-air balloon, carrying away my hopes and dreams. I had to do something, and quickly.

"Hey." I tapped the table abruptly.

"Listen, I get it. Ok?" I paused, my voice clawing its way back to its confidence. "You're here as a favor. It's not ideal." I sighed, "It's not ideal for me either to have to beg someone to read just ten pages of something I've put my entire soul into." I cut through the bullshit and broke through the façade we'd both had up.

"The truth is… Well, this could be shit." The honesty took her by surprise. "Or it could be literary gold." She arched her eyebrow at the contrast. "You'll never know unless you read ten pages." I struck a deal. Her ever-so-slight grin told me that she was amused. I'm unsure how people often spoke to her, but I needed to talk to her heart, not her business brain.

"All I've ever wanted to do was write." I lowered my voice as I waited. The decision hung between us, floating like a fleck of dust or a small feather caught in the wind.

She tapped her perfectly manicured nails on the table, her face unflinching. Every second she didn't speak felt like a lifetime had passed. I shifted in my chair, shoving the napkin on which I'd scribbled a poem before she had arrived further out of sight. The black ink smudged along the table as I attempted to conceal it.

"Ten pages?" She questioned me and opened a small planner with scribbles of illegible notes inside.

"That's all it will take. I promise." I, too, let only a grin slide out so as not to appear overly eager.

"If I read ten pages and I don't…" She didn't have to finish.

"Then, I'll work on it more and see you in a year?" I asked. Giving up wasn't an option. I wouldn't give up on my dream because some *agent* didn't like ten pages of my heart and soul.

But she would. I knew she would.

"I'll reach out when I have a decision." Her tone was curt but not entirely dismissive. She tossed a twenty down on the table, stood, and smoothed the creases in her blazer.

I watched her leave, the click of her heels fading into the café's chaos. She didn't take the manuscript. No, she left it sitting on the table, like a rejected offering, and now both of us are left abandoned, uncertain of the future.

"She said she'd read it," I huffed to myself as I grabbed my things and scooped my untouched muffin from the table.

"She said she'd read it."

I smiled as I took the copy I'd printed just for her. I walked back through the door I'd come in through *nervously.* I gently passed my fingers over the gold bracelet on my wrist, letting it ground me as I walked out excitedly.

✳✳✳

The chime of my iPhone startled me awake, and for a moment, I cursed the nerve of it. It had interrupted my dream just as Ryan Gosling and I were about to fall in love.

"Hello," my voice cracked as I answered the call with a subtle frustration.

"Taylor Turner?" The sturdy male voice on the other end was unfamiliar.

"Halethorpe, I go by Halethorpe." I rolled my eyes.

"I'm sorry, Ms. Halethorpe," They corrected themselves.

"That's me," I answered as I sighed and fell back onto the pillow. This was already taking too long.

"I'm Cassandra Lopez's assistant, Christopher."

His words jolted me upright. I sat up so fast that the room spun, and the tangled mess of sheets wrapped around my body fell to the floor as I stood. My heart was pounding against the inside of my head. The red digits of my alarm clock glared at me: noon. Was this real? Or another layer of my dream? A slight wave of nausea in the pit of my stomach confirmed I wasn't dreaming.

"Ms. Halethorpe?" His voice pulled me from my spiral.

"Yes, sorry. I'm here. Poor signal," I lied. The words sprang from my mouth as I curled my hands into fists to stop from shivering.

"Ms. Lopez read your manuscript. She's willing to represent you. Can you meet tonight—9 pm? The Whitmore."

The Whitmore. I pushed back the uncertainty creeping up my throat. "Yes," I answered, too eager, too fast... even I knew it.

"She'll see you then."

The call ended before I could thank him. I stared at my phone in disbelief.

She's willing.

I crawled back into bed, clutching my phone against my chest, afraid that if I let it go, it would fly away and disconnect me from the dream that was becoming a reality.

I can do this.

I would do this.

CHAPTER 3

GLASS HEELS
2011

It hadn't been a year since I sat at The Whitmore with Cass and made a deal to publish *Glass Heels* 'untraditionally.' She'd told me that she didn't think it would sell to a traditional publisher, but she felt a closeness to it. She loved it so much that she didn't just read ten pages. She read the whole thing... twice. *Intentionally.*

I recall that moment so well, even though we'd let the martinis take over as the night passed. She wanted it to work out for me, but she believed in my writing and the story.

So we sealed a deal and self-published *Glass Heels* using every resource we'd compiled in the industry, and she took off her agent hat to become a marketer, an assistant, a salesperson, a brand ambassador, and a *friend.*

The shoes, the bag, and the fancy watch had fooled me. Cass knew how to pull up her sleeves and *work* like no one I'd ever met. She had a relentless drive that, on most days, exhausted me just looking at her calendars.

I remember the day she handed me the first physical copy, a hardcover.

"Close your eyes," her excitement almost uncontainable.

"What? *Cass,* what is wrong with you?" I laughed and reluctantly closed my eyes.

"Hold out your hands."

I did, and she gently placed the glossy book in my grasp. I opened my eyes and, at first, was washed with panic. I'd given her creative liberties on the cover and, for a split second, regretted the decision.

"It's so..." I squinted, my faux smile cracked into a funky shape.

"Pink," I added, turning it curiously from side to side and flipping the pages until a small gust of air hit my cheeks. The sweet aroma of a freshly printed book splashed over me.

"I know, it's *perfect.*"

The silver foil that accented the cotton candy pink twinkled in the sunlight. But in a flash, I watched the pink turn dark, twirling into the familiar patterns of wallpaper from the Estate. I blinked, and the phantom darkness had faded from the cover, and only the cotton candy shade remained.

A small reminder that no matter how far I ran from the Estate, from the Halethorpe legacy, a part of it would always follow me.

"Yeah, exactly what I was going to say," I lied. She knew this industry better than I did, and I trusted her. She knew how to get this book into the hands of those who'd read it and rave about it. A pink vessel was the least of my concerns.

A moment where I held this *pink*, cartoonish cover in my hands, and even though it looked nothing like what I had imagined, it was a tangible manifestation of my dream.

It was the bubble gum pink, *'suck it'* to Edward Turner. May *he rot in peace.* I'd taken every doubt, laugh, and bad thing I'd ever said about myself and turned them into success.

Life had ambushed us since that very moment. We seemed to gain so much traction that we began flying at warp speed. Every new event was a surreal experience that turned into reality, and I became increasingly comfortable being on the inside.

Cass and I scored a lucrative traditional publishing deal and endorsements, and *Glass Heels* was even considered for a big-screen movie deal with an all-star cast.

The royalty checks were flying in, and I regularly made National TV appearances. I'd even been photographed by paparazzi leaving a hotel in Chicago once after the rumor of a *Glass Heels* cast broke the internet. Jennifer Lawrence had signed on as the female main character, and I had practically peed myself at how exciting that was.

✷✷✷

I met Dante at a local charity event. Cass didn't have to convince me that giving back to the writer's community while *Heels* did so well was essential. I was excited to be there.

Through the mission, I had the opportunity to interact with many independent and self-published authors—authors who would have outwritten and outworked me *any* day of the week. Independent authors have humility that makes them genuine, and being around and supporting them came easily.

It was always about the words and the sentences, the characters, and all of their flaws. They *always* did it for the plot...

I'd just given a seminar on making the most out of self-publishing when a handsome man approached me.

"You're a natural up there," he nodded toward the stage and smiled casually, a dimple creased on one side of his mouth.

"Honestly, public speaking scares me," I joked. "No one told me it was part of being an author." I finished as I jostled some of my papers into my leather bag.

"They never tell you about public speaking," he sighed. "No one electively chooses that part." He smoothly grabbed two drinks from a passing waiter and graciously handed me one.

"Oh, I was just about to head out. Thank you, though," I said with reverence.

"Just one? For a *big* fan?"

He caught me by surprise, "You've read *Glass Heels?*" I questioned, amused at the idea.

"Is that so surprising?" He grinned handsomely.

"You're not my statistical target audience, *so yes.*" I returned his smile and gently took the glass from his hand, our fingers grazing one another gently. The touch lit a small fire inside my chest. One that I'd thought I'd let go out a long time ago.

I'd had *lovers* and relationships in the past, but nothing consistent or steady, and certainly nothing strong enough to withstand this whirlwind of a world I was a part of now.

Attraction was a strange force. You could think nothing of it for years while you focus your energy elsewhere, but in the time it takes for your heart to beat once, it could come crashing into your well-laid plans and take you unwillingly on a perilous journey.

It made you weak to seduction, and it pulled down those mile-high walls you'd mortared and reinforced. I was fully attracted to this delectable man feeding me his best lines, and I knew, yes... *I knew that it was a game.* I was becoming a feminist icon. It wasn't lost on me that the number of male suitors who believed me to be a conquest or something to *achieve* was uncountable. But I wanted to have my cake and eat it, too.

I didn't care if I was someone's bragging rights. I cared about a fleeting moment of human connection where I felt feelings other than those that had become so mundane and regular.

I wanted a thrill.

If a blonde-haired, blue-eyed man—with what I can only imagine are abs of steel under that perfectly tailored suit—wanted to take me to his room, I would let him.

"Dante Graves." His smile distracted me from his name.

"Taylor Halethorpe," I said as he took my hand to his lips and kissed it like we were at a ball in 1892.

"I know who you are, Taylor Halethorpe." He whispered.

He leaned in, and I caught the slight scent of leather and... amber. It was intoxicating and indulgent, taking me out of the moment in an almost euphoric sensation. He gently removed the drink from my hand, setting it on the table with a clink.

Dante laced his fingers into mine as we walked toward the hotel elevator.

CHAPTER 4

AN AURORA
2013

"When I wrote 'Glass Heels,' I'd never imagined it would end up here, on this stage."

I took a deep breath, settling the fear of the audience by pretending I was in my old two-door coupe, driving up and down Rt. 2, a honey Dutch in one hand, and nowhere important to be.

I'd given this speech a thousand times in that car, pretending to win this exact award, in front of far less and a far more invisible audience.

A dream that became a reality. Something so few ever see in their lifetime. Something I couldn't take for granted.

"I don't think many authors ever do. You see, we limit ourselves to protect our little artist hearts. We determine what we're worthy of or the value of our creativity, and we only imagine up to that point. Nothing beyond it is possible. Until it is."

I forced myself to remember to smile, to pause, to breathe.

"If there is one thing that Glass Heels taught me, it's that anything is possible." I playfully huffed. *"A cliché, I know. How dare I?"* Following the planned joke with a wide smile.

I suddenly became aware of the audience as a loud wave of laughter stretched through the theater. I placed my hands gently on the podium, and a flash from my wrist caught my eye—my bracelet. The momentary recognition allowed me to take a deep breath, and I resumed my speech with poise and a gracious smile.

"Truthfully, I wrote 'Glass Heels' as a way to work through my frustrations with the world—my doubts, fears, and the beliefs that had been pushed down on me about what it means to be a woman."

As I planned the last line, I paused, a natural break to catch my breath again.

"The idea that it's resonated with so many of you, too... Well, I'm still trying to process that when I thought I was alone, I was with so many of you." The applause started as I finished my speech. *"Thank you, Cassandra Lopez, Everbound Press, and Dante Graves, for your endless support. Oh, and thank you, Edward."*

The musical cue to exit blared toward my flushed face, and I carefully stepped down the stairs in my too-high Louboutins. A picture of composure and class as I gently held the railing and smiled effortlessly in my return to my table.

When I reached my seat, Dante stood and carefully helped me collapse into the comforting hug of the faded fabric chair. A sigh of relief plummeted from my mouth—it was all over. My heartbeat could finally slow down.

"An *Aurora*, Tay," Dante's face gleamed with pride through his smile. He wasn't a writer, so he didn't know why he was excited. If he were, he'd fear the power of this award the way I did. Its omen was a burden that only I carried now.

Too many writers have won this same award and then fizzled off into nothing. When I found out I'd been nominated, I asked Cass if we could decline, and she said it would be career suicide, to which I replied, "So is accepting it."

Creative writers tend to believe in curses, burdens, spells, fate... the unknown controlling our trajectories while we're hurled through space on a flaming rock. Anything can happen so long as it can be written, right?

We were perhaps told too many times as children that *anything is possible.* And, well—we may have taken it too seriously.

The Aurora Prize was cursed. Of that, I was confident.

And The Aurora Prize for Social Literature wasn't just a beautiful statuette—it was a testament to the transformative power of words. Established in the early 1970s during an era of global upheaval, it had grown into one of the literary world's highest honors, awarded to authors whose works had sparked change, provoked dialogue, and left an indelible mark on society.

The ceremony carried a mystique. Each winner was invited to leave an inscription in the Aurora Journal—a living archive of reflections from past recipients. It was said that many of those who had won before were haunted by the weight of the legacy it bestowed, some unable to write another word, others consumed by the pressure to consistently be better than their last written word. Many lamented in the throes of writer's block and never resurfaced.

As I stood there, clutching the iridescent glass trophy, I couldn't shake an all-consuming thought:

What if this was my peak?

I squeezed Cass's hand as I blurred out the rest of the presentations, waiting until I could take myself politely to the women's room and vomit from the anxiety of it all.

She glanced at me, recognizing the overwhelming horror this moment was, and she gave me back a soft smile and a squeeze as if to say, "I've got you."

After the theatre had cleared, we returned to a luxurious dining room. There were scattered clinks of glasses and periodic pops of Cristal bottles permeating the open air. A long room with a faded, outdated pattern filled with extravagant spreads of expensive foods and desserts.

I saw past the sparkle and glitter for what this event was: waste. Glasses abandoned, yet still filled to the brim with champagne at easily two hundred dollars a bottle, the sight made me cringe. Full dinners filled with expensive cuts of steak and fish left untouched. Their smell permeated the room as they cooled to an inedible mush.

There were high-profile *someones* in every corner of the room. Some recognizable actors and actresses were even parsed in little cliques, distributed evenly, and many of them were writers themselves. Small clusters of those who knew each other and felt safe enough to let loose were closely accompanied by comrades they trusted to keep any little secrets. Secrets that might be easily dislodged with a bit of wine or something stronger.

It's hard to hide my expression of my discontent while they slam open a new bottle of something expensive before the last one is even finished, shout, and laugh at stories told by dry, cracked lips and inflamed rosy cheeks. The sickening announcement of "remember that one time" fills the air repeatedly.

It really *was* the lowest form of conversation.

I smiled as I floated from crowd to crowd, ignoring the outlandish ones whose laughs were too loud to be genuine. I grazed over a small plate and sipped from my water glass. Events like this always dehydrated me, and I was cranky without hydration.

"You okay there, Tay? You're staring at that steak like it owes you royalties."

I startled slightly, glancing up from the untouched plate of Wagyu. Cass leaned against the table, a glass of something not-so-bubbly in hand, her eyes narrowing as she looked me over.

"Just soaking it all in," I replied, mustering a smile.

She snorted. "Sure. I know that look. That's your 'Oh God, I'm trapped in a Jane Austen novel and everyone's drunk' face."

I let out a genuine laugh. "Better than a Stephen King novel," I jokingly admitted.

She grinned, clinking her glass lightly against my water. "I'm sure that would be a hell of a lot more fun. Now, stop worrying about impressing these people. You already did that. More than once. Enjoy your moment, Tay. You deserve this."

I wanted to believe her. But when she squeezed my hand and leaned in, I knew she'd caught the unease in my expression.

"Don't let this room get to you," she said softly. "This place will eat you alive if you let it. Just stay *you*. That's what got you here in the first place."

But was it?

CHAPTER 5

A REGRETFUL LOSS
2014

"It's a rock, but the words engraved into it mean more to me than any I'd ever written," I mumbled, sitting cross-legged in the dew-soaked grass just before sunrise. My jeans were damp with the world's morning tears as I scribbled fragments about feeling this moment onto the back of an elongated pharmacy receipt from my pocket.

"How ironic," I murmured with a bitter smile, noticing it was the receipt for the Xanax prescribed to cope with her death.

VIVIAN ADELAIDE HALETHORPE-TURNER
1953 - 2014
Beloved Mother, Keeper of Tradition
"A legacy endured within the walls of her beloved Estate."

I rubbed the gold chain along my wrist, feeling the texture collide with the softness of my fingers. My best memory of my mother was attached to me. The day she gave me this heirloom, I swore to protect it like it was my *only* legacy. Like there wasn't a two-hundred-year-old Estate bearing my last name. Like there wasn't a reasonably large trust fund, either. No, that wasn't the *Halethorpe* I was. I was the one who treasured a small gold bracelet.

This morning, I had already shared my sorrow with her. Whispering recollections and regrets against the cool granite of her new version of existence. A rock in place of the smile lines around her lips, the glow of hope in her eyes. Engraved letters instead of the honey sweet voice of her saying my name.

I felt *nothing* when Edward passed. It was another day. But my *mother*. I hadn't done right by her. I let Edward keep me from having the relationship I wanted with her, and I'd always imagined there would be time.

Maybe when I had my children, maybe when I came back to live at this Estate someday after I retired. But I'd waited too long and missed a chance I'd never get back. Something that again haunted me even when my eyes were open.

I remembered my last conversation with her, and the regret slammed into my chest, taking my breath away.

It was a phone call.

My phone buzzed in my hand, and when I saw "Mom" glowing on the screen, I hesitated. I always hesitated when she called these days. It was too easy to make excuses—deadlines, meetings, premieres. But I swiped to answer, pinning my phone between my shoulder and ear while sipping champagne I didn't need.

"Hi, Mom."

"Hi, sweetheart." Her voice was warm, but it sounded faint.

"You okay? You sound tired," I asked, not really listening, just saying what I thought I was supposed to say.

"Oh, I'm fine," she replied, her tone gentle but strained. "Just... a little under the weather, I suppose. Nothing to worry about."

"Then rest," I said automatically, scanning the room for Cass. "Let Miriam bring you some soup or something. Isn't that what she's there for?"

She chuckled softly, but something in it panged my stomach. "Miriam's been wonderful, but there are things she can't do for me, Taylor."

I started to ask what she meant, but before I could, she kept going.

"I was just thinking... It's been a while since you've been home. I thought maybe you could come for a visit. It would be good to see you." She stalled a response, and her words lowered into a depth that didn't sound much like her.

"The Estate misses you." She said.

Something cold threaded through my spine.

"The Estate misses me?" I said, laughing a little too loudly. "Should I give it a call?"

A strange pressure built in my chest, an old discomfort clawing its way back up. I swallowed it down.

"Mom, it's a house. It's not waiting for anything."

"Maybe," she murmured. "Or maybe it knows you belong here."

A prickling unease crawled across my skin, but she sighed before I could say anything, and the silence was long enough to feel wrong. "Maybe I miss you too," she said like she was confessing something.

I sighed, glancing around the set as if someone might give me an excuse to hang up. "Mom, you know how crazy things are right now, and Cass is hounding me for the next book. I'll come soon, I promise."

"You've been saying that for months," she said, not angry but somber. "I don't want to push you, but time... it gets away from us."

"I know, Mom. I'll make time." I could hear the impatience creeping into my voice. "Maybe for the holidays, okay? I'll fly out, and we'll spend a week together. Just you and me. We can decorate and drink cocoa."

"That sounds nice," she said, but there was something in her tone—it left me feeling guilty.

"That's Good. I'll let you know as soon as I book a ticket. I love you, Mom."

"I love you too, sweetheart. Take care of yourself."

I hung up before she could say anything else, my focus immediately snapping back to the chaos around me. Whatever it was in her voice—the pain of her words, the pause before she answered—I pushed it aside. But for the rest of the night, I couldn't shake the feeling that the Estate really was waiting.

I didn't know that would be the last time I'd ever hear her voice. And now, here I was.

Not two weeks after her passing, the lawyers read her will, and as her only child, I was given the responsibility and, let's call it for what it is, the *burden* of that same *Halethorpe Estate*. I sat across from the lawyers, thumbing through the arranged documents. A glossy pamphlet with photos from easily twenty years ago caught my attention.

"Once a pinnacle in this town's history. The Halethorpe Estate... a sprawling, historic manor nestled on the outskirts of Baltimore, a relic of the mid-19th century that echoes the grandeur of a bygone era. Passed down through generations of the Halethorpe family, the estate is as much a repository of secrets as it is a home."

Or that's what the Chamber of Commerce says about it in this advert, which I'm now financially obligated to sponsor, according to the suited grim reapers sitting across from me.

"Secrets, eh?" I grumbled.

But now, I was reliving it all while I finally slowed down enough to sit by her side in the beautiful silence of a new morning.

I lifted myself from her burial site, right here at the Estate. It's just a short stroll if you're into hiking. All of my mother's family is buried here, including Edward, who I chose to ignore on this visit, ensuring it stays cordial.

I returned to the dusty foyer of the Estate's main house, a mansion in every aspect. The ceilings felt hundreds of feet tall, the architecture impossible to recreate today. I noticed something I hadn't seen before each time I walked into this room.

Although it was old, smelled old, and looked old, seeing it from this perspective, the *ownership* perspective made it shine in a certain way. It wasn't just a dusty, decrepit money pit. It was a legacy I had been born into. There was an honor in it that I'd never before felt. Was I finally proud to be a part of this place?

"Taylor Halethorpe, last of her name, owner of Estate," I joked as I moved a sitting chair covered with a sheet into the corner. It honked as the feet rubbed against the original plank floors.

My phone began violently buzzing in my hand, and when I saw the name, I cringed and panicked.

"Cass," I said out loud, taking a deep breath in as I swiped to answer the call. "Hey there, Cass," I said in the most chipper phone voice I could muster.

"Cut the shit, I know you're sad,"

"I'm working on being *positive*, remember?" I lied, though Cass probably saw through that, too.

I was merely existing somewhere in the lowest pits of despair. Positivity felt impossible, like being waist-deep in a pool of concrete, too heavy to climb out, and with a deep desire to become one with the ground.

"Look, I know you're hurting. I'm so sorry. I know how important your mom was, but... Listen—Everbound won't take these chapters without a plan." Her voice softened, but I prepared for the kick.

"Or, like… a plot?" she added. "Do you even know what you're writing about?" It sounded like concern, not her managing me.

I let the question hang in the air as I studied the delicate filigree of the wallpaper. The sun finally caught up with me and washed bright beams across the faded patterns. No one could tell me this hellhole wasn't at least beautiful, picturesque even.

The silence grew a voice and began to scream at me, making it uncomfortable. Ignoring anything Cass had said up to this point, I blurted it out.

"I'm giving up the penthouse and moving back here to Halethorpe." I knew it would shock her, but it had to be done.

"Fair enough. I don't care where you write, Taylor. Everbound just needs something, *anything*. A plan. A plot. Hell, a first chapter that doesn't scream 'meltdown.'" She took a deep breath. "Or that extremely lucrative, earth-shattering, never-before-seen deal that we have is going to be in breach, and we'll both be living in that crumbling estate, ok?"

She constantly ranted when she was nervous.

"I get it. I'll send something cohesive. I promise." My promises *usually* always landed. I'd promised her ten pages of *Glass Heels* was all she needed, and I was right. I could promise some cohesive chapters… *that* I could do.

"Hey, Tay, before I go, have you…" she stopped, hesitating. Whatever she was about to ask was going to cross a line and she knew it. "Have you talked to Dante about anything?"

"No, why?" It hit harsher than I wanted, but also, *why?*

"If my fiancée decided to move across the country, I'd want to know…" And just like that, she was wearing her 'friend' hat. I could tell she was coming from a place of love. Her voice came through with a subtle warmth she didn't have when talking business, but her words didn't anger me any less, even when I could identify her intent.

"I'll talk to him, he's just... I don't know, distant lately." Instead of avoiding the subject, I paced as I said it, finally admitting to someone that I knew something wasn't entirely right with him.

"I think you need to talk to him."

"I will, I will..." I was about to promise but didn't want to sign up for too much commitment in one conversation.

"Ok, I have to go. *Please write something*," she begged, something she'd started doing shortly after *Glass Heels* was fading from public relevancy. That's the neat thing about our society... We move on from fads faster than Hollywood couples move from 'soulmates' to 'irreconcilable differences.'

The movie was shelved after the pilot scenes bombed in testing, and the buzz surrounding it faded within months. We'd waited too long to capitalize on it, missing the sweet spot entirely.

In 2012, it was a national phenomenon. Nearly two years later, those same people can barely remember it. A few weeks ago, I did a signing at a big chain bookstore, and the coordinator asked me if I'd written the "slipper" book.

It was a mortifying experience, to say the least.

Cass, the woman I once imagined never having to beg, *regularly* begged me to write. Her words echoed in my mind: "It doesn't even matter *what* you write at this point, just something that makes sense. People will buy it. It's got your name on it."

I looked at my phone and debated whether it was worth the argument, but Cass was right about at least one thing: I needed to talk to Dante. I took a deep breath and let it out in a therapeutic sigh.

"Hello?" He answered—I'd hoped for voicemail.

"Hey, it's me," I said, smiling at the sound of his voice.

"Hey, what's up? I'm about to walk into court. Is everything ok?" The chatter in the background deterred me from offloading everything immediately. Now wasn't a great time for him or me.

"Oh, everything's fine. We just haven't talked." I paused. "Maybe call me tonight?"

"Yeah, of course. Sure." He was distracted and disconnected. He didn't even sound happy to hear from me. His grieving fiancé.

"I love you." But the call had already ended.

"Odd," I said as I shoved my phone into the back pocket of my jeans and reluctantly made my way up the grand staircase. I walked on the delicate runner, my hand gently grazing the massive banister, hand-carved by someone with my last name so many years ago. This was the first time I had been to the second story since my mother had passed.

I felt the eerie hold the second story had—the shadows pooled in places they shouldn't, the groans and creaks of the floorboards called out when you'd thought you were alone.

I felt a definite shift in the air as I made my way down the long, dark hallway. Without even trying, it looked like a scene from an M. Night Shyamalan movie.

"I better not see dead people," I whispered as a quick shift in the light grabbed my attention.

This house had too many bedrooms to count, close to fifteen. Some were empty, and some were still fully furnished with the same ornate furniture that had existed since my ancestors had walked through these halls. I imagined them in their nightgowns and nightcaps, holding candle trays and wearing loafer slippers made from cowhide tanned on this very farm.

If generations of Halethorpes could keep this Estate alive, why couldn't I?

I hadn't fully decided against selling the Estate. But it cost me nothing to live here, as my mother's inheritance was explicitly left to maintain the estate and cover Miriam's paycheck.

The Housekeeper, Miriam, was born here at the Estate and has lived here her entire life. In fact, all of the women in Miriam's family served as housekeepers at the Halethorpe Estate, dating back to her great-grandmother.

Royalties from *Glass Heels* still trickled in from time to time. As an Aurora Prize novel, it was added to curriculums in specific college courses, and I'd get a surge of sales just before classes would start. Not enough to survive on, but I also had substantial savings. It wasn't enough to be sustainable long-term, but by reducing my expenses, I could focus on writing my next project and have more time to do it by living *here* instead.

As much as it felt like I was avoiding sending Cass any of my work, I was trying to figure out how to follow up on a legacy like *Heels.*

I wanted to write, but the words were hard to find. When I was angry, my words seemed riled and ready to flow freely, but my sorrow was a reserved thing, something I felt private about, and it made stories harder to find.

No, it made them impossible.

I rattled the handle of a locked door. My mother had hidden the old skeleton key that unlocked most of these doors somewhere in this house where I would never think to look. A locksmith would cost a fortune, considering these locks were two hundred years old.

I'd tried almost all the doors at the top of the staircase, but they were all locked. I stopped when the light diminished. I wasn't walking down into the dark bits where electricity was scarce.

I had no plan of getting swallowed by the darkness of the massive arched hallway. This house was a living ghost, a maze of decay, beautiful once but now tragic. The metaphor tickled me a little as I reached for anything to write on and found nothing. *Another one lost to inconvenience,* I thought to myself.

I had far too much in common with an inanimate *mansion,* which was enough allegory for today. I really needed to find that key before I came back up here. There could be anything living in these rooms, including some unsavory critters. The thought of the added expense of an exterminator crossed my already worried mind, but I let it go.

Perhaps a little too swiftly, I made my way down to the room I felt most comfortable in, *my childhood room*. A bed too small, but the most modern room in the house, updated by Edward for me in 1999. A TV, a CD player, and old posters are plastered on the wall. It was a time capsule that took me back to a time when life was annoying but far more straightforward, that was certain.

It was a time when the Estate's pressure in my life felt far less ominous and real, and this thought made me realize how suffocating this house had become ever since I'd *grown* up.

This house wasn't just mine now—it was my *responsibility*, inheritance, and burden. A burden I wasn't ready to come to terms with, but one I was hesitating to let go of, much like my mother had. Perhaps all Halethorpe women faced the same struggle, the curse of our name...

CHAPTER 6

BREAKING POINT
2015

After hours of battling the sketchy dial-up internet, I finally sent Cass twelve chapters of my Beauty and the Beast reimagining—one where the roles were reversed. The story was destined for tragedy: the inventor's son, incapable of seeing past the beast woman's monstrous form, ultimately rejects her. She remains forever trapped in the shape of a bear-like creature, doomed to maim and murder everyone she has ever loved.

I wasn't thrilled with the outline or the core writing, but she told me to write *anything*.

Dante still hadn't called back, and as I looked at the large ticking clock from across the massive sitting room, the hands told me it was closing in on 11 pm.

Earlier, Miriam had lit a fire and served a buttery Italian pastina soup that tasted like my childhood. It was undoubtedly a recipe she had handed down from her mother, as it immediately reminded me of sledding down the hills on the property and building snowmen with Mom.

I was fortunate to have a childhood worth remembering. Even if my ascension into adulthood was marred with my feminine rage toward my misogynistic and overly traditional father, I had a great childhood.

The nostalgic memories were something I hoped to hold onto forever and maybe someday share with my children.

The sofa and settee in the living room were firm as if filled with cardboard and hay. This was nothing like the luxurious sectional I knew was sitting in the center of my high-rise penthouse apartment in LA. The stiffness reminded me of a few things I'd put off during the day. I swung my laptop open and kicked out a few emails while the hotspot was still connected.

I had made my decision final—moving back to the Halethorpe Estate made too much sense. I broke leases and organized transport and delivery of all my personal belongings from LA. I didn't think that flying out there was necessary until I heard back from Dante. Not when I had a hauntingly close deadline to meet and a very uptight agent breathing down my neck.

A flicker in the lights that felt like a flutter of agreement, a subtle sign that perhaps the Estate had recognized my intentions to stay and found them acceptable.

Was it my imagination, or was this place alive?

But when the fire in the hearth surged, its wild tendrils of flames licked ever so slightly too far toward me like something otherworldy was beckoning me to write here, to stay.

I had my answer without hearing it for what it was.

***

After a few days of cleaning the Estate with Miriam, we moved the old furniture out and donated it to a small historical museum in Baltimore County. I'd pulled down the old linens and drapes and sought someone locally to sew custom, more modern replacements.

The dust that plumed off the old rags as they smacked against the floor felt like someone had tossed in a smoke grenade. It was impossible to breathe, even with our masks on. A musty smell permeated the room and sent us running for fresh air. Hopefully, the odor would follow the old heaps of old fabric as I tossed them onto the front lawn.

Miriam teetered on the very top of our tallest ladder as I held the base. "Be careful!" I shouted up to her as she nodded consistently, growing tired of my worry. She was *fearless*, and the woman had grit.

I still hadn't heard from Dante. It had been days since I'd called him.

The thought speared into the moment and sent a sharp pain into my gut. Something wasn't right. I'd left him another message but didn't want to overwhelm him with my excessiveness. He hated it when I was over the top. I looked down at the emerald-cut diamond glinting on my left hand, remembering when wearing this would have been shameful.

But I missed him.

I missed his smile and how he was my biggest fan and supporter. I won't go into how this mansion seemed to drop below freezing even in the summer and how the absence of his warm body tangled with mine left me remorseful and yearning. An ache in my creative mind that relived some of our most intoxicating nights over and over to replace the void.

The nightmares... were becoming more frequent and always in *this* Estate, and it always ended with my incapacitation. I couldn't tell if I'd died or if I was reborn into a new life, but every time I dreamed it... I woke up wishing I could remember more details. I rushed to write it down, but by the time I reached for something, *anything*—the thought had been lost in the cold, dark night.

Dante used to comfort me through those rough nights. I'd even felt as though perhaps his just being *near* me staved them off—protected me.

Despite trying to catch the wisps of flying nightmares out of the sky and get them on paper, I'd been working on something—my latest story, and after I put some finishing touches on Act 2, I carefully sent it to Cass and my editor.

It wasn't my best work, no... absolutely not, but it was on brand, on the theme, and it would be a nice tie into *Glass Heels*. Perhaps, somehow, I am staking my claim as a re-imaginer of public domain stories. Maybe that was my *thing*.

I'd heard the loud beeps of a truck at the long driveway end before I saw it backing its way up to the entrance of the Halethorpe Estate. The anticipated arrival of my belongings from LA wasn't for another week, so it was a surprise to know I might sleep on something more comfortable than an old spring mattress from 1998.

I closed my laptop, opened the giant doors, and stepped out to meet the movers and driver. The drivers barely confirmed my name before they pulled the large ramp out from the rear of the truck. The clang was so loud it made me flinch.

My face dropped when the trailer door flung open, and tears collected in the corners. The movers eyed me for a moment and then looked away.

This trailer was filled with things that belonged to me, but these were things I'd kept at Dante's place, not mine.

He—he shipped me my things?

No wonder I hadn't heard from him. Was this his way of breaking off our engagement? It had to be... All of the signs and the uneasy feelings I'd had in my gut since before I flew home to bury my mother.

The asshole couldn't even tell me to my face. He'd broken my heart without so much as looking me in the eye. Coward.

I had spent years with him, and this was how he thought he should do this? Rage pulsed through my veins, and I clenched my hands into fists, but slowly, the anger was replaced with morsels of sorrow.

As the moment weighed me down, and I felt like I might fall to the ground, I saw the sparkle of the ring I'd started wearing on my finger just a few weeks ago. It made me sick to my stomach. Vomit sizzled in the back of my throat, but I swallowed it back with my tears and sobs that were violently trying to escape me.

I'd finally started to take pride in my engagement with him, shifting my career backward in the list of priorities, putting *us* first, but perhaps I'd forgotten, in all the madness, to tell him how important he was to me. I thought I had. I thought that's why people were *engaged* to each other.

I started bargaining as I saw *our* stuff roll off the ramp. If only I could *talk* to him, explain everything, tell him I'm not grieving anymore, and get back to writing.

We could be happy again. We could be everything again.

I didn't know if I was trying to convince myself or if I genuinely believed it. I didn't know what to do. I grabbed for my phone and found it tucked into my back pocket. I was shaking as the screen unlocked, and I saw the email notification: "I'm sorry," from Dante Graves.

"No!" I shouted while the movers kept unloading the perfectly packed and labeled boxes and totes of my clothing and furniture. I gazed over art I'd bought and sculptures we'd selected together at gallery visits. There was the bedroom furniture we'd picked out together encased in protective shrink wrap... *My God...* this was his entire apartment, everything we'd picked together.

Even a painting packaged in a lumber frame rolled off the metal ramp. I knew what it was the second I saw the box. It was "*The Bookworm*" by Carl Spitzweg, the 1884 third version that Dante scoured the world for and found in a private collection. This painting was worth more than the Estate itself.

I closed my eyes and let myself get lost in the vivid memory of the day he surprised me with it. He presented it to me with a grin that couldn't grow wider. He held my hand as he revealed it and said that it reminded him of me.

I was enthralled by it. I ate all three meals, sitting in front of it, staring at its intricate details. After a few weeks of it on the gallery wall, I'd barely noticed it again. I'd forgotten we'd even owned it.

I snapped from the memory, "He'll buy me a $1.5 million painting but email me our breakup?" My angry voice was an intense rumble. The disconnect tones chimed into my ear, striking a chord.

'We're sorry, the number you are trying to reach has been disconnected.'

He changed his number. He sent an *email.*

The sadness and sorrow that I'd felt just moments ago were morphing into madness and vehement anger.

"What a fucking prick!" I shouted at the phone. The two movers stopped mid-carry of the priceless art and looked at me with concern.

"Oh, no. not you—*sorry.*" A flush of embarrassment grew on my face. They steadied their stare as if they were waiting for something.

"In there, through the big door," I gestured toward the giant entrance to the mansion. Miriam could show them where to put things. I started walking toward the rear garden, where Mom was buried. I needed a minute. I needed air.

But before I could make it to the graveyard, my phone's chime pierced my thoughts and interrupted me. I answered the unknown number swiftly, almost ignoring the call instead of answering.

"Hello?" I only said one word, for if I let more come out, the tears would ride along with them.

"It's Cass. I'm in the office with Pete and Chris. You remember them, right?" She didn't even give me a chance to tell her that right now wasn't a great time.

"Hey Cass, yes I remember, hey uh—" I started to explain, and another voice interrupted me.

"Hey, Taylor, It's Pete. We're looking over these chapters. This is good stuff," he paused. The 'but' was coming. I felt the tension building. "But this isn't something we want to get behind right now. We're trying to steer away from re-imaginings. They're... overdone."

The same feedback I'd heard all those years ago when Cass sat across from me at that café in Baltimore. It's like they're programmed to say things like "overdone" or "frequently explored."

"Yeah, I've heard that before. " This was a dig directly at Cass, and I hoped she'd heard it.

"Listen, since you're having a hard time conceptualizing, we were thinking—"

"You were thinking what? That maybe you'd try your hand at writing a national best-selling, societal phenomenon?" My anger was poking through at the audacity.

"I'll tell you what: You stick to selling books, and I'll stick to writing them." I paused. "Don't call me like this again."

I hung up the phone, slamming my finger on the red dot. It wasn't the same as it used to be when you'd slam a phone down on a receiver, something technological advancement took away from us that I'll never forgive them for.

An injustice I'd need to fight another day because my world was crumbling apart. I'd started to tuck the phone away when I saw Cass's number flash on the screen.

"Damage control," I mumbled as I answered it, bringing it to my ear but refusing to greet her.

"What the actual fuck, Taylor?"

To say she was mad would be a gross understatement.

"Cass, why don't you try not to ambush me without checking first?"

"What is your problem now? You've had plenty of time to figure this shit out, and now, it's time to return to reality. Our *jobs* are riding on this, Taylor. And you're off... fucking around!"

"First, *Cass*, I'm trying to organize my life, considering my fiancé just broke my engagement off over an email and shipped an entire trailer of my things to a mansion I can't get into any of the rooms of."

I was out of breath, the anger was taking my composure, and within its absence, the sobs and cries infiltrated the vacant space.

"Oh, Tay... I didn't know." The instant regret in her voice was nice to hear, but I was still seething.

"Because you didn't fucking ask," Oh, I was definitively *still* mad.

"Look, they don't like the Beauty and the Beast thing, that's all."

"You told me to write *anything*. How do I write anything except for what they don't like?" I questioned. It sounded unbelievable even to say it out loud, but I wasn't interested in becoming a mind reader. "I am not a mindreader..." I barely breathed out, lost in my collective sadness and anger.

"I'll talk to them. You've gone through a lot. We'll get an extension."

There it was—the thing I'd been waiting for. My shoulders relaxed the second she mentioned it.

"An extension," I repeated. It was music to my ears.

I stepped back into the Estate, out of breath. The unraveled madness felt unreal, like a joke or a dream. I looked around, and for a moment, nothing made sense.

The wallpaper didn't look the same. The wood was gleaming in an ethereal but melancholy way, its grains darkened but not by light or shadows. The lighting pulsed and rattled with my breaths as if it were alive, feeding off my energy—off my sorrow.

I closed my eyes and shook my head, and when I reopened them, everything was normal. Miriam made her way toward me with a cup of frothy dessert coffee.

Now—*she* was a mind reader.

CHAPTER 7

BAD DECISIONS
2016

I'm not sure what witchcraft Cass used, but she inevitably renegotiated my contract when I failed to write anything substantial after the Beauty and the Beast chapters were passed over.

I'd send in an idea and a few chapters and get a rejection almost instantly. It was like they were purposefully rejecting everything I wrote. Of course, nothing would ever be as good as *Glass Heels* was to them, and the irony of the entire thing...

Was that *I* didn't think the book was good at all.

It was viral writing, not artistic writing. It had shock value at the time. It wasn't poetry. It was twenty-something-year-old Taylor's perception of a world she knew *nothing* about... If only she had known how the world would chew her up and spit her out all these years later. *Glass Heels* might not be what it is today, but maybe if it weren't, I'd know my own voice when I heard it.

In the absence of creativity, I'd done a few freelance side gigs that Cass sent. They weren't a breach of contract, and I got paid for them. She was always looking out for me, even when I wasn't her primary source of income anymore.

Along with the expensive habitual drug use, there was a string of random men, sometimes at the Estate, sometimes in public spaces, and some nights, I was too drunk to remember their names.

I'm pretty sure there were women, too. It was hard to be entirely sure of the messes I was creating. I wasn't concerned about the dangers of the little fires I was lighting in the world. No, they were necessary to feel the warmth of being *alive* when I watched everything burn down.

My, how I'd fallen so far to the bottom, below even the ground. I was in a pit, and it was *suffocating* me.

Cass all but fired me as a client when I showed up drunk to one of the face-to-face meetings with Pete, the villainous publisher executive, who didn't like it when I called him out on his shit. After that, they managed their expectations better and removed my headshot from their website as a signed author.

Fuck Everbound Press. I left the Baltimore office that day and dragged myself to a bar in Fells Point—a way to avoid feeling the eerie judgmental presence of the Estate, and I wasn't in the mood to face the crushing reality of my loneliness.

I'd never tell anyone this, but I thought that by moving into the Estate, I could feel closer to my mother. Instead... It only widened the hole in my heart where the guilt was festering.

The way this place had started to crumble, and I hadn't so much as *offered* to help with maintenance. The way my mother lived in dust-covered madness, and I hadn't once thought that perhaps, like me, she had been a prisoner of the name *Halethorpe,* and she wasn't happy, either.

Did my mother feel this alone in her last days because of me? Did that fucking house kill her, or did I?

God, I hated myself.

And the only thing I hated more were sports bars, especially in Fells Point, but they were right there—a whole strip of them for me to get myself kicked out of.

I found the least pretentious one, and I sat at the far end of the bar. For the first two glasses, I felt comfortable. The noise was low, and the light was lower—my favorite, I thought to myself. Everyone here was like me, *thirty or older*, and it oddly made me feel secure in my presence.

The bartender had a heavy hand, and my third glass felt like it was also my fourth, too.

I'd need to get a ride home after this one.

And as I pressed it to my mouth, a group of unruly college students rushed in. *Oh great*, I thought as the never-ending train of them crammed the counter stools, filling in around me like an ironic game of Tetris.

They were loud, and their fun was almost *abrasive*, with laughs so egregious you felt forced to wonder if you'd ever found anyone else *that* funny. I'd never laughed at anyone's joke loud enough that an entire bar needed to be subjected to the cackle I'd let free.

I'd attended events shoulder to shoulder with philanthropists, attorneys, TV personalities, and A-list celebrities, but somehow, a group of college students made me nervous.

I was ready to leave... But it was a shame to waste perfectly good wine. I'd stay until the last drop of this cabernet hit my lips. But the universe had other plans for me tonight. The universe, a cunning and devious thing, sent me a not-so-subtle message when the dark-haired mysterious girl plopped all her notebooks onto the table, and a paperback copy of *Glass Heels* slid down off the stack.

"Are you still reading that book, Mer?" The handsome boy asked, gazing at her with yearning eyes and the smile of a flirt.

Oh, he had a thing for her.

"It's an *assignment*. You'd know what those were if you ever came to class." She said, smiling back as he leaned in. Their attraction was palpable, straight from a romance novel.

Ick.

"It's not a bad book, just kinda arrogant if you ask me." The girl announced as her friends all shifted their attention toward her. I squirmed uncomfortably and moved slowly to conceal myself from accidental eye contact. Nothing was more mortifying than being *present* for a face-to-face one-star review of your most prized work.

It also didn't help that my photo was plastered all over the backside of that book. The black and white headshot from all those years ago that I thought was elegant and chic. My young, collagen-filled face was now a sunken, hollow version of what it used to be. The stranger's face on that book was a haunting reminder of how far I'd fallen.

"You don't look like you're having fun," a voice tickled my entire right side. Too close to be anything other than a vile attempt to hit on me while I drowned not one but all of my sorrows in my wine.

I glanced up to see a man leaning his entire body against the bar. His hair was tousled just so, and he had a half-smile on his face. "Rough night?"

"They're all rough," I muttered, taking a larger sip of wine.

"Let me guess," he said, sliding onto the now empty stool beside me, uninvited. "You're here because you hate being alone." A pause. "But you're crammed in this dark corner because you hate people more? Am I right?"

I raised an eyebrow. *He was one of these guys.*

"Do you always hit on women with cheap psychoanalysis or just me?"

He laughed, a low, effortless sound. It was nice.

"No, you're special. I'm Nick."

"Ashley," I lied.

"Ashley?" he questioned, tilting his head to the side

"You sure?" he smiled.

"Are you?" I asked him back.

"Not entirely."

"Then neither am I." My stomach twisted momentarily as a brief vision of Dante crossed my mind. Nick was attractive enough, probably more so than Dante, because it was natural and not fabricated with endless luxury and money.

He had a rural grunge to him, a roughness that Dante would never have, and it felt like something I needed. His smile was sharp, and it warmed a part of me that I was embarrassed to admit I might have let get too frigid.

I'd kept my promise and escaped that establishment as soon as the last drop of wine hit my lips, but I didn't leave alone. Nick and I went back to the Estate, and usually, that drive and the arrival would have scared some people off, but Nick found the whole thing amusing and entertaining.

"You live *here?*" his mouth gaped open as he gazed out the backseat window of the rideshare.

"Unfortunately," I groaned as I pushed open the heavy door and nodded to the driver, handing him the last crumpled cash I had in my bag.

"It's like it's from a movie." His eyes fixated on the old Estate. "You're not going to murder me or something?"

"Or *something,*" I replied with a taunting, seductive tone.

His gaze caught mine, and he met me halfway, pulling me into his arms and kissing me like it was the end of the world. The Estate's lights flickered faintly behind us, darkening the landscape in sporadic pulses.

Nick's thirst to be great made him a pleaser. One I willingly invited into the dead air of the Estate. Our moment came to an abrupt pause when, finally, my back thudded against the massive solid wood door. While pressed against it, my legs tangled around his perfect body. I grabbed clumsily for the knob, enthralled by the taste of this drunken delirium.

I found the latch, and with a clink, the door opened. The creak that announced our arrival was barely noticeable over the gasps for air and the pounding of our hearts. Tonight, Nick and I were tethered together. Two damaged souls that found momentary solace basking in each other's pleasure.

I thought I'd never see him again, but Nick became a main character in my story. Sometimes, he played the hero—rescuing me from myself, forcing me to feel something other than regret and self-loathing.

Other times, he was the worst kind of villain. The one who didn't know all the wrongs they'd done and vehemently denied their existence. As quickly as he could build me into the Taylor Halethorpe I longed to be. He could rip that foundation down and turn me back into *nothing.*

Before Nick, it had been months since I'd even scribbled a note or tried to piece together my thoughts into prose. His introduction flickered an excitement for me to write.

I was also facing dire financial ruin if I didn't write something, *anything.* The royalties were becoming non-existent, and the inheritance was quickly drying up.

I still managed to get comped wine from a few oblivious Maryland wineries that thought the Halethorpe Estate was a *wedding venue* and sent cases upon cases as trials.

We certainly tried them, alright.

We tried them all *regularly*—for breakfast, lunch, and sometimes two different pairings at dinner.

Nick encouraged the spiral. He glorified and justified staying intoxicated with me. Our binges were adventures that took us to the farthest parts of alternate realities, knowing we didn't want to be a part of this one. We imagined a different existence for ourselves. He and I knew I would find the next *Glass Heels* at the bottom of one of these bottles.

Of course, I would find my next masterpiece.

Until I didn't.

✳✳✳

The room smelled like stale wine and takeout that hadn't made it to the trash. Nick sat sprawled out, his feet kicked up on the expensive furniture. His hand rested on my neck, deceptively gentle as his words seared me.

"I don't know why you're upset." His voice's hollow poison sunk deep into my skin. "I was just helping..."

I scoffed, my anger flailing like the flames of the violent fire in the fireplace.

"You told Cass I was too unstable to meet with the publishers."

Nick let out a sigh, his impatience with me completely audible. He ran his hand through his dark hair and gave me a look—the one that meant to say, *you're overreacting.*

"Because you are, Taylor. Look at you. Do you remember the last time you didn't need to sedate yourself to sleep?" He stood and started to raise his voice.

"Do you even see how people look at you?" he shook his head, and his lip snarled upward in disgust.

"Cass is trying to make you something you aren't. You don't owe her anything."

"I owe her my entire career," I snapped.

Nick snickered under his breath, "You're delusional. Cass doesn't write your stories. You do. It's all you, Tay."

I should have argued back. I should have defended my friend, but... *was he right?* Nick knew precisely where my insecurities lived—how to crawl inside them and make them feel like they were things I'd thought of myself.

"Cass wants me to write another *Glass Heels*," I whispered, my voice feeling as small and insignificant as this conversation made me feel.

"Exactly. They don't care about you. They care about what sells. You're letting them break you over a book you don't care about anymore." He leaned in, pressing his forehead against mine like he was saving me from myself.

"Fuck them," He snarled.

I clenched my jaw. I wanted to hold onto my anger, to remember that he'd still gone behind my back and told Cass *I was too unstable* to meet with my own editors and publishing team. But his eyes were soft, and his voice was a sweet song whispering my heart into resignation.

"C'mere," he murmured, pulling me into his lap. "You know I'm the only one who cares, right?"

I swallowed hard, forcing my head down onto his shoulder, forcing myself to relax against him. If I pretended hard enough, maybe I could make his words the truth.

Because if they weren't—if the way he looked at me and the way he reassured me... The way he knew I was more without them...

If this wasn't love, what the hell was it?

∗∗∗

Nick had a way of making goodbyes feel like punishment. One minute, he leaned against the counter, arms crossed, watching me like I was the problem. The next, his keys were in his hand, his jaw tight, and eyes narrowed in a way that made him look unrecognizable.

Especially when he finally pushed me too far, and I asked him to leave the Estate.

"You'll call," he let the words slither out. "You always do."

Then he was gone.

The door slammed, and the silence he left behind was deafening, but it also held a sliver of hope—the reassurance of my safety, the start of my peace. I let out a sigh and let myself melt to the floor, finally able to let my guard down.

When he left like this, I never knew when he'd return. It would always be on his terms, never mine.

Days, weeks... sometimes months. I could only hope that this time was the last.

***

Unexpected headlights shone directly into the living room. I hesitantly stood. I often received visitors to the Estate— sometimes, they were just tourists or solicitors. Occasionally, someone looked for Taylor Halethorpe to comment or to sign a copy of *Glass Heels*.

I darted for the door, but not before I snatched the six empty bottles of wine and frantically hid them in an empty cabinet in the kitchen. Miriam would likely find them later and take care of the mess. She was used to cleaning up the messes I so often made, which she concealed from me, preventing me from realizing how disgusting I had become.

I opened the double doors and immediately recognized the beat-up sedan. He stepped out, and his faded denim jacket, too-tight pants, and polished leather boots played in my head like a scene from a movie.

Ick.

"Nick," I said woefully, "You're supposed to call first," I warned as I stepped onto the porch.

"I did," he replied, holding up his phone. "But you blocked me. Rude, by the way."

"What do you want?"

"What? No 'Good to see you'? or, 'How have you been?" He sauntered toward me like a low-budget Jack Sparrow leaving his sinking ship. I didn't find it as whimsical as he was playing the scene.

Nick was an actor. His most significant credit was a toothpaste commercial five years ago. Since then, he's only ever been an extra, or the shows he's worked on go unreleased. He attempted a narrative podcast but struggled to get listeners.

"I came to check on you. Maybe you need some company in that big, creepy house?"

"No, you wore out someone's couch and need a place to stay." I corrected him, and I saw through his motives. Actor or not, I knew Nick. I could see the truth through the disguised lie every single time.

"You wound me, Taylor." He placed his hand over his heart and smiled as he closed in. I pulled my sweater around my body as the breeze prickled my skin.

"Maybe," I marginally conceded as he stepped up the stairs with a sensual grace. Long gone was Jack Sparrow, and instead, I had the quiet intensity of Noah Calhoun. He pulled himself in close, and he kissed me with the same intoxicating passion he always had for me.

I hated how he could turn it on and off and decide how and when he wanted to love me. It was harmful and hurtful when he'd decide I wasn't worthy of the love he had to give. It made me wonder if Nick was capable of love, or perhaps... he just wasn't capable of loving *me*. He had enough love for himself, that was certain.

One night, that's all I had with him before he disappeared again.

I better make it worth it.

We stepped into the Estate and sat casually in front of the fire, the raging hole of flames that Miriam made sure roared every night, even in the hottest summer months.

I sat cross-legged on a cushion close to it. The glass of wine had miraculously returned to my hand, as I didn't remember picking it up. But I knew I'd need to keep pouring it in since I let him stay.

"You ever think," I started, slurring just a little, "maybe this is it? Like, maybe we're not supposed to be anything more?"

Nick tilted his head, studying me. His lips curved into a familiar smirk, the one that gained him entrance to my life that night in Fells. "Tay, you're the one with a mansion and a Pulitzer. Don't drag me into your existential crisis."

"An Aurora," I corrected him, rolling my eyes as I laughed. "Living the actual dream in my big hollow, crumbling mansion." I paused and walked toward him. "None of that means anything, Nick." I tilted my head back and finished my glass.

"Then let it go." He said it so simply, like it was easy. Sometimes, I hated, no, *despised* his casual confidence.

"Why are you really here, Nick?" my voice cracked. I was officially out of wine, so we were either going to do this, or he was going to leave.

"I just want to feel something real." He said, "You are always that for me." He admitted carefully. His words were selected from a carousel of things he knew would cause me to drop my guard.

Without saying a word, I began to walk upstairs. I'd finally put together a room up there with my furniture from before. It was the *only* responsible thing I'd done in a while.

He followed, his eyes over my body like I was a meal he was getting ready to devour.

No sooner had I closed the door, Nick was upon me, slowly unraveling me like a gently wrapped present. He kissed me like he was trying to make amends for something—his failures, my grief, how we've never worked out. And I let him. I let the heat of his hands on my waist draw out all of the calamity in my mind. I let the taste of the whisky on his breath intoxicate me into a fantasy where this worked out in the end.

With Nick, he always worshipped me in intimate moments.

I let the wine make another bad decision at the end of a string of even worse ones, but I was ready to let the guilt and Nick go.

Nick was gone before the sun had even risen. The only evidence he'd been in my room was a little scribbled note on my nightstand: "I'll see you soon."

But I knew better.

After that night, I fully descended into a dark string of violent indiscretions, mistreating my body by letting him use me for his temporary love.

To quiet the thoughts that hammered back at my atrocious behavior, I smoked myself into oblivion with the finest, delicate sativa, letting it chase away my anxiety and unleash the creative thoughts of someone who was always woefully under-thinking.

When I ran out, I let the free wine wash over my body to blur away my regrets and mistakes, and it felt good to do so. I loved things that tantalized and awakened my soul and wanted to follow them until I perished.

I never loved Nick more than after I devoured an entire bottle and begged him to sleep next to me. His body was just another one of my vices, a drug I couldn't quit. His harmful words toward me or his jealousy were easy to ignore, so long as between his evil sentences, his mouth was somewhere else.

Writing did not feel good in my soul. It irritated and frustrated me.

If I never wrote again, it would be too soon.

Nick was enough.

THE LOST YEARS

THE DOWNWARD SPIRAL

2017-2019

CHAPTER 8

NO MAGIC OR CURSES
2017

Every night, the same terror would wake me, and I'd shake it from my body, pretending it hadn't made me cower in fear and that I wasn't somehow intertwined and connected to this Estate in a visceral, alive way—*like it was talking to me.*

But maybe this is what happens to the brain when the way that it's worked for thirty years is suddenly not an option. When all that you've learned to cope, to escape, to *deal* with the inconveniences of life is barred away behind a path of obstacles you can't pass?

You grasp at straws, and you blame the world. You cry into the darkness and scrape together the few small remnants of humanity to make it to the other side. You have nightmares of being suffocated by ancient vintage wallpaper flowers.

And then, you find a new normal.

My new normal was empty nights with strangers, trying to collect their stories and turn them into my own experiences. I'd gone back to scribbling notes on tattered papers, but by morning, the thoughts I thought were magic had turned into bits of wasted effort.

The unruly and untamed always have the best ideas.

It was haphazardly scratched onto a faded receipt from a local tavern. "What the actual fuck was I thinking?" I shook my head at the distaste the words left in my mouth. While I wasn't a perfect writer, I took pride in being intentional and precise with my words. I scoured my brain and the thesaurus for the perfect combination that would shoot to a reader's heart.

Whatever it was, this was not the writing I'd once taken pride in. There wasn't much these days that I took pride in at all. I was still ashamed to be loosely associated with Everbound, but Cass wasn't my agent, at least not unless I cornered her with a masterpiece and she'd reconsider.

She'd told me she felt it would complicate our friendship if she kept representing me during this time of...

She couldn't say it, so I said it for her: "Failure."

"You're not a failure... You were just dealt a weird hand."

"I was cursed by the Aurora award. I *told* you we should have rejected the nomination." *And this was bargaining.* I was fighting for someone, *anyone*, to believe that this rock-bottom writer's block wasn't my fault. It was everyone else's.

"Taylor, you can't honestly believe that a *curse* is why you haven't written anything?" Cass scoffed at my audacity. These days, I'd had so much of it that I didn't think anything I could say would surprise her anymore.

"Actually, yes," I answered, crossing my arms and staring at her pixelated face on the other side of the video chat.

"That's insane. You know that, right? Curses... they aren't *real,* Taylor." Her tone descended from humor into concern. I released a sigh as I brushed my hair behind my ears. It had grown out, and my dark roots faded into what used to be my perfectly maintained platinum blonde.

"I'm worried about you, Tay," Cass calmly confessed. But I already knew she was. She didn't have to say it. It was in her tone and the way she hesitated before she said anything. Weighing on whether or not it would be the thing that broke me. It was in the way she delicately danced around things she would have once let loose from her abrasive mouth. She was treading lightly and carefully twisting words so that they didn't disturb what little peace I had left.

"Why don't you visit me for a while, stay in my guestroom?"

I heard the desperation hiding in the words she didn't say.

"Get out of that funky place and into some warm weather."

Weather.

Not the real reason she wanted to see me. Although the offer was kind, I could tell it was a surface-level attempt that she didn't think would ever be accepted, so I didn't.

"Now's not the right time, Cass," I breathed. The words sounded familiar—the exact words I used to brush my mother off all those years ago.

"There's never a right time for anything," she paused. "Hear me out. If you start talking about magic and curses again, I'll book the flight myself, okay?" I nodded and grinned.

"No more curses, but... are aliens off the table?" I let out a breathy giggle, a peek of hope in the darkness of this conversation. Something that hadn't happened naturally in a long time.

"I love you, Tay. I gotta run." She crinkled her nose. "No aliens. Ooo—unless... you're writing about them and making them kiss, okay?"

I nodded again. "You got it, one sci-fi alien dark romance coming right up." I teased her as she shook her head, and we disconnected the video call.

I sat for a minute, letting the silence tingle my ears. What if I did write a story about a writer who'd been cursed by the award she'd won?

It wasn't an *awful* idea...

I thumbed over my bracelet, as I always did when I needed comfort, a reminder that I'd make it through these dark times.

"No curses," I recanted as I grabbed my now frigid coffee and wandered to the second level for an adventure.

CHAPTER 9

FLIGHTY STORIES
2018

I told myself it was the *last time* and, every time, I would let him back in. At this point, there was no longer a yearning for him to be more than just someone who fed my needs. Nick had proven that he was only good to have around to stave off the chill of lonely nights.

I was a woman in her early thirties. I was at the height of my sexuality. It felt wrong to waste these years sitting idly and letting *it* accumulate dust.

Exactly something a person with an addiction would say, and I knew it.

Nick was my addiction, and I was a fiend for the high.

When he disappeared, the withdrawals would force me to fill my nights with reckless nobodies whose names I didn't bother to remember, or I'd drink myself into trouble and wake up in whatever room I'd found at the peak of my intoxication. Miriam always worked around me.

Miriam.

Perhaps an angel on Earth, maybe even too good to be true. She lived in this Estate and ensured I didn't crumble like these walls. She never took a day off, and she was a relentless force that couldn't be stopped when she sensed a bit of dust lingering too long on any surface.

Her entire legacy was tied to the Halethorpe Estate. She walked through these halls as if she was meant to be here, and she certainly was. I'd never imagine this place without her dutiful humming while she tidied and cleaned after hurricane Taylor had assaulted every room night after night with gale-force winds.

One night, I stared at the bottom of an empty wine glass for the fifth, no... sixth time, and I wondered if anyone else could see Miriam too or if she were a ghost that haunted the Estate. Her unfinished business kept her tied here, forever brewing the perfect cups of coffee and wiping down the mantle while she chased after me with a rag drenched in polish.

The Housekeeper of Halethorpe. An idea for a story I couldn't let go of. I fell to my knees, fumbling around in my mess, trying to find a paper where I could catch the fleeting idea before it flew off into the air.

I didn't make it.

I found myself far more comfortable pressing against the fibers of the imported rug. I lay there until morning when I realized where I was—a pen in hand but not a single paper with a viable note around.

And the nights like this multiplied. Each idea that surfaced was lost to my drunken addiction. Each story I started conceptualizing was swallowed wholly by the self-doubt that made me forget it.

As if the walls had swallowed it up.

CHAPTER 10

BEST FRIENDS FOREVER
2019

Cass was coming to visit.

It had been over a year since I'd seen her in person, and her promise that this visit was "just as my friend" rather than my agent had left me cautiously hopeful. In the five years I'd holed myself up here in the Estate, I'd done the bare minimum—an article, here, a short story there. Just enough to keep Everbound Press engaged but away from the idea that I'd ever have another bestseller.

Nothing I'd written had come close to *Glass Heels*, and I think somewhere along the line, we'd stopped pretending it ever would. I kept a few short stories for myself, afraid that the world wasn't ready for that Taylor yet.

The distant sound of gravel crunching under the wheels broke through the morning silence. I set down the cup of creamy coffee, and tendrils of its warmth billowed from the top.

My heart thudded as I glanced out the window and saw the sleek black Escalade rolling to a stop. Before I could overthink it, I swung open the front doors, the air outside crisp and biting against my uncovered skin. The porch creaked under my weight as I stepped out, and for the first time in months, I felt a flicker of anticipation.

Cass emerged from the vehicle, her hair glossy, her heels sharp, and an absolute vision of class. She always carried herself like she was meeting the Queen of England, and arriving at my disintegrating mansion was no exception.

"Cass!" I called out, uncharacteristically bright. I jogged toward her, my boots skidding slightly on the gravel.

She met me halfway, a tiptoe run in her impossibly high heels. "Tay!" She said, wrapping her arms around me in a hug that smelled like her signature vanilla. Her hug had the comfort of a warm chocolate chip cookie.

When she pulled back, she held me at arm's length, her manicured fingers gripping my shoulders as she gave me her typical once-over, judging every decision I made when I got out of bed. She did it out of *love*. This I knew.

"You're losing weight," a disappointed stare gleamed at me.

"I've been... busy?" I responded, but it came out questionable.

"With what? Brooding in your giant mansion?" She looked toward the Estate. I'd done some work to the exterior with what little remained of the inheritance. For now, it no longer appeared as if a harsh wind would tip it over, but it was still easy to confuse with a haunted house. But I could see Cass's disappointment that I hadn't done the same for myself.

"I'm glad you're here," I said, much quieter and with a genuine honesty that I knew she felt.

She slipped her arm through mine as the driver from the Escalade brought her bags in, "Of course you are. Now, I want a grand tour of this Estate and expect to see *ghosts*." She paused, her eyebrow raised.

"You know, I read a manuscript once about a lady who had a ghost in her house and was *sleeping* with him. It was slightly spooky smut..." Cass joked as we stepped inside.

I looked at her and let out an uncontrollable laugh, a sound I hadn't made in *years*.

"Cass, do you want to fuck a ghost?"

"Hey, never say never."

✳✳✳

Cass and I walked along the busy streets of Baltimore. This was her hometown, too. This was as much a homecoming as it was a rekindling of a friendship on fire. We'd met here in this city. She started her career at an agency and was racing to break her next big author. Somehow, she ended up at a café with me, a scoundrel of a writer, begging agents to read *just ten pages*.

She'd been here for a week, but time was a thief, and the week had only felt like a few short hours. We hadn't talked about work for even a moment. Cass made it a point to avoid discussing our careers almost entirely, and it was rather *suspicious*.

It had come down to her last night, and we were *going out*.

Since she'd arrived and stayed reluctantly at the Estate instead of in the five-star hotel she'd reserved, I was forced to change some of my worst behaviors so that she couldn't see exactly how far I'd fallen, but she also saw through nearly *all* of my bullshit.

On her second night at the Estate, Nick had shown up *again*, unannounced and uninvited. When he tried to forcibly invite himself in to meet her and *'chill out with us,'* I'd recognized something that I hadn't before.

His demands of me were becoming so frequent that it took this out-of-body experience of watching him hatefully interact with Cass for me to realize how abusive his behavior was. Thankfully, Cass sent him on his way after I painfully admitted to her that I thought he was all I deserved.

It wasn't until her last night here that we finally cracked each other open. And after such an emotional series of confessions, it reminded me why we always need a *best* friend. I was finally able to tell her about all that collapsed inside of me when my mother died, the guilt that had manifested, and how it devoured the parts of my soul that felt free to write.

Finally, letting out that I ended up buried in trauma and was too helpless and broken to dig myself out or ask for help. And then, to pour salt in my already gaping wound... Dante didn't just end our engagement—he fled and ran for the hills without a *goodbye.* The whole thing, it was a crippling moment for my ego, and for what little confidence I had left.

It made it hard to chase creativity, or perhaps I believed my talent to be a finite thing that I had exhausted. Maybe I had no more left to give the world. Edward was right, and writing was a stupid dream.

"I used my magic up on *Glass Heels,* and I had nothing left to give the world, let alone myself," I said to Cass, and it hit me, so I repeated it.

"I didn't have enough to give *myself.* How would I give anything of value to the world?" I grabbed a piece of paper from the table and scribbled it. It was the first time I'd done it in longer than I wanted to admit. But Cass interrupted my spiral before I could say the next self-loathing thing about myself.

"I knew Dante, wasn't it... but it's hard to say anything when you know your friend is just living their best life." She looked sad, a rare expression for her.

"I didn't see the harm. There wasn't any *yet.*" She'd added, "And when he left the way he did, I felt so guilty that I didn't tell you I'd seen *signs.*" She paused and took my hand into hers.

"That's why I worked so hard to get your deal restructured. I felt responsible for this... decline you've descended into."

"Cass, you're not responsible for my actions, ever. You aren't at all to blame for my fall from grace." I reassured her.

"Taylor, never let anyone keep you a secret."

She looked at her watch, "*Shit*, we're going to be late." She grabbed her coat off the back of the chair in the lounge we'd waited at. She gulped down the last watery sip of her drink as we rushed for the door.

We were attending an exhibition Cass got us exclusively invited to across town—a group show where a collective of East Coast artists auctioned their work. Apparently, there was one blond, Viking-like man she occasionally saw when she made it back toward Baltimore who would be there.

"The Skarsgård," I cooed jokingly in the back of our Uber.

"His name is Erik," she corrected me.

"I'm pretty sure there is an Erik Skarsgård... You know, there's like eight of them."

She laughed hysterically. "Better than a Skarsgård."

"How *fun*." I felt a little giddy for her, at least someone had something to look forward to.

The exhibition was standard, with lots of white gloss and a polished dress code. I always found it ironic that we came to these things in suits, ties, and expensive designer dresses, but most of these canvases looked like someone vomited on them and called it "art."

My heart ached at the mere fact that some of these canvasses looked carelessly painted, with splatters and mistakes of paint—splotches and smears haphazardly coated in no particular pattern or shape. They made a mess and called it abstract, and the world ate it up.

As a writer, I received no such grace.

I could word vomit thousands of pages, but it would be called a nightmare. Writers needed to do the sentences justice and place each word perfectly in its order. We needed a plot and plans. We needed to know the end before the words of the beginning had ever been written. We were creators of universes that hadn't existed before we'd scribbled them down or typed them out.

Perhaps I didn't get '*abstract art*.'

I let Cass wander off to play *Vikings* with her Norwegian prince, and I stood before another splattered mess. I wondered for a moment if this was how some people felt about my writing. If you didn't 'get it,' then it was just nonsense, but if it spoke to you, you connected with it on another level.

If I'd connected with this piece, would I see it? A dog running through a field, a bird perched on a lamppost. A tortured man staring longingly out a window, waiting for something that may never come.

I twisted my head slightly, staring at the lines and colors, looking for something that perhaps wasn't there. I became instantly aware of the many observers nodding intellectually at the composition, pointing and engaging... At the risk of looking uncultured, I nodded like everyone else and hummed with an astute tone, like I'd made my observation.

A sip from the sangria I'd been handed before Cass left tingled my lips with its overly sweet peach taste.

"It looks like a toddler painted it, right?" A voice from beside me, playful and endearing.

"That one's called *Rebirth.*"

I turned to see a woman standing there, her curly hair in a messy bun, but her dress was form-fitting and plain. She had a casual confidence about her.

"You painted this?" I asked, nodding toward the canvas.

She smiled, wide and unguarded, and extended a paint-streaked hand. "Yes—Emma Delacroix."

I hesitated before shaking her hand, the rough texture of dried paint brushing against my skin. "Taylor," I said, then glanced back at the painting. "I don't think I get it."

Her smile turned, knowing. "Do you always let other people tell you what to feel?"

I blinked, completely caught off guard. "What?"

Emma stepped closer, folding her arms as she studied her work. "You're looking at it like there's a right answer. There's not. It's not about what anyone says you *should* see—it's about what it makes you *feel*."

I stared at the painting again, my mind frazzled. "I'm...I'm not sure what I feel," I admitted, my voice quieter now.

"Good," she said, "That's a start."

I glanced at her, frowning slightly. "I guess I'm more into art that... tells a story."

Her laugh was soft, the kind that made me want to smile. "And I guess I'm into art that screams into the void." She looked at me again, tilting her head like I was one of her paintings. "Guess we're both artists in different ways."

Her words caught me off guard. Artist? I hadn't thought of myself as that in a long time. Not since *Glass Heels* stopped being relevant.

"You should let me paint you," she said, still smiling at me. "You're beautiful," she added.

My face flushed, and I felt the heat rise to my cheeks. Embarrassment? No, it was something else... desire?

"Will I look like that?" I pointed back at the canvas.

"Depends on how long you make me wait." Her voice was low, a seductive whisper, as she handed me a slip of paper with a phone number smeared on it. Even the digits looked like they were painted with expertise, the numbers bubbly and hopeful.

I stood, holding my drink in my hand, looking back at the painting in complete disbelief.

✳✳✳

"So, something weird happened last night." I paused as Cass devoured the plate of French toast in front of her.

"Oh?" her mouth full.

"I got a phone number," I smiled hesitantly.

"You did?" she grabbed the napkin on the table and pressed it to her face.

"Emma." I grinned, thinking about her request to paint me. A memory I'd keep all to myself.

"Oh." Cass's eyes lit up with intrigue. "And are we going to call... Emma?" she asked, slightly nuanced, navigating uncharted territory.

"Hadn't decided." My uncertainty lingered in the vowels of my words. "Aren't you going to tell me to worry about more important things like my sinking career?" I questioned Cass for a moment. It was miraculous that she still hadn't brought work up since she had arrived, so I opened the door for her.

There was something she wanted to say, but for some reason, she was reluctant. Hesitation that wasn't normal for her—unless it was something big. I felt it in the thready bits of tension that crept into some of our moments together. An odd stare that lingered too long, or her right eye twitching slightly when we'd had a genuine moment.

"About that," her face scrunched up with the sour taste of what I knew was bad news. "I do have to talk to you." A frown carved its way onto her face.

She patted her mouth with the cloth napkin. "Everbound wants to drop you... This time, a complete severance." Cass stood and walked over and put her hand on my shoulder. "And, if it happens, I won't ever be able to work with you. Something about it being a *conflict of interest.*" Her eyes rolled deeply back into her head.

"It had to happen at some point," I reassured her that I wasn't shocked. I felt like it made giving the news easier. She'd already blamed herself for so much. This wasn't her fault, too.

"They'll give you one more chance if you can come up with something by the end of the quarter," she said, looking me in the eye. That's a little less than three months away, and I know you can do it."

I loved that she was confident in my abilities, but I wasn't sure I had a novel hiding in me that I could write in three months.

"Honestly, if you can send me even half a *high-quality* novel by then, I can make that work." She was always wheeling and dealing with Everbound.

"I'll see what I can do, Cass." I didn't want to disappoint her, but... I was still so disconnected from my passion for writing. I hadn't thought an original thought since... I grabbed through the pockets of the jacket I'd worn last night. The crumbled paper had my drunk handwriting swirled across it.

"I didn't have enough to give myself.
How could I give anything else to the world?"

I looked up at Cass, who was watching the cogs of my brain spin away in sheer delight.

"How long does it take to find a muse?" I asked her, fiddling with the paper between my fingers, its low crinkle distracting me.

"Depends," Cass smirked. "How long until you call her?" Cass winked at me as she headed to her room to pack her things. The car to take her to the airport would arrive within the hour. As the bittersweet feelings of her departure crept into my heart, I also realized that I had something to look forward to.

CHAPTER 11

UNLOCKED DOORS
2019

The locksmith dropped off the key early on a Friday morning. Leaving the archaic-looking metal piece with Miriam, who wasted no time opening *every* locked door in the Estate. I assume my mother kept them closed to save money on heat, but Miriam couldn't help wondering what had been in them all these years.

Most were empty shells of rooms, clean but cloaked in layers of dust, something Miriam wouldn't be able to stop herself from tackling.

I heard her clanking open what felt like every door in the long hall. When I slowly creaked mine open to peek out at whatever chaos she creating, I saw her panicking from room to room with a cart of cleaning supplies and four dark black buckets of murky water.

I wrapped myself in my robe and stepped out into the hall, staring wildly. My hair was disheveled, and my face was swollen from too much wine and sleep. "Miriam!" I shouted, "What on Earth are you doing?" She froze, looking around at the mess, and shrugged.

"The key! It arrived, these rooms... A mess." The concern on her face was genuine, and I almost laughed at it for a moment.

"Miriam, you don't have to clean these rooms right now. Let's take our time and just... have a look." I said calmly. This was already too much thinking and problem-solving before I'd had any coffee. I rubbed my forehead, and she smiled at me.

"You want me to make coffee?" Setting down the mop and the dusters, she didn't wait for me to answer before she started toward the stairs.

"Actually, yes, please. Anything that will stop you from... whatever this is." I mumbled as I receded into the darkness of the large primary bedroom. "They've been dirty for probably fifty years, Miriam. They can certainly be dirty for one more day!" I shouted as I closed the door, and she trotted down the stairs.

I pulled a heavy sweater over my aching body. I definitely drank a little too much wine yesterday, falling back into bad habits after Cass had gone home. Life was just so much more colorful when she was around. She made me feel less bad about being an absolute *nothing*.

I pulled my jeans over my hips, and instead of being too big, they lay perfectly against my waist. I ate like a normal person while she was here and continued to make sure I ate at least one meal a day, and it seemed I had put back on some healthy weight.

Imagine that.

I stepped out into the hall, and Miriam brought a tray with a cup of creamy coffee for myself and a cup of dark tea for her. We lifted the handled mugs to our faces simultaneously and breathed in the smell, almost a mirror image.

I giggled, "Some might think we spend too much time together, Miriam."

She scowled at me. "Well, if you'd leave every once in a while, we wouldn't."

I almost spit out the sip I'd just taken.

I let out a sigh of satisfaction as I enjoyed the first half of my coffee. I nodded at Miriam as we walked into the first room— together. She'd already started to clean this one. A bedroom with a massive four-poster bed and a fireplace that probably hadn't seen a flame in a hundred years.

Miriam and I finished cleaning it, top to bottom. It took an hour, but it made me feel strangely awake. Doing something human instead of forever sliding down the avalanche of existential crisis.

We moved on to the next one, and I unlocked the door with the metal key. There was a clank, and the door creaked open with an eerie groan that almost sounded like a yawn.

Inside, a desk in the center of the room faced a big, wallpapered wall. To the far left, the massive arched windows were adorned with long gossamer drapes that let in all the natural light.

The room looked spotless. I looked at Miriam. "Did you clean this one already?"

She eyed me with suspicion. "No? Did you?"

I scoffed. "Miriam... you watched me unlock it."

"You never know!" She threw her arms in the air like it wouldn't have been impossible.

I stepped in and sat on the leather chair positioned at the desk. A typewriter was perfectly positioned in the center, and a blank page was placed inside. The room looked ready for someone to sit down and tell a story. It looked as if it was waiting for... *me*.

I'd promised not to think of curses and magic, but there was something haunting about this room—something that made it feel *intentional*.

I hovered my hands over the keys of the typewriter, and a vibration traveled through my fingers, begging me to type, to press any combination of letters that might form even one word. But a sorrow washed over me as I realized that even if I wanted to find words, I didn't have any to give this typewriter.

However, this did feel like *the* room. It felt like the place I could start trying. I reached out and pressed the 'T' key on the typewriter. The arm slammed the paper abruptly, and Miriam jumped back as if it were a scene from a horror story.

A single, solitary 'T' now viciously impaled the paper.

It's an eerie detail that even though this typewriter sat untouched for who knows how long, the letter I placed on the page was in glaring black ink. Not dried out and crusted, the ink was fresh and hadn't turned to dust like almost everything else in this Estate.

It was as if it were freshly replaced and waiting to be used.

I quickly brushed aside the oddity I'd discovered since weirder things had occurred here, of which I was sure.

'A-Y-L-O-R.'

They say all it takes is one.

This room had a magnificent view. Why the desk was facing the big blank wallpapered wall when there was so much to take in near the window was beyond me.

I stood and looked at Miriam. "We'll do more tomorrow."

She shrugged, flung a towel onto her shoulder, and left the room with her supplies.

The discovery of this room excited me a little. I felt a building of anticipation and, for the first time in what felt like years, a little bit of *hope.*

I went into my bedroom and dug out my laptop, charging cables, notepads, and pens. I dragged anything I'd boxed up from my LA office across the hall to the room I now called 'the Study.' I set up what I could and piled up the boxes that didn't need to be opened into the corner against the wall.

I was busy admiring the intricate details of my new writing desk when I glanced over and saw the time. It nearly slapped me in the face. I had become too used to the days blurring together.

Time was a miserable concept *before* Cass had come to visit, but now I was regularly keeping track of where my days had wandered off to.

I grabbed my phone and started making the calls I should have made months ago. I put in a requisition with the local internet service provider to get high-speed internet and cable. I called two contractors to see about making some upgrades and enhancements to this old mansion, including ensuring the wiring and electricity were solid and safe.

My productivity made my head spin, and as I sat reveling in the day's accomplishments, I found myself thumbing over a small scrap of paper containing a phone number I had thought about calling every hour since she'd placed it in my hand.

But I hadn't called.

I'd feared her finding out that I was a fraud or no one special, that I wasn't worthy of her time and, clearly, on the verge of full-on alcoholism. I was a liability for whomever I chose to pursue, and I knew it... Someone else would eventually figure it out, too, and it would be Dante all over again.

I called the number anyway.

"Hello?" There it was, that voice that went with a smile I couldn't get out of my mind.

"Hello, it's—T-Taylor," I slipped on my own name. Admittedly, I didn't know how people talked on the phone anymore.

"Taylor." She repeated my name back with affection, I could hear the smile in her tone. *She remembered who I was.*

"I was wondering when you'd call."

She had been waiting too.

"I hope you are ready to take me up on that offer?"

"Offer?" I asked, slightly confused.

"To paint you."

"Maybe we could start with dinner? At my place?" I asked, knowing it was an insane invite. But I didn't know how to *be* with her in a public space. I'd never done anything like this before.

"When?" *Oh, shit... She didn't say 'no'. What was I doing?*

"When are you free?" It blurted out. I felt like something had taken over, and I could no longer control my actions.

"Tonight?" she asked.

My heart raced at the idea that Emma could be here within a few hours, with me... alone.

"I'll text you the address." I had to remain calm. That was the most relaxed thing I knew to say. I felt a rush of lack of control squeezing into my mind. I didn't want to start acting on impulse— I wanted to be intentional with her.

"See you later."

Thank God she hung up.

The tone of her voice made my knees weaker with every vowel. How was I going to get through dinner without bursting into flames or becoming a full-on feral maniac?

I waited a few moments to avoid seeming overly eager and then pressed send, unleashing the address to the Estate.

The anxiety jostled my mind as I ran down the list of things that could all make the evening go terribly wrong. If I am lucky, she doesn't *Google* the address. Otherwise, she will find the Halethorpe Estate and all the articles about my inheriting it.

However, those stories will then send her careening straight for all of the old TMZ posts about the decline of my book, the failed movie that never saw the light of day, and, worst of all, the video of when paparazzi accosted Dante with his new fling leaving *our* condo before the world knew we'd ended things.

"Artists don't use Google, right?" I said it aloud, even though I was alone. This room made me feel like someone else was here to answer my questions. It made me feel as though I had a real friend—that I wasn't alone.

∗∗∗

Of course, I'd been waiting. I'm gnawing at the skin on the side of my thumbnail, picking at it. I'd paced enough that I'd started to break a sweat. If I stayed in place any longer, I'd wear a pattern in the perfectly preserved plank flooring.

I watched the long drive for a flash of light for at least forty-five minutes before I saw her. Her car—a beat-up hatchback—pulled up to the porch, looking absurdly out of place against the Estate's towering façade. My breath caught as she stepped out, dressed in loose linen pants and a tank top, her bag slung over one shoulder, paint-splattered like everything else she owned.

I met her at the door, my heart racing.

"You found it," I said, forcing a smile.

"Hard to miss," she replied with a grin, brushing past me into the foyer. Her eyes went wide as she took in the space, the high ceilings and dark wood paneling, the chandelier that looked like it might fall any second. "This place is—"

"Yeah," I said, closing the door behind her. "It's old."

Emma turned, her head tilting as she studied me. "It's beautiful, though. Do you see it?"

I laughed, a sharp, humorless sound. "Maybe, a long time ago... It's falling apart now."

"That's part of what makes it so magnificent," she said, walking further in. Her fingers grazed the edge of the staircase banister. "She's tragic, but she's so much more than that." She faced me, looking into my eyes. "God, you must write beautiful stories here."

I stared at her, caught off guard by the observation. "Not quite," I said, my voice wavered.

She turned back to me, her gaze steady. "Well, you could."

She darted off, her curiosity pulling me into rooms we'd only just unlocked this morning. She marveled at the ornate wallpaper, the cracked molding, and the forgotten furniture cloaked in sheets like ghosts waiting for something to haunt.

When we reached the sitting room, she stopped, turning to me with a smirk. "You're going to let me draw this, right?"

"Draw what?" I asked, confused. "It's a room…"

"The light's perfect in here." She dropped her bag and began rummaging through it, pulling out a sketchbook and a box of charcoal. "I'll make it look how it feels. You'll see."

I leaned against the doorframe, watching as she crouched in the middle of the room, already lost in her work. Her hand moved quickly, smudging and shading, her expression focused but free.

"Do you always do that?" I asked after a long silence.

"Do what?"

"Throw yourself into things."

She looked up at me, her charcoal-streaked fingers still moving. "Life's too short to second-guess everything."

Her words felt like they had a double meaning, both meant for me. I stayed silent, watching her work until she held up the sketch. It was far more detailed than I could have imagined in such a short time.

"What do you think?" She asked, holding it out to me.

I hesitated before taking it, my fingers brushing hers. "It's beautiful," I said honestly.

She smiled, the same knowing smile she'd given me at the gallery. "I know she is," she said softly.

She stepped closer toward me, close enough that I could see the slight smudges of charcoal on her cheek and the flecks of gold in her hazel eyes. "Taylor," she whispered my name, and my body jolted at it falling off her lips.

"Yeah?" My voice, breathy, and my tone an uneven whisper.

"Stop overthinking," she murmured, and before I could think of another thought, she leaned in.

Her lips brushed mine, tentative at first, to see if I'd pull back, and after a heartbeat, she was warm and confident. The moment unfroze me, and I took the advice.

I didn't second-guess, and I let whatever was holding me go, deepening the kiss. Her hand brushed against my cheek, and she tickled my jaw as I breathed her into me. I didn't want to stop.

She slowly pulled back and smiled. My entire perspective of her had changed in an instant.

"See?" she said, her voice still soft but back to its airy tone. "You don't have to *get* everything to feel it."

The Estate felt impossibly quiet after Emma left. She had a way of breathing life into everything. I'd stood in the living room for what felt like hours. My stare locked on the dancing flames of the fire.

My phone buzzed violently.

Thirteen missed calls

Nick.

CHAPTER 12

AN ADDICTION
2019

His only text was short and clipped.

'OMW. Don't ignore me.'

Suddenly, the sound of a door slamming echoed through the foyer, rattling the stillness and peace of the Estate.

"Taylor!" He called out, his voice brash, ricocheting off the plaster walls, scattering the peace like a stone tossed into the glass surface of a lake.

I stepped into the main hall with my arms crossed. He stood there, his leather jacket slung over one shoulder, his signature smile unrelenting.

"*Jesus...* You could have told me you were there," he sighed. "This place gives me the creeps. I thought you were a ghost."

I shrugged. "It's just a house."

He let out a sharp bark that made my skin crawl. "A house? Taylor, this is a fucking castle." He laughed a little. "You're so delusional about your entitlement sometimes. It's sick."

"I'm not entitled, Nick." I stiffened. "What do you want?"

He didn't answer right away. Instead, He poured himself a drink from the sidebar like he owned the place. His glass hung casually in his hand as he walked toward me.

"You," he said, his voice falling into a low growl, his smile shifting into something darker,

Before I could respond, his lips were on mine, heavy and demanding. My hands pressed against his chest to push him away, but part of me froze. Old habits, old feelings—too tangled for me to sort out.

He grabbed my wrists with an aggression that heated my soul. A visceral yearning that made me feel *seen*. I felt my bracelet press into my skin. He was clamping down with a pressure that made it hurt, but the ache was a reminder that I was still alive. I could still *feel*.

"No one is going to care the way I do," he whispered against my lips, and again, I believed him.

"I hate you," I murmured back, my voice weakening to the physical desire I had for him.

"No, you don't," he replied, still smirking.

His hands released my wrists and slowly slid to my waist, pulling me closer with a firm tug. I let myself fall entirely into his familiarity.

I knew the void I'd have in the morning, but I didn't care. "Stay," I heard myself say, the words fleeing from my mouth before I could hesitate them away.

"Of course," he said, as if he'd known I'd give in.

He always knew.

✳✳✳

Miriam's loud clatter of cleaning broke the stillness of the morning *again*. I opened one eye, squinting against the sunlight streaming through the curtains. The sheets twisted around me and my clothes in a precise path leading from the door.

Nick was gone. Thank God.

The guilt had settled deep into my chest overnight and pressed into my ribs, shortening my breaths. Despite Miriam's calamity in the upper hall, my room felt quieter than usual. It's like it was waiting for me to acknowledge the mess I'd made, *again.*

I groaned, rolling onto my back and staring at the cracked ceiling. The kiss. Emma's kiss. Her hands on my face, her whispers telling me to stop overthinking. For a moment, I'd believed in the possibility of something new.

And then Nick.

I let him in... again. I closed my eyes, and vivid images flashed behind my eyelids. I cringed. I pressed the heels of my hands into my eyes, willing the shame and the visions to disappear. I wasn't in love with Nick. I didn't even really *like* him. He was just a bad habit I couldn't quit, the thing I reached for when I was getting too close to recognizing myself.

And Emma... God, Emma. She was so alive.

Instead of leaning into her warmth, I'd crawled back into the dank hole that was Nick, the darkness I deserved, and I felt cold all over again.

I grabbed my phone and saw a missed call from Cass about an hour earlier. I straightened myself out and walked across the hall to the Study. Miriam brought me a cup of perfect coffee, and I called Cass. I stared into the swirling steam from my cup, how it danced with the bursting sunlight in the Study. It was miraculous how this room got the best sunlight, given its position in the Estate.

"Hey," I said before she could say anything.

"I..." I paused. "I need help."

The silence on the other end was deafening. It stung.

"What can I do?" She broke the silence. "I'm sorry, I've just never heard you ask for help before." She wasn't hesitant. She was in disbelief.

"Can you get me a few ideas that Everbound would be *more* willing to entertain, and I'll use them? I'm writing, but... I'm coming up with *nothing.*"

"I can get you a list of hot novel ideas. Pete just sent an email for priority manuscripts. If you send me something for one of these, it's a guaranteed win." A clattering of keyboard clicks in the background.

"Sent. Check your inbox."

"Thank you—I don't say it to you enough."

"Hey, Tay?" She paused. "Are you really okay, or... do I need to call someone?" I heard the worry in her tone.

"No, I'm not there yet." I choked back the tears fighting their way from the back of my eyes.

"What happened? Tell me."

"What hasn't happened?" I joked as I sipped my coffee.

"Give me the TLDR because I'm about to walk into a meeting." I heard the muffled attack of her ripping into someone for not giving her a minute.

"You're busy..." I pulled back.

"No, give me the two-minute DL, and I'll text you back while in this meeting." She laughed at herself. "It should have been an email."

"I kissed Emma, and I practically fell in love, and then, immediately after she left, Nick came over, uninvited—again, and I didn't make him leave, and I feel dirty about all of it." I sniffled as the tears rolled down my cheek.

"Oh—my—you weren't kidding..." She paused. "First, we're going to get a little thing called a protective order on Nicholas—what's his last name?" she asked.

"Foster," I said jokingly, "I *am* okay. I need somewhere to start."

"You've got the perfect setup for a great story right there, Taylor. That house of yours? It's practically alive. My God, if those walls could talk, they'd probably write a damn book for you." I heard the muffled rush in the background. There was an eerie chattering as if the air around me had agreed with Cass.

"Tay, I have to go, but I'll call you back tonight. We'll drink wine, and you can tell me all about Emma."

"Ok, ok, go. Bye." I ended the call and sat for a moment... The email she'd sent buzzed through, but I flipped my phone screen face down.

Her comment lingered in the air long after the call ended.

If only these walls could talk.

I leaned back in the chair, staring around at all of the details of the Study. The whole house was silent, the kind of silence that unsteadies most people, but I'd become used to it. It was the Halethorpe Estate's signature voice.

My gaze drifted to the blank wall opposite me—the one the desk so oddly faced, positioned across from me like it was ready for its interview.

"What would you say, hmm?" I playfully teased the inanimate wall that stared back at me blankly.

"The strong, silent type, eh?" I joked as I tossed my pen onto the blank pad of paper. Just then, the air seemed to shift. A soft creak echoed through the room, but nothing had pressured it to move. It felt like someone was standing in front of me. A presence that made itself *very* apparent.

And I froze in a moment of panic.

"Miriam!" I shouted as I stood quickly and rushed out of the room, my chair spinning wildly from my momentum.

CHAPTER 13

HAUNTED
2019

I chased Miriam down after the moment in the Study. I'd known this Estate, in part, my whole life, and I'd never considered the Estate haunted or that it ever *felt* haunted.

Eerie, yes. Creepy? *Sometimes,* I can admit it.

But haunted—a dangerous, demonic dwelling?

A place where I felt unsafe or feared for my life?

Never.

Well, not until…

But it was also safe to say that I spent so little time here as an adult. Manifestations of ghosts, apparitions, haunts, or things of that nature weren't something a child or a teenage girl would regularly consider.

Perhaps, like other things in my life, I'd merely ignored the fact that the Halethorpe Estate was haunted. It was the avoider in me who'd refused to admit it.

If I were going to ask this question to anyone, it would have been my mother, but with her untimely departure from this world, Miriam would be the next best connection to the Estate.

She'd spent as much time here as I had, years more even since she was older than myself but younger than my mother.

"Miriam," I paused, hesitating at the weight of my next question.

"What do you know of this Estate?" I was intentionally vague to let her steer the conversation.

"The Halethorpe Estate is a legacy. It's been here for many years in this community. It used to be the epitome of luxury and glamour. My grandmother used to tell me stories of the grand balls, social events, and parties." She flashed a reminiscent smile. But she was holding back. This was the run of the mill advertisements I saw too often. I wanted to know something deeper.

"I think I remember my mother telling me about those too. She was just a girl when they stopped having the social events."

A memory that I hadn't recollected buzzed through my mind. I watched the vivid images play back like an old film strip of my mother disappearing for days, leaving me with Edward. But she'd tell me these magical stories about princesses and heroes when she returned.

I shook away the distracting, irrelevant memory.

"I'm looking for something else... Something more... ghostly?" I targeted the question using my tone.

Miriam's eyebrow arched, her lips pursed together, the outlines turning a pale white with the pressure.

"What are you asking, Lady Halethorpe?" She wasn't playing my game, which is something I appreciated about her.

"Miriam." My eyes met hers. "Is the Estate haunted?" The words tumbled out.

"Haunted?" she smiled, "You read too many books, Taylor." She stood, walking toward the sink in the kitchen.

"You mean to tell me that you've never felt the breeze the wrong way or like the house was listening to you?" I paused. "Never?"

I stood from my stool, and she stopped, "Sometimes."

My eyes widened. "I knew it!" I playfully shouted at her.

She turned briskly towards me and shook her head. "If we don't acknowledge it, it isn't real."

"Ha! Miriam, that's nonsense." I shifted in my chair, thinking about the extent to which the Halethorpe Estate could be haunted.

"When did you first notice it?"

"Lady Halethorpe, I don't think it's wise to speak of such... evil." Miriam's face was broad with concern.

"Are you afraid of this Estate, Miriam?"

"No, not afraid, I just know better."

⁂

The sun had just started to set when it felt like I finally had something to say. I loaded paper into the antique typewriter, looked around the room, and began. The first sentence was all I needed. The words started to flow out of my fingers like a river once held back by a dam. They were liquid and fluid, dancing around the page in an elegant tango.

Until they weren't anymore, and I came to a dead stop.

My finger hovered delicately above the spacebar, my heart pounding inside my head, rattling against my skull. I had stopped mid-sentence of my story, entered a few lines down, and interrupted my writing with a rogue thought.

How do I find a story inside me when I am still hollow?

And I meant it.

The sun began to creep below the far distant horizon. Its last gasps of breath lingered on the dust-covered window of the study.

I took a deep breath.

"Who is Taylor Halethorpe?"

My fingers moved without thinking, as if the words had written themselves on the paper. I was merely the vessel that carried them there.

Who was I?

Where was I?

It was a turning point in my life. I left behind the wreckage of failed success and looked toward what kind of artist I wanted to be. I had arrived at a crossroads where an indelible line was being drawn for me—in this room, right now.

Write whatever comes next. I thought to myself.

"Evelyn Halethorpe used to say that you are what you read." A voice clattered the room with a deep, orotund voice, almost... aristocratic.

"My internal dialogue is just dying to be male," I thought as a joke and let out a soft chuckle. I'd always said I wished to approach confidence like a middle-aged businessman. I guess my subconscious was taking such desires seriously.

"Taylor Halethorpe, you are not a middle-aged businessman. For that, we should thank the good lord." The voice bickered back to me.

"Yes, it's certainly the *good lord* we should be thanking," I scoffed.

I didn't want to lose the momentum, so as the thoughts flew, I clattered them down onto the typewriter's keys. The rattle and the typewriter's limitations were the only things slowing me down.

I stopped after I keyed the last punctuation mark.

A strange thought hit me, like a plot hole I'd discovered too late into editing. How would I have known that Evelyn Halethorpe said anything? She died before I was born.

"You didn't know, obviously. I told you. That is what we call a *quote.*"

I tilted slightly to the side, and my eyebrows dropped on my forehead in confusion.

"Who?" was all I could muster as the creeping, slow-rising suspicion infiltrated the back of my head, the thought growing and blossoming like a flower in the night, odd but miraculously beautiful.

"Are you... a ghost?" I asked the ridiculous question in fear and exhilaration all at once.

"Heavens, no. Ghosts smell terrible."

"That's enough." I stood and exited the room with a speed I didn't realize my legs had. I ran for my room across the hall, thrusting the doors open, leaping into my bed, and crawling under the covers as if they were something that would protect me from the apparent apparitional experience.

I heard the grandfather clock on the lower level chime and knew that it was eleven o'clock, and somewhere shortly after that, I fell into a deep, restorative sleep.

✳✳✳

I'd nearly forgotten what had happened the night before, and despite not having more than a single glass of wine, I credited the interaction to my loose overindulgence. I was drunk. That was all.

I met Miriam in the kitchen for breakfast. She'd made homemade bagels, and as I smeared the soft cream cheese onto one side and began eating it like a sandwich, she eyed me with curiosity.

"You worked late last night, no?" Her eyebrow rose like it did when she was about to say something off the wall.

"Yes. It's my new thing, *working*." I responded sarcastically, with my mouth full.

"Write anything good?" She was digging for something.

"I'm writing a very hedonistic novel, where a woman... has *experiences* with the ghost that lives in her house." I'd pulled the idea straight from Cass.

Miriam's interest was piqued. "What kind of experiences?" she asked, not realizing what I meant.

"Orgasms, big, earth-shattering, scream out in pleasure... orgasms," I said as I smiled wildly at her.

Her cheeks immediately blushed a deep red. "Taylor! The more you write, the further from the Lord you stray..." She started to panic and cleaned the kitchen as I sat, holding my ground with a playful smirk.

"You know I'm only joking, but also... why are you so interested in my writing, hmm?" I paused. "Something you want to say?" I let the question hang in the air, and it seemed she had no desire to answer it.

I finished the last bite of my bagel and walked toward the sink with my plate, but she swooped in front of me and took it from my hands.

"Go... *work*." She eyed me with defiance. "We both need a place to live." She smiled at the slight dig at my crumbling finances.

I took her advice and returned to the second story. I creaked the Study door forward, and it howled its usual yawn as it slowly opened. I hesitantly peered around the corners of the room without stepping in. I searched behind the door and focused on the distant window to see if the curtains had been disturbed.

Nothing.

The room looked unremarkable and precisely as I'd left it last night. Or so I think it did. I didn't take an inventory before I scurried away like a scared cat.

"Hello?" I asked gently in a soft voice.

"Hell-lo-o-ow?" Dragging out the ending vowel in a melody. *Nothing but silence.*

I stepped into the room, pulled the tan leather chair out from the desk, and found everything I'd written exactly where it was before. Untouched and, hopefully, *un*-haunted.

I found the free thought paper still lodged in the typewriter and released it. Sitting back in the chair and swinging my legs onto the desk, I reread everything I'd pulled together last night.

"Evelyn Halethorpe says, 'You are what you read.'"

The idea that I didn't honestly know much about anyone who'd ever lived in this Estate hit me harder than I'd imagined. I live here *now.* This was my family's legacy, and I'd never learned to respect it.

I might have realized I was sitting on creative gold if I had.

"The Halethorpe Chronicles," I said aloud as if I were trying on a new dress or pair of shoes.

"By Taylor Halethorpe."

Something I didn't think would happen again in this lifetime. But that was already too many *Halethorpes* for one book cover, and I'm not sure that name carried so much weight these days.

I snapped out of my daydream with a mission. "You are what you read," and this Estate had hundreds of books. There was an entire library that I never went into, for Christ's sake.

But first, I'd look a little closer. I pulled at the handles of the writing desk, but the first drawer was *locked*.

It's the same for the second and third. I arched my eyebrow and stuck the skeleton key that locked almost every room in this house, and the drawer lock clanked open.

Aha.

A single leatherbound book lay in the drawer, nothing surrounding it except air that smelled of decay and mildew. I reached down, slowly lifted the artifact from its spot, and opened it up, expecting to find finely printed words, the way words were printed on a press when bookmaking was a proper art form.

I flipped the pages, and to my surprise, this book was *blank*.

The pages were worn... like someone had tossed them through their oily fingers thousands of times. It looked like a well-read book, enjoyed and held tightly as a prized possession. But it wasn't a book at all. It had no story.

"Am I empty, too?" I whispered, the thought slipping from my lips. I saw these blank pages as a mirror, and I couldn't escape the idea that this was the story of Taylor Halethorpe, *empty and wordless.*

'You are what you read,' and the first book I open to read is blank, empty. It is *nothing.* I set the book down in frustration, grunting, "I guess I'll order something from the internet." I closed the drawer with a finite anger that I couldn't or wouldn't process.

I exited the room, and my phone buzzed in my hand.

Emma.

✳✳✳

Emma insisted on returning to the Estate. She'd said it opened her creative mind and had an 'enjoyable aura'. A thought I'd once found ludicrous, but the Estate itself was starting to grow on me too.

I found more things about it daily that made me marvel at its magnificence. I'd asked Miriam to help me find more information about its history and legacy, something more than what was written on the internet and in old newspapers.

I wanted to know what kept it alive all these years, what mysteries were inside, and what secrets it held. I didn't care much that an architect named T.L. Hamilton built it in the early 1800s. I didn't want to know about the generations of farmers who co-farmed this land alongside my ancestors. All of that was public knowledge. I wanted what was between the lines. I wanted what was buried deep in the foundation.

Miriam was on the hunt for journals. She said most of the Halethorpe women were writers and kept meticulous journals.

Were they writers? My mom watched me struggle against my father about my writing and my desire to be a writer, and she failed to tell me that I came from a long legacy of women who'd felt the same. The thought was jarring, and for a moment, disdain for my mother danced across my mind.

"So there's a pile of dusty journals in this mansion somewhere?" I asked Miriam.

"There could be, yes." Her eyes widened a little as she said it.

"Where did they write? Do you remember?"

"Your mother wrote in the room you call the Study. Evelyn often wrote in the garden, sometimes on the terrace by the library... Sometimes, she wrote in that same room, too." Miriam squinted her eyes like she was trying to recall more details.

"Come to think of it, *my mother* told me once they'd all written in that room, at least for a time."

"So the journals could be in there?"

"There's nothing in there, Taylor. You saw it. It's a desk and a wall."

"One I'm going to beat my head against," I grumbled. I'd felt like we were getting somewhere, but we'd just detoured through scattered remnants of an old lady's poor memories.

"I'm sorry, Lady Halethorpe. I know this is not what you are looking for." Miriam said as she polished a dish before putting it in the decorative cabinet.

"I'll find my story, Miriam. You wait and see."

CHAPTER 14

PAINTED PICTURE
2019

Emma arrived with her arms full of supplies. I stared at her, leaning against the wide front door frame. "What is all of that?" I asked, knowing I was going to get an off-the-wall response.

"My paints." She smiled as she dropped a leather pouch.

I walked out, meeting her halfway, and picked it up as she brushed past me. She smelled like clementines and daisies in the spring, and I closed my eyes, relishing in the comfort of it.

I took one last look at the setting sun in the distance before I closed the doors of the Estate. The calm winter sunset was sometimes even more beautiful than a Maryland summer setting. The kaleidoscope of chilled pastels looked like a painting themselves. Perhaps Emma brought such beauty along with her.

I met her inside, and Miriam was already bringing a cup of something warm and steamy, setting it delicately on the table and quietly disappearing.

Emma crossed the room in a single fluid motion, her arms sliding around my neck, pulling me into a kiss before I could protest—or even breathe.

I almost instinctively wrapped my arms around her, combing my fingers through her wild, dark hair. My hands reached each other, and my bracelet slid down. A tickle that grounded me in the perfection of the moment.

We'd kissed before, but I wasn't sure if it had been a stray entanglement or something more. I leaned into it and savored the moment. I let my mind release all of the uncertainty and owned my desire to kiss this woman—her soft lips, gentle touch, and the heat of our bodies pressed against each other.

As she pulled herself back, she smiled at me, "You are..." she didn't finish, "You are something else." I let the minor fact that she couldn't tell me what I was *either* meddle with my expression.

"Something else," I repeated mockingly.

"Where can I paint you?" she questioned.

I softly stared at her, not answering the question.

"You're not serious, are you?" I finally asked, cracking the silence she always felt comfortable in.

"I'm doing this, Tay, and you're coming along for the ride." She said it with a certainty that couldn't be denied.

I let out a sigh, indicating my resignation.

"The Study." It flew out. Did I want to be painted in my mother's office? In the administrative center of the Halethorpe legacy? In a room that was inexplicably haunted?

"Sounds like you," Emma giggled.

"Upstairs. Let's carry this stuff up." Picking up her massive bags and portfolio case, we hauled them up the grand staircase. We arrived at the top, nearly out of breath from carrying supplies and laughing at the clumsiness of the moment.

My eyes caught her smile as she laughed back at me, and I realized I didn't laugh as much as I used to. The sound felt foreign. This moment felt slightly uncomfortable as my heart fluttered around its innocence.

The lights were dim in the hall. Old wiring and barely bright light bulbs in sconces lined both sides, casting bright bursts of light over the patterned, aging wallpaper.

I gestured, "That one," to the tall door of the Study, and as it creaked open, the room revealed itself with an eerie stillness. I walked in and clicked on the lamp, and instantly, the brightness burst over every surface, gilding it in gold.

This lamp looked like it belonged in a museum, but oddly, it was one of my favorite things about the room. Arguably, it wasn't even as old as the house. It was probably a later addition, maybe by Evelyn herself.

"This room, Tay... It's..." Her sentence faded off as she paced around it. "It's incredible."

She was fascinated by a room, which I found hard to understand, but I suppose that's just how visual artists worked. Everything they put their eyes on was a work of art. I was envious of such an ability since nothing I'd thought of was a story worthy of telling.

If only every word I wrote was *incredible* for Everbound Press. I wouldn't be fighting so hard for my credibility back. I wouldn't be battling demons and bargaining with the Gods to restore my flailing career.

Emma set her easel at an angle that caught the desk facing the wall just right. I was surprised she didn't position herself toward the desk and the distant window, as it felt like something beautiful an artist would want to paint.

"Why not toward the window?" I asked as she kept diligently setting up her supplies.

"The window's nice, yes." She nodded and smiled, "But this wall is a blank slate."

She set her brushes on the folding table and slowly stepped toward me. She brushed a piece of my hair from my face, "Like you." She kissed me again, and I realized this was going to be something that would happen regularly.

"Now, sit here, and... write," she pulled the chair from the desk while her face was still close to mine. I could see the glow in her eyes and hear the beat of her heart.

"Write? I thought you were painting me?" I whispered.

"I am... while you write."

"What if I don't have anything to write?" I knew I didn't, but I didn't want to appear as an artist who couldn't make her art in front of an artist who *lived* to make hers.

"You do, Tay, you do," she disappeared behind the canvas while I prepared for something I wasn't entirely ready for.

"You overthink," she continued, "and it stops you from feeling everything you've locked inside." I heard the brush swipes against a textured canvas.

"I think far less than you might believe," I joked, my fingers hovered ever so slightly above the old typewriter, still unwilling to commit to even a single sentence.

Her soft voice came from behind the canvas, "Have you ever been in love?"

The question stopped me cold as it was unexpected and too personal for the moment. I blinked at the typewriter. Having Emma stare at my finest details to paint me cracked open my vulnerability, but now she was asking immensely personal questions, too.

"I'm sorry?" I asked, keeping my expression calm and collected despite wanting to squint in disgust.

"Have you ever loved someone, non-platonically, the way they write it in novels?" She clarified, and I felt the tightness in my chest ease slightly. Still, it wasn't a question I wanted to answer.

"Like Shakespeare's love? Or like, modern-day Romance novel love?"

"Aren't they both love?" She asked, ever the philosopher.

"I've never wanted to poison myself to death over someone if that's what you're asking." I quipped, breaking the weight of the conversation. My fingers almost touched the keys, but nothing made them move.

"So, Romance novel love?" She pressed, ignoring my deflection.

"I've had passionate engagements," I answered, hoping it was enough for her to move on.

"But not *love.*" Her response was quick, like she saw through me.

I hesitated as a lump in my throat started to rise. I reached for a glass of water to take a sip. "I thought I was once," I admitted. "I was engaged, actually."

"Really?" her tone softened, perhaps, now sorry she'd asked.

A memory of Dante scampered across my mind. His sharp jawline and confident smile appeared like a ghost that still haunted me. "I'm not talking about this."

Emma's brush stopped, but she didn't lean out from behind the canvas. A moment of silence passed, and her brush hit the canvas again.

"It's in the past, Tay." She said gently, "You can stop feeling bad about anything that's happened before this moment because it's already over."

Maybe she was right, or perhaps it was my past that made me who I was. Taylor Halethorpe was the collective trauma of her life, *and* she was a writer.

My fingers hit the typewriter.

'But maybe *Taylor* Halethorpe says, "You can write anything you want."

And I kept going.

THE MIDDLE YEARS

AUTHOR ERA
2020-2024

CHAPTER 15

A VOICE, UNRELENTING
2020

On every news channel, they were calling it a global shutdown. We weren't supposed to leave our homes unless it was essential. When we did, we wore masks, stayed six feet apart, and tried not to breathe too deeply in the presence of other people.

The world had never felt lonelier.

The streets were barren and abandoned, like a ghost town that stretched across the country. Houses were darkened without hope. We'd taken our big, wide world and shrunk it down into just a tiny space for us to survive in.

For all its horrors, one thing comforted me during those endless weeks of isolation and uncertainty: People were *reading*.

Books became a solace, a way to escape the madness. Stories became the only way to reach each other in a world where the circumstances tore away our human connection. I watched sales soar, headlines praised the renaissance of the written word, and lists of "must-read quarantine books" flooded the market.

But I hadn't written a damn thing.

Cass calls more frequently these days. Video chat check-ins disguised as virtual happy hours, and sometimes *just because* calls where she doesn't even mention work. She'd tilt her glass of white wine and laugh, but her eyes searched my face, looking for signs of anything… weakness or progress.

Her deadline loomed two weeks away, and I had nothing to give her. No concepts, no pitches. Certainly not an outline. Just a growing collection of discarded notes and the ashes of the ones I'd tossed into the forever-burning fireplace.

But then there was the moment when everything changed.

In the blink of an eye, on a cold March night, even the fire at full rage couldn't knock the chill that permeated the Estate.

Every hearth was wildly burning, thanks to Miriam. She always ensured the property had enough firewood to last through an apocalypse—and, well, *surprise.*

We shared a cup of tea and watched the muted TV. The news without sound was louder than ever, with death counts and survival statistics on replay. It was nothing but somber stories of loss and regret.

I'd had enough of the onslaught and retreated to the Study, giving Miriam a nod before making my way up the grand staircase. As I moved through the door, Emma's supplies sat lifeless in the corner. The room began to glow for a moment, and I pictured her peeking out from behind the canvas with her sultry smile and wild eyes.

But it was just a trick my mind played. Her supplies were still there from that night she'd painted me, evidence that it had genuinely happened but a reminder that it wouldn't happen again soon.

I sat at the desk, staring at the notebook before me, and sighed. Cass had forwarded Pete's list weeks ago, and while I'd walked it a hundred times, nothing felt right. Nothing felt *mine.*

The world needed to be inspired. They needed a story of great love and hope that reminded them there was still something left to fight for in a world drained of its color.

The only one on the list that came close to hope...

Historical Romance.

Something so far off the beaten path of anything I'd ever consider writing. I knew as much about history as this pen in my hand. Or this wall in my office, I thought to myself.

"If these walls could talk," I muttered under my breath, "Maybe they *would* just write the damn thing for me." I chuckled, remembering what Cass had said that had tickled me with some inspiration.

I pushed the notebook away and tossed the pen at it. It rolled across the desk before it stopped. And then continued and clattered to the floor.

Odd.

"You're looking for love in the wrong places." A voice, one I'd heard before. Deep, rich, an aristocratic air to it. Coming from the very foundation of the Estate. It was like the *walls* were, in fact... talking.

I froze. No one was in the room. I knew that to be true.

My own internal dialogue wouldn't be able to startle me, would it? I would be thinking it, and because it was me—thinking, how could the thought startle me?

"Wh... who's there?" I said, my body chattering in a wave of fear.

"Love," the voice repeated, "It's what the world needs, isn't it?"

I hadn't had a single glass of wine tonight, just tea. This was *not* a hallucination. It couldn't be. It was too real.

"This isn't funny." I grew some confidence and said it louder to the room.

"Oh, that too. The world needs laughter."

I shot up from the chair and slowly backed away from the desk toward the door. My eyes snapped from corner to corner. I glanced behind all of Emma's supplies, a bare corner.

A crackle from the fireplace grabbed my attention, and my eyes swung to it without being asked.

"What... do you want?" My heart was pounding, and I felt it throbbing in my ears.

"Want?" The voice laughed, "It's not about what I want, Taylor Halethorpe. It's about what you keep asking for." The voice paused, "And are too afraid to take."

The candle on my desk flickered violently, but the air reached a stillness that made the small pants of desperation I was letting out sound like a roar.

"Start with Evelyn and Charlie."

I froze. "How do you know, Evelyn and Charlie?"

There was no answer.

I stood, waiting for an acknowledgment.

I slowly pulled myself back into the chair. I loaded a paper into the typewriter, and the clang of the load rattled the room.

I typed, 'Evelyn Halethorpe and Charlie Whittaker,' and slammed the enter key violently.

If the walls wanted to talk, I was going to listen.

CHAPTER 16

THE DEADLINE
2020

I fought the layers of exhaustion for hours last night while sitting completely still in the Study. In a battle of wits, I held out as long as possible, waiting for the voice to return and reveal its origin. I had to know if it was the isolation, a mental breakdown, or something far worse.

I'd fallen asleep somewhere after 1 am.

I woke to an almost blank sheet loaded in the typewriter. 'Evelyn Halethorpe and Charles Whittaker' was scrolled across the page's header, but the rest was blank.

I wiped my face with my elbow as my head raised and took in where I'd ended the night. My glass of water was still half empty, and the fire in the hearth was a slow sizzle as it took its last dying gasps of life.

It was a rainy day, and the large, fat drops slammed against the single-paned window and slowly crept down until they disappeared behind the sill.

I sat up straight, finally acknowledging that I was awake. I looked around at the Study like I'd never seen it before, waiting for something... anything.. to be different.

But again, it was unremarkable. Unscathed. It was the same room I'd walked into; before that, it was the same as the last time I was here. A light knock at the door startled me, and I yelped as the door swung open with its usual ringing groan.

"You're up early. Coffee?" Miriam asked, knowing the answer already as she placed the mug and saucer on the desk. She glanced at the sheet of paper in the typewriter and saw the familiar names.

"They had a beautiful marriage," She paused, "Full of adventure and love." Her smile widened as she silently recollected memories I could only wish to have.

"I wish I knew more..." my voice cracked as the day's first words crept out of my mouth with an uneven tone.

"You know, they were married for many years, and Evelyn... she passed on, and Charlie... he was left to learn to live a new life without her."

I scoffed. "So much for a *love story*." I pulled the paper out of the typewriter and tossed it into the metal trash bin next to the old desk.

"Ah, but it was... the way he *lived* after she was gone. He carried her spirit and made the most of every day." Miriam spoke like she was singing a love song, the way it flowed off of her tongue.

"Not all Happy-Ever-Afters end with riding off into the sunset, Taylor. Don't be so naïve." Miriam crossed her arms, her brow furrowed in a look of disappointment.

"I just wish I could find her journals," I said with longing as I took a big sip of the perfect mix of coffee and cream. Holding the cup's warmth in my hands, I was colder than I had realized.

"You'll find her story, Lady Halethorpe," Miriam said as she tossed an oak log into the hearth and meandered through the door, mumbling a list of reminders for herself.

I leaned back in my chair, reflecting on what it meant to write a love story when you were not so sure you'd ever truly experienced love before. There were moments when I loved things, but had I ever been in love? It was an honest question and one I felt I already knew the harrowing answer to.

Happy ever after had only looked one way to me. The industry standard of dying happily next to the person I loved. *The Notebook* style.

My phone rang before I could answer it.

Cass.

I answered, "Hey!" I tried to sound overly confident to hide the impending doom that I would miss her deadline and let her down one final time.

"How's... *everything?*" she asked, as I heard her turn the sink on and clatter dishes in the back.

"Still isolating, but I've been writing something spectacular. Alright, I'll tell you. It's a historical romance, if you must know." I said before she could even ask.

"That was on the list!" There was a glint of pride and excitement in her voice, and I didn't have the heart to break hers. Not now, not today.

"I can't wait to read it, Tay. It's going to be great." Her faith in me was woefully misplaced, but I let it remain because, for a moment, it felt good, even if I lied to get it.

"We'll talk soon." The lie began festering, as they often do. "I'll send what I have by the deadline."

"Dragging that one out 'til the last minute, eh?" As if she expected I'd be done early.

"When have I ever been on time for anything?" I asked jokingly as I heard my phone beep with another call.

Nick.

"Hey, Cass, I'm getting another call. I'll call you back."

I switched calls quickly.

"What do you want?"

"I'm unblocked! It's a miracle." His snappy tone sharper than usual.

"I didn't block you, Nick. You lie about being blocked when you don't call me for weeks." I wasn't playing this game anymore.

"Hey, I need a favor. I wouldn't ask if... I had some gigs fall through because I'm not *essential.* I need a place to crash." The request hit me like a brick in the chest.

"No, absolutely not," I said with certainty.

"Please, just a few nights, I—"

"You wore out your welcome. It seems to be happening a lot." I paused. "No, Nick. Absolutely not." I doubled down.

I hung up the phone before he could say another word.

***

I finished a scavenged dinner of whatever I could find in the fridge that required little effort and returned to the Study. I pulled my glasses down onto my face and determinedly approached the chair, the desk, and the typewriter. No formal introductions were needed.

I wasn't leaving this room until I had enough to send Cass. Not until I had something that would make her proud. I loaded the typewriter with another blank sheet of paper and typed out the words I'd left here with the night before.

Evelyn Halethorpe and Charles Whittaker.

I took a deep breath, and as my pinky finger reached for the next key, I was met with the voice I'd been waiting to hear. It was like a melody that had been stuck in my head. A song I couldn't stop repeating. They were talking again, and this time, I was ready.

"Evelyn wasn't a woman you could ignore." The Walls began slowly. The tone and tenure of the deep voice was rich with a grand reverence. "She sailed across the rink as she owned it, the mirror ball reflecting bits of light onto her blue dress as she danced on her skates."

I started tapping away at the blank page, filling it faster and faster with the recollections of Evelyn and Charlie, of how they met, their courting, and how they fell desperately in love with one another.

"And then, there was Charlie," The Wall continued, with an adoration for him. "The poor boy couldn't stand on his skates even while holding the railing, but he had a smile that made you forget, or... made *her* forget. No matter how foolish he looked, she saw something more."

I looked up at the blank wall. It had no shape or mouth. It was unclear how its voice rumbled through the Estate, but only I could hear it. I whispered, my voice low so Miriam couldn't over hear me talking to *myself.*

"Is that really how they met? *Roller skating?*

"Does it matter?" The Wall replied bluntly. "What matters is that they did."

For hours, the Walls spun the tale of Evelyn and Charlie—a love story so rich it felt like it had already been told. They were the perfect couple of their time, not because they were flawless—in fact, their marriage had many flaws, but because they chose to fight for one another relentlessly through trials and tribulations.

But as you can recall, Evelyn passed away in 1985. Leaving Charlie with a void that could never truly be filled. Through their forty vivacious years of marriage, they experienced all of the moments that made life beautiful—starting a family, traveling abroad, and hosting community events in the grandeur of the Halethorpe Estate. Together, they faced anything the world threw at them with a grace that was to be admired.

When Evelyn fell ill, those they had invited into the warmth of their friendship and marriage rallied around them, proving they'd done it the right way.

However, their love story didn't end there.

No, Charlie wasn't ready for it to be over.

After her passing, Charlie made it his mission to honor her by living each day with purpose and intention. He became an even bigger pillar in his community, giving more than he took and always seeking to make others feel seen.

He turned the Halethorpe Estate into a sanctuary for wandering souls, allowing them the freedom to grow and heal from their broken parts, and he did all of this in Evelyn's name, in her honor.

Charlie took his work nationwide and left the Estate in the hands of Vivian, my mother. He spent his last years shepherding lost souls to their destinies and was laid to rest next to the love of his life, his muse, here at the Halethorpe Estate. A Whittaker by name, but a Halethorpe by heart.

✳✳✳

The Walls chattered away with vivid details of a story that hit me in the chest—a story about my own family. I'd been searching for evidence of love like this my entire life, and Evelyn, my mother's mother, lived the experience.

This was my legacy—*All Good Years.*

The typewriter clattered and snapped as my fingers went faster than it could handle. I became incredibly aware of the loudness of it all, and then, slowly, it distracted me, vibrating in my entire body with each keystroke. My mind was racing too fast for the keys, and for this typewriter, I was losing good material at the cost of the raging river of thoughts running through my mind.

With a frustrated sigh, I lifted the typewriter and carried it to the empty closet, leaving it on the floor, alone. I returned to my desk and pulled out my sleek, glossy laptop. Half of my story was written in the authentic elegance of the Halethorpe Estate, and the other half was on cutting-edge technology with a processor faster than twenty of my minds put together.

I thought to myself, guilt tugging just slightly at my disappointed artistic heart, that I would have to transcribe it anyway to send it to Cass.

I'd tapped away for hours, the glow of the screen lighting up my face, the brightness stinging my eyes, making me fully aware of the exhaustion creeping in.

The chime from the grandfather clock burst through the entire Estate. Usually, I'd tone out the sound, but as it chimed five times, I looked out the grand window of the Study to see that the world had started to brighten.

Despite it being morning, the full moon was still pinned in the sky, like a button lost among the finest pastel silks. Opposing it, an amber blaze of sun threatened to devour it by igniting the horizon.

The Walls had given me a story, and I had written at full speed for an entire night. I hadn't written with such passion in years... probably since *before Glass Heels*.

As that hungry sun rose fully over the Estate, the Walls's voice receded, and a silence hung in the room.

I let out a sigh of relief. I'd done it. I met the deadline.

And I'd finally written a story worth telling.

FROM ALL GOOD YEARS

CHAPTER 34

They made it to that hospital room, out of breath with sweat pouring down their faces, and it was at that moment that they realized life had left Evelyn's body.

Charlie didn't stare at her. Instead, he looked up as though searching for something to hold onto, trying to process the weight of what had happened. His expression was confused, his soul visibly distraught, and the blatant fact lingered: there would be no recovery for him here in this room, either.

He would leave his heart behind in this room... just like hers.

The only difference was that he would have to walk out on two feet, carrying death where his love used to live.

"Forty years, and not every one of them was great. But most of them were." He paused. "They were all good years." He nodded as a single tear fled from his cheek.

That's what he said while staring adoringly at his deceased wife, Evelyn. Her wedding band was still placed on her tiny finger, and as he ran his hands over hers, his fingertips lingered on her diamond.

I measured his expression and tried to locate a quantity of sorrow. Instead, I only identified the pensive recollections of a well-lived life and the untimely death of possibilities.

I could see that he had realized that this would be the final time he would hold her hand. Every moment he would hold her from this point on would live only in memories, all of which would soon start to decay and fade as they seemed to do once their muse had passed.

Despite the sudden separation of two great lovers by meeting life's ultimate end, this was a pinnacle moment for Charlie in a different way. This was the absolute recognition of the true meaning of loving someone. Forty years beside someone is longer than some people's whole lives separately.

A commitment so strong and a bond so special is created that you are only faced with one lone truth: if you can outlast the temptations of being human and overcome the obstacles of partnership, the inevitable... death will still eventually rip you from one another with no remorse.

Of course, the irony will be that you are surrounded by your friends and family who bring their own variation of love—but nothing, not a single thing, will fill the emptiness left behind.

This moment, for him, was like a bullet into a glass heart. Unmanageably shattered. A hole that penetrated so deep, an impact that hit with so much force, the bullet, an invader, sinking into this once healthy and thriving vessel, paralyzing it.

I could see the tiny fractures pushing outward from the point of impact. I saw his discontent when he realized that all he had to do was sign a single white sheet of paper, and it was all over. He'd walk away and leave her alone in that hospital room.

In this place, a Baltimore Hospital, on a day so beautiful that your skin bathed in the sun's gleaming warmth when you stepped out of the shadows... in this place, death was uncomplicated.

Do you know what it's like to drive home for the first time without the love of your life in the passenger seat? The hum of the road on the tires drowning out the soft groan of the speakers from the radio... It's a song that you know, but all you can hear is deafening silence.

There's a ringing as if, before the arrival of this silence, you had heard all the world's sounds at once. A silence that you will have to befriend because from now on—it's all you'll hear. It won't be cracked or interrupted by the voice of your soulmate.

For Charlie to hear what his heart yearned for most, he'll have to travel down memory lane, where he can recall life's sweetest moments and hang on to every detail. The drive home was only an hour, but an hour is an eternity when you can replay a memory of a weeklong vacation in seconds.

Your senses are heightened, and these memories almost feel real, like you could reach out and hold their hand one last time. This drive is a torturous form of time-travel trickery, for when you come to and are pulled out of your visit—your loss will hit you again.

Charlie pulled into the driveway of the Halethorpe Estate. He had left so abruptly to catch up with her that he noticed the front doors weren't closed completely. He sighed deeply at the idea of walking into the Estate without his wife by his side. He gazed up at the mansion with a deepening scowl of disappointment.

The sun was setting behind him—the day was over. The day that Evelyn left... this awful day was finally ending, and Charlie could only hope that tomorrow, when he woke up, it would all be a bad nightmare.

CHAPTER 17

BEST-SELLER
2020

I started my morning with a cup of vibrant citrus tea. The first tangy sip hit my tongue and snapped me out of a daydream.

"What the hell?" I stared disgustingly at the cup. *This wasn't like me.* After digging in three cabinets, I finally located the mugs, something I had done so infrequently, and it showed. A stranger to this part of the Estate.

I poured a freshly brewed cup of coffee from the full carafe. I felt an instant relief as the deep, roasty smell swirled through my senses.

I tapped my phone screen again, and the blue glow revealed no notifications. None. That meant there wasn't bad news, but also, there wasn't good news. An overwhelming feeling of being stuck in the in-between of perceived success or ultimate failure had me making orange-flavored tea, acting out in rebellion of my good sense.

A moment of nothing had me reaching for my wrist to thumb over the golden tether to my mother, who never left my side. It was the only thing that I felt connected me to her anymore. The Estate felt devoid of her, as if she'd gone from it completely. But this bracelet was my only chance to say I was sorry.

It was my way of carrying her with me every day.

I sat back at the kitchen island and clicked refresh in my inbox. Nothing new from the last time I'd smashed the button with the same contempt not even five minutes before.

While I waited for my future to reveal itself, I meticulously organized every unsolicited coupon and piece of unwanted junk mail. I'd even taken the time to unsubscribe from every retailer's mailing list that I'd joined for a welcome coupon.

The stagnant arrow from my mouse stared back at me, an unspoken digital taunt. A world un-romanticized by the instant gratification of technology. If this were 1820, I'd need to wait for a handsome messenger on horseback to bring me the news of my impending doom.

There was passion in anticipation, and while I longed for the slow-burn romance of *patience*. I also wanted a damn email.

I scribbled down three words, 'Handsome Messenger—Horseback,' on the notepad beside me and smiled.

I glanced down at my phone again. *Emma*. I let out a melancholy sigh. She had grown increasingly flighty during the mandatory isolation. I didn't blame her. These were strange and uncertain times for most of us.

I'm not sure how I missed the call. It was as if it hadn't even rung. No voicemail, either. I couldn't lie. I undoubtedly missed her, but I also didn't think much about her while writing *All Good Years*. Perhaps that wasn't the worst thing in the world, either. Distractions had only ever proven to impact my writing negatively, and without her, I had been focused.

Through its spoken word, I had let the Walls take me to places I could only dream of seeing in real life. I'd explored parts of my grandmother's life I don't believe even my mother knew about.

Over the days and nights of relentless chatter from the Walls, I'd slowly built an immense closeness to my heritage and the Estate itself. With each sentence, it became a definite part of who I was—who I was becoming.

The Walls—They were speaking to *me*. They had chosen *me*. Perhaps the Walls once talked to my mother, too. I see it now. I couldn't see it then... the signs. If only I could have asked her about them. About this Estate. If only I hadn't pushed her so far away.

Is this why Edward hated *writing* so much? He saw my mother wrestle with the never-ending pressure of the next story. Maybe he watched my mother's identity become the one the Walls gave her, too. This is why he fought so hard for me—to protect me.

The Walls weren't evil—indifferent... yes.

Powerful, even.

But vengeful or dangerous? Not quite.

Not Yet.

There was a distinct difference between my mother and I, though. I was doing *something*. I was using whatever this magnificent magic was for good. That's more than I can say for anything she had done. She let my father bully her into silence when she could have even been a miraculous storyteller—a famous one, even.

I returned Emma's call after I decided that I was safe to be distracted. In fact, a distraction was welcomed so that I didn't continue to refresh my email compulsively. I worked myself up to reconnect with the soft voice of my favorite wildflower and pressed the call button with a moment of hesitation.

No amount of pause could have prepared me for the wildflower encased in ice. Her petals frosted over and hardened. There was no small talk. She just wanted back the supplies she'd left that night in the Study. I tried not to read too far into it. After all, she was an artist, and I'd be a wreck if I were separated from my writing supplies. It wasn't a sign that she was withdrawing from me.

It couldn't be. Things were possibly about to take—

'All Good Years – Positioned for NYT Best Seller.'

The subject line took my breath away. I hesitated, my hand hovering over my mouse. "Not a taunt anymore," I whispered. The warmth of anxiety heated over my face. I'd waited all morning, incessantly refreshing, hyper-fixated, and now that the answer to what I'd been waiting for was staring me in my face, I was frozen in time. *Did I even want this?*

This was another realm of responsibility that I'd proven incapable of having.

I let out a deep breath and pressed down.

Taylor,

I don't know what you did or how you did it. But this is brilliant. Even the rough draft you sent had the entire publishing office hanging on your every word.'

I skipped the blurry, unnecessary details in between.

'Pete's fast-tracking it. It's with your editors. They're pushing production in less than a month. Advertising is starting today.'

I let out a sigh with my eyes closed.

Five years of stress slid off my shoulders, and the permanent tightness in my chest lifted. The entire weight I'd been carrying around, dragging me down, forcing me to measure myself against a person that I assumed didn't exist anymore...

'You did it, and I am so proud of you. Check out the first article...'

A bold blue text string glared at me, waiting for me to click it to unwrap the introduction of my grandparents' love story to the world. I clicked, and the large black headline made my heart leap delightfully. For the first time in a long time, I felt wild hope growing inside me. It was hope.

'Taylor Halethorpe is back!'

Words I had only dreamed about someone writing. Words I'd fantasized about seeing for years while I disintegrated into nothing here in this Estate. Words I thought were so far out of my reach that I'd never see them except in dreams alone. Today, in reality, my heart beating ferociously out of my chest, Taylor Halethorpe *was* back.

An abrupt knock interrupted me. I quickly closed the laptop and rushed to the door. Peering through the small box, I saw Emma's car, unattended and still running. The headlights pointed away from the Estate as if she positioned herself for a speedy getaway.

The realization caused a slight wince of disappointment to climb into my expression. I'd thought she'd want to talk or stay for a bit, but the idling car in my driveway showed that Emma had far different intentions.

I took a deep breath, cast the negative thoughts aside, opened the doors on my exhale to hide the nervous sigh, and forced a smile. But the expression that met me was far from the same. Emma's eyes told a story of reluctance, firmer than her usual jovial self.

"Tay," she said with only a hint of an obligatory smile.

"Em, come in." I gestured and allowed her space to pass through, closing the door with a loud clank behind her. I stood holding my hand against the center seam before I turned around. This was a critical moment for Emma and me, and I needed to play it right.

"Just here for my stuff, is all." She said in an incomplete sentence. I could tell she was throttling. She didn't want to accelerate into a whole conversation. A hesitation sparkled in her eyes, reminding me of her distance.

"It's been a while. Are you sure you don't want to stay for a bit?" I raised an eyebrow and smiled. "Miriam can make dinner?" I added, knowing how Emma felt about Miriam's cooking. I immediately regretted asking, as it felt like I was manipulating her by doing so.

"I really shouldn't." Her eyes lowered to the ground, masking something... different. Shame or regret, both appearing tragic in Emma's glowing hazel irises. I'd never seen her so *distant*.

"I'm not sick. I don't leave the Estate."

"It's not that, it's... I'm just thinking...." The pause... *she'd* been thinking. "This is too serious." She admitted, her face flush with the conflict.

"I thought..." I started but realized I didn't think about *what* Emma and I were. We were just something but hadn't had time to grow into anything. It seemed the world always had another plan for us.

'We're new?" I said, questioning not only her but myself.

"We're not supposed to be anything but fun," Emma said as if I had been a mind reader.

"I want you to stay," I said, reaching for her hand. When I touched it, she sighed. I could see her wanting to reciprocate my touch. Maybe it was my uncontrollable, sad eyes welling with tears, but I was making this decision difficult.

And honestly, I wanted to. I wanted to make it hard for her to walk away from whatever this was. This beautiful, flighty artist had never grounded herself, ever.

I wanted her to pick me.

"Please promise me you're not... like falling in love or anything." She tilted her head. "I can't do love," she finalized the thought.

"I am not in love," I reassured her with a chuckle, uncertain if I'd just lied, but I'd deal with the fallout on my own. I did know that I didn't want her to leave, not like this. I wanted more from her, even if it was one last night.

"Then I'll stay for a little while." She smiled. What's on Miriam's menu tonight?" Her devilish grin spread across her face as she looped her hand into mine, and we walked toward the kitchen. For a short moment, I took my mind off the excitement of my new career news and focused on the thrill of a fun night with the exhilarating artist who convinced me to believe in myself and my art form.

***

I was awake before the sun could barge into the darkness of my room. I didn't want it to interrupt this fleeting moment of bliss. Sleeping next to Emma had brought a comfort that had been missing from my nights here at the Estate. Her presence made me forget about what was happening outside of these walls. While she was here, I abandoned the possibility that the world could wake up today saying awful things about Taylor Halethorpe.

But now, in this dark office, I was ready—after a night of discovering my lost confidence, after being so vividly reminded several times that I was alive, I was prepared to handle what came next.

What awful things would be said about my attempt to reintroduce myself to the writing community? Would I see the attack of comments about my washed-up writing style or that I wasn't relevant in the historical romance genre?

Inbox: 250 Unread

It wasn't junk or spam. No, these emails were from real people: readers, sponsors, business owners, and reviewers, all excited for *All Good Years.* There were positive comments and words of encouragement. Some people even cited me as their favorite author.

"I know that's a damn lie," I mumbled to myself as I clicked through email after email. The feeling was more energizing than the cup of coffee missing from my hand as I let the world and its thoughts about me shine in.

"You did the story justice, I suppose." The voice interrupted my internal celebration.

"I would have made different artistic choices, but... I can't write. I can only sing the stories of the Halethorpe Estate to this sad writer with her shallow voice." It added.

"I resent that. I'm not sad. And my voice... isn't shallow." I replied, still clicking wildly through the e-mails, ignoring the Estate's bold insults.

"Then why is your heart aching for the woman who lies so gently in your bed? The one afraid to love you back?" The thought stung with honesty.

"We're reciting poetry now. How cute! Let me get my pen." I closed the laptop and stared at the blank wall with a searing glare.

"What do you want?" It was a direct question.

These Walls gave me a story that made my wildest dreams come true. It wasn't free... and certainly wasn't from the kindness of its heart, whatever shape it took. It was for a reason, and I'd just now thought of asking.

"What do you want?" I repeated myself with a sharper tone.

"I want to tell my stories," A pause, "I want to be heard."

I sat with the confession. The Walls were staging a bargain, a deal... A *curse*. But perhaps it could be mutually beneficial. I was a writer. The Walls had lived through decades of stories and secrets.

"I could write your stories," I blurted out but stopped.

I needed to select my next words carefully. "You give me the stories, and I will turn them into novels." I offered hesitantly.

The insanity of the moment wasn't lost on me. I was making a deal with the talking walls of my crumbling Estate, a mansion that had seen a life far grander than I could ever imagine.

The bargain hung between us for a moment while the Walls carefully considered what this agreement meant.

"Such a deal requires rules, Taylor. You should know that." The Walls rattled in response.

"And what rules would you find fitting?" I asked.

"I have two for you to consider. For a hasty decision could come at too great a cost for you." The Walls speaking in riddles sparked annoyance deep in my gut.

"You must never tell anyone of my existence. Speak of me, and I will disappear as quickly as I appeared."

"Easy enough, no one's going to believe the Walls talk to me, anyhow." I replied with confidence, "And the second?" Curiosity overwhelmed me—what could a wall demand from me that would result in an immense cost?

"One story for one sacrifice." The Walls recited the rule like they were singing a hymn.

"Sacrifices?" I questioned. "What is this, witchcraft?" I teased.

"The things in this life that you hold most dear, I will exchange one for a single story. Only you can decide which one is more valuable. The story, or *it*." The Walls clamored and chattered with an odd vengeance. A chill lingered down my spine while I considered what vile implications they were insinuating.

It was a chaotic deal. Sacrifice the things that I held most dear? "Emma?" I whispered.

"If I should decide she is worth one of my stories." The Walls answered, the voice changing abruptly to a mischievous tone.

"*People?*" I was stuck on what this meant. Did these Walls mean... what I thought they meant?

"Sometimes people, sometimes things... it really depends on what is important to *you,* Taylor."

"If you want your stories told, why take such costly things from the person willing to give you a voice?' The question was valid.

"A story without sacrifice is hollow and empty. When you've given up something to tell it, you will write with your heart. *You will leave a part of yourself in the words.* "

"I can write a story without *losing* anything," I answered. I wasn't entirely ready to commit to this deal. It seemed too costly, too dangerous. This felt like a dance with a devil.

"Can you? Your last novel required your father to die."

I scoffed. Are you saying I *killed* Edward?

"Not at all, but a sacrifice was made. Your father's end for a Best Seller and... an Aurora." The Walls were bold, insinuating that Edward's death had something to do with my success.

"That was *my* hard work and relentless work ethic," I answered.

"You have written *nothing* of value since, an empty thing you are—with no heart and no mind, nothing inside."

The rhyme awakened an anger inside of my chest. I wasn't empty or hollow—in fact, I was full of angst and thoughts, filled to the brim with trauma and twisty darkness that I knew would tell a magnificent story.

I wasn't empty. I wasn't *nothing.*

Oh god... was I?

I would show these Walls and this world that Taylor Halethorpe was more than nothing.

"Deal," I said quickly, understanding that if the cost became too high, I might never write another story inspired by these Walls again. But did that mean I wouldn't be able to write again?

No.

The room vibrated with a seductive excitement that pulled the breath from my chest. Almost instantly, it looked as though the Walls of the Estate had changed their appearance. Areas that were once dim and cracked, nearly crumbling, had healed from the decay, and the wallpaper had a brighter, more colorful tone—as if it had just been pasted to the wall today.

These were Walls that looked prim and proper. Walls you'd have tea next to or use as a backdrop for a family portrait. They'd become vibrant and *alive.*

Before the Walls could respond again, there was a creak in the floor, and the office doors slowly opened. Emma walked in, wrapped in a silk robe. "Who were you talking to?" she asked, and my breath hitched.

"My Aurora." I gestured to the sparkling statue on the mantle. "I talk to it when I outline my stories, sometimes." My answer was a joke but secretly laced with more truth than Emma would ever understand.

"As long as it doesn't talk back," she smiled. From behind me, she leaned down, wrapped her arms around me in a half embrace, and whispered, "Come back to bed. It's too early to write." My skin prickled with the warmth of her words.

"Only if you promise not to fall in love," I teased as I stood and pushed the chair in, giving the wall in the study one last stare as I closed the doors.

✻✻✻

The following weeks blurred together as if they were merely a single day. The world had changed so much that most of the book tour for *All Good Years* was virtual. I spent more time with the Walls in the Study than I had planned, knowing it was watching each smile and each perfectly rehearsed answer to the questions about its origin and historical legitimacy.

Interviews that were ironically the most inhuman I'd ever done, on discussing a novel that spoke on the depth of our humanity and how death inevitably comes for us all. But the glimmering hope that we can *live* despite the truth of death.

I plastered a fake smile on my face as I discussed the inspiration for such a beautiful story. Interview after interview, the thought that plagued the deepest parts of me was discussing the vastness of my grandparents' love. At the same time, I was drastically underloved in each of my prominent relationships.

Regularly used for what I offered by Nick and held at arm's length by the free-spirited Emma, both harmful in their own ways but impossible to let go of when what was waiting for me was compounding loneliness.

I was unable to face the fact that I feared being alone, so I carried on, but with each online appearance, with each discussion diving deeper into *All Good Years*, I thought more about freeing myself from these bonds that held me in such an uncomfortable place, for I had *no good years* to consider my own.

Nick sniffed out the shift in my career and weaseled his way back in with his charm. A few of his acting gigs had worked out, and he ended up on TV in a national food chain commercial, ballooning his ego into thinking he now brought something of value to the table.

Although his career had been at an all-time low for as long as I could remember, he thought we were rising stars *meant* for one another. He'd referred to us as a power couple once, and I had to choke back the bubbling vomit in my throat.

He even dared to comment when a popular literature magazine reached out to him for an interview. He *suggested* to the interviewer that we had been dating for *eight years.*

He was a bad habit that I let linger in my bed, on my lips. I don't think I ever made it clear to him that we were nothing more, but I'd thought it was implied.

When Emma wasn't around, Nick filled the empty hole in my heart, waiting for her to miss me the way I missed her.

Despite all of the toxicity of my love life and the demoralizing treatment of my heart in these conditions. *All Good Years* still became a New York Times Best-Selling novel, making waves not only for its beautiful message but also as *Taylor Halethorpe's* meteoric re-entry into the atmosphere of literature.

All Good Years broke barriers on social media, garnering attention from the stay-at-home mom to the blue-collar uncle. It brought people together in a way that only a good book could.

Nick stood in the kitchen, shirtless—as always. He took a gulp straight from the orange juice container when he saw the headline flash across the local morning show. We kept it on to fill the awkward lulls of silence in our conversations. Sometimes, we even used it as a reason *not* to speak to each other.

"Bestseller, eh?" He smirked as he wiped his face with his arm. "Guess that makes us a power couple for real."

The sound of it made me cringe. We weren't a couple, and neither of us contributed to the term *power.*

"Maybe I should do an interview about you," he said nonchalantly, reaching for his phone. "I mean, I was there for the whole thing, right?"

My stomach clenched. That's precisely what he'd do. Attach himself to my name, spin a story where he was the muse, the backbone, the unsung hero of my success.

I didn't even fight him. I was too busy realizing that it should have been Emma sitting across from me. She should be here grinning across the breakfast table, proud of what I'd done.

She wasn't. And that was the problem.

CHAPTER 18

FIRST

2021

The Walls had bargained with me only *after* they'd told me the story of Evelyn and Charlie. I thought I'd found a way around paying the cost, but as the story's success took off, the Walls incessantly reminded me that we hadn't landed on an agreeable *payment.*

The Walls were willing to negotiate this time since the story was already alive with a heart and soul.

"For the story you've already told, the fee shall be paid in *gold.*"

"No." I calmly replied, knowing *exactly* what the Walls requested.

"You do not get a choice, for you took my story without asking what I'd want for it," The Walls snapped back.

"I didn't bargain. You gave me that story before the deal."

"And look at what it did for you, Taylor. A bit of gold can't take away the *fame* you've accumulated."

"No," I repeated, crossing my arms. "Find something else," I warned.

"Ok then—Miriam." The request struck me in the gut.

"What?" I asked again.

"Your Housekeeper, surely you know her name. How rude it would be if you didn't."

"This isn't funny," I replied. "She's not my housekeeper. She's my friend."

"It's your gold bracelet or Miriam." The Walls sent a bold wind through the office that startled me. I almost found it frightening. I didn't want to upset them, and I didn't know the true extent of their power.

Could they kill me? Or worse?

"Fine." I slowly unclasped my bracelet, thumbing over it one last time, and threw it violently at the patterned paper on the walls. In an instant, it was like I'd thrown nothing, for it vanished into thin air.

Gone, as if it had never existed.

My only tether to my mother was stripped from me at the cost of a single love story.

I stood silently, wondering what had happened and how these walls had infiltrated my life. It's a bracelet now, but what next? My vision? Memories? Money?

What gave these Walls their power?

What curse? What witchcraft? What mechanism fueled their selfish desires to be heard? I shattered into a million pieces as I realized I'd paid their price. I'd done it. And it felt easy. Giving them something that I thought was a piece of my identity felt simple. Was I a sell-out, or was I something worse?

Just then, a glint—a flash from the mantle in the office.

The Aurora. The iridescent glass reminded me of something I'd known for too long. It was this blasted trophy—*the curse of the Aurora*—that animated these Walls. It had to be.

It glittered in a beam of light that seemed to come from nowhere, which alone confirmed my suspicion. It was a haunted thing, that trophy.

Maybe I should destroy it?

CHAPTER 19

THE CLOCKMAKER'S WIFE
2021

Before Evelyn fell in love with Charlie, Isobel loved Henry. Isobel Halethorpe-Stone was a rebel with a cause, a woman with a purpose. Isobel was the Clockmaker's wife, but she was also... so much more.

The Walls had given me just enough to tantalize my artist's heart, to suck me in and make me beg for more. But the stories did not come for free, something I'd later wish I'd never agreed to. But, while the intoxicating rush of finding the next story hidden in the Estate was thrumming through my veins. I made that bargain.

"The Clockmaker's Wife is a story of a woman without bounds, without restraint. The courage to do the right thing in the face of imprisonment and possibly death." The Walls teased a story that put fire in my heart. That made me eager to discover what other secrets the Halethorpe family had hidden in this estate.

"I want, more than anything, to tell Isobel's story," I said, becoming the willing recipient of whatever these walls dared to bestow on me.

"More than anything?"

"I know... a sacrifice. Name your price," my anxiety forced me to rush to the part I didn't want to hear. The Walls could ask for anything. I'd given them that freedom. They'd taken my bracelet. Perhaps it would be something disposable again. I couldn't measure how greedy these Walls would be.

But I *wanted* this story—No, I needed it.

It was my heritage, my ancestors. It was my birthright to tell the story of any Halethorpe who came before me. I was the last one left to let our legacy live on.

"Nicholas." The Walls cackled back.

"Nick?" I sat with consideration, in silence, in the study. My fingers hovered over the laptop keys, deciding whether to relax or press on.

Nick.

My mind screamed, "Do it!" reminding me that Nick would sell me out for an extra role on an obscure foreign show in a heartbeat. But my body and heart craved how he catered to my needs and made me feel whole when he focused on me.

There were times when he made me feel like I was the only woman in all of existence and that if I perished, he'd die without me. He wrapped my body in a bubble that made it immune to outside pressures and released a feral part of my heart that raged at the world's unfairness.

What would my life without Nick look like? Would I grow and blossom without this toxic distraction? Or would I find that a piece of my heart was lost along with him?

Without another second of thought, I disposed of Nick.

"Take him." The words flew from my mouth, and I regretted it as soon as I'd said it. I gave him up so easily for a guaranteed win. But I held him in my life for all these years, trying to quit him. My hands clapped against my mouth, wishing they'd arrived sooner to stop the name from escaping.

I guess I'd finally found what I wanted more than Nick.

The story.

"Let's begin, for this tale has waited too long to see the light of day. Isobel can wait no longer, and I grow tired of your heavy breathing." The Walls interrupted my sobs, disregarding the pain of my loss.

"I just gave you someone who has been a part of my life for almost a decade. A moment of panic is expected, is it not?" I chuffed at the Walls, sniffling away my tears.

"A decade is nothing." They answered, "When you've lived as long as we have, that is but a blink of time."

"I won't live as long as haunted wallpaper. But isn't that the point?" A tear formed in the corner of my eye.

"That's why you *have* so many stories. We are only here for a moment, and you take ours and hide them inside you—under the layers of that aged wallpaper and paint."

I sniffled, the stream of tears pouring down my face, "You'll sell my story to the next person who sits in this study," I mumbled the thought out but let the silence linger before I asked *the* question that was flapping around in my head like a bat stuck in a room with no exits.

"Is he... gone?" I asked, curious about what a *sacrifice* truly meant.

"No. We're not murderers, Taylor."

"Then how did I sacrifice him?"

"He has never existed in this life, nor will he in the next." The Walls hummed with an eerily calm tone for the weight of their revelation.

"What do you mean?" I asked hesitantly, my pulse rising and my face heated with rage.

"He exists not. How many ways shall I tell the story?" The Walls were becoming more brazen, bold even. I felt like I'd been tricked. I'd never considered their motive to be so dark.

"I hope when I whisper the legacy of Isobel, you pay more attention, for if I must tell you twice, I will take something more."

An entity I had imagined to be a friend was darkening into the villain I hadn't expected.

I stood mere inches from where I perceived the Wall's face was. My breathing was erratic, my fury nearly uncontainable. Could I take a sledgehammer to them? Would that end their magic? Would I regret it the moment I struck out its life?"

"I realize now that instead of making a deal with the magic Walls of my Estate, I've made a deal with the devil himself." With fiery anger, I slammed the insult out at the blank space I stared into. "Now, I haven't called *you* any names, Taylor."

✳✳✳

The Walls recounted priceless details of my Great Aunt Isobel, The Clockmaker's Wife. In 1940, Isobel and her husband, Henry, owned a clockmaking business in Massachusetts. When World War II threatened the lives of her husband's Jewish relatives in France, they began an operation that ran until the declaration of the end of the war. At the start, they sent clocks and timepieces into Europe to be received by the Resistance.

These clocks and timepieces were no ordinary time-tellers, no. They contained manufactured parts and pieces for counter-weaponry to fight the German Nazis.

They were critical pieces of explosives, firearms, wires, and rare filaments expertly crafted by Henry to look and function like regular clocks. When passing from country to country, the American woman who protected each shipment distracted those checking the inventory enough for them to be *just* clocks.

When their shop was burned to the ground, Evelyn begged Isobel and Henry to return and stay at the Estate where they could continue their work under the protection of the land and authority of the Halethorpe name.

Evelyn would have said anything to get her sister back, for their bond was stronger than any metal or iron.

The Nazis tragically captured Henry at the height of the War, and he never returned to Isobel, but she continued their mission and made the clocks herself under the name of her husband. She worked under the darkness of the night, cloaked by her chain of Resistance contacts.

Henry and Isobel's baby was born on a cool Saturday evening in the west wing of the Halethorpe Estate, in the apartments now occupied by Miram. The birth of their son didn't stop Isobel from the mission. She came and went like a phantom in the darkness.

Isobel relentlessly served her husband's legacy, and when the war was declared over, she disappeared. Only the Walls knew where she'd planned to go, *to France*, to live among her late husband's family and to raise their son in a heritage struggling to rebound from mass murder.

Isobel never returned to the Halethorpe Estate, leaving it to Evelyn when their parents passed away. There was never again a sign of the woman with the heart of a warrior and the patience of a Clockmaker.

FROM THE CLOCKMAKER'S WIFE

CHAPTER 31

Isobel ran her finger along the edge of its casing, smoothing it over and checking for any rough edges.

Henry would never leave rough edges, she thought to herself. The faint ticking from its mechanisms was steady and *innocent.* But beneath the expertly imitated faceplate lay a detonator no larger than a coin, surrounded by wires so thin they felt like the finest silk threads.

"Not bad for someone who failed her studies *twice."* Isobel teased with a short, bitter smile. She slowly lifted the final gear between the tips of the tweezers, her hand as steady as a surgeon, her heart racing wildly like that of the patients.

The babe stirred in the makeshift crib only a few feet to her left, within reach of her to rock him when he cried for his next meal or needed the warming comfort of his mother. Isobel paused, waiting for a soft coo or a breath from his swaddle.

She should have let someone else take Henry's place, but she *couldn't.* This was now her burden to carry. She carried the full weight of her husband's legacy. He was a man who sacrificed himself to save thousands of his family and friends. This was the legacy of a man whose son would be proud someday.

If she didn't see this through, his story would be one of the hundreds of thousands of losses, a story that would disappear in the sea of deaths orchestrated by the Germans.

She would *never* let him be lost.

Henry's name was still etched on the tiny plaque at the clock's base—Henry Stone was a household name in clocks and watches. There wasn't a house without a Stone timepiece. The Nazis couldn't know he had been captured, that it was his business that had been sending such weaponry.

He had been given fake papers when he'd made his trip. He'd be imprisoned as someone else, someone Isobel would never know, and so she never learned the fate her husband met.

But his new identity was the only ghost she'd know, for *she* kept Henry alive by continuing to produce his clocks and watches. Not a single tick or tock had been skipped since Henry's capture.

A sharp rap on the door sent her heart into a panic. She slowly reached for the pistol she kept loaded under the workstation, the clocks around her ticking, reminding her of how little time was always left.

"Who's there?" She called, her voice steady, calm.

"Julien," a muffled, familiar voice, "I have news."

Isobel let out a sigh of relief and opened the door just enough to reveal a hooded face, pale and colorless... a familiar look that many in the business of secrets adopted.

His eyes looked into the small, warm room lit with a fire he was yearning to stand next to. He scanned her workspace and saw the masterpiece sitting on the bench. "It's perfect." He whispered, enthralled at her imitation, "It's just like the real..." he stopped himself from finishing. Anything more would be an insult.

"It's perfect," he repeated, leaving it at that.

"We don't have the luxury of mistakes," Isobel said, her mind walking the instructions on her directive again for the thousandth time.

"You'll need to leave soon. Shift change is in only a few hours, and they're doubling checkpoints near the border."

She glanced at the crib. Her son hadn't stirred again, but a soft coo from the swaddling was enough to shake her voice, "No mistakes." She repeated as if she were trying to convince herself.

"Henry didn't, and neither will I."

CHAPTER 20

MISSING

2021

The Walls weren't liars. I searched for Nick on every social site and found nothing. I scoured search engines for any evidence of his work or new articles. When I looked up his previous roles or parts on IMDB, I saw they were all credited to someone else.

The photos on my phone of us together were not as I remembered them, or they were gone completely. I even went to the places I knew he frequented and asked bartenders I knew he was friends with if they had seen him, and they'd said they didn't know who I was talking about.

Nicholas Theodore Foster no longer existed.

I stayed in bed for three days after I'd confirmed it—after I'd let my heart finally understand that he was gone. A loss that I'd so easily inflicted on myself. I'd taken him from this world.

I was a *murderer*.

I'd let the endless questions and concerns flood my entire body. Did he feel pain? Is he here, on this Earth, just invisible, screaming out to be noticed?

I'd even questioned whether Nick was real, to begin with, but then I remembered Cass staring him down that night he showed up at the Estate.

But he had never actually got out of his car. I recollected that she had shooed him from the door, and his car drove away. But he never came face to face with her. I couldn't make a fool of myself by asking Cass if she remembered him. I didn't want her to think I was on the edge of another meltdown. Was anyone in the car, and did I manifest the entire thing?

I closed my eyes as I lay in the darkness of my room with the curtains drawn. I let out a deep sigh of air. Nick was real, and what we had, no matter how toxic, was real, too. I let myself rot in bed and play through the reel of memories that I had of him in my mind, the only thing the Wall couldn't take, and to me, it was both a blessing and a burden. Nick now only lived through me and through whatever story I could write for him... *someday.*

Yes... he had been real until I hastily sold his existence to my possessed Estate, the one he always found *creepy.* What an ironic demise.

***

After a week of mourning, I was awakened inside by a text from Emma. I texted her once last week to tell her I was thinking of her, and she waited six full days to acknowledge the sentiment.

'What are you doing tonight?'

I let the question sit on my desk while considering what would happen next. If I continued to see Emma, the Walls could want her too. If I decided now to refuse her, she could be safe and stay in this world.

A world without Emma was a world I didn't want to live in, even as a miserably successful author. Emma was light when there was darkness. She was heaven when the world was hell. She was all of it, and I was hopelessly in love with her.

"One more night with her, and then I'll let her go," I whispered the promise to myself, hoping I wouldn't find a way to break it.

***

I walked into the study and glared at my laptop. I had no intention of speaking to the Walls today. I fine-tuned The Clockmaker's Wife, adjusting word usage and tone, changing pacing, and doing my standard once-over editing.

I cried rereading.

The sobs were relentless, a reminder of how powerful Isobel's love for Henry was. She loved him so much that she kept him alive through the fight, through the danger.

I cried because I'd never had a love so powerful.

And when you considered the comparison, I hadn't much of anything like this at all. And because of this, I also cried.

I sent it to editing and copied Cass. I'm sure she would be thrilled to know she didn't need to beg the next story out of me and that it wouldn't take another seven or so years for me to keep my momentum. It wasn't a minute later that my phone rang. 'Cass' lit up on the screen.

"Hello?" I answered, guarded by the surprise call.

"What are you doing?" She wasn't asking me as a friend but as a concerned agent.

"We weren't expecting another project from you for at least a year. Everbound is so thrilled with the *All Good Years* residual sales that they praise you at every top executive meeting.

"Then hold onto it until you're ready?" I paused, "I can't control when the motivation strikes, but The Clockmaker's Wife is even better than *All Good Years*, honestly."

"I'll read it tonight, but Tay..." Cass's concerned voice took over.

"Listen to me, do not—*Are you listening?*—Do not burn yourself out." She demanded.

"I won't. Oh, hey, do you remember that guy Nick?"

"Who? Who's Nick?" Her response is almost immediate. Cass's entire business was remembering people's names.

"Did I... forget someone?" Cass panicked, and I heard papers shuffling around on the other end of the line.

"No, I wasn't sure if I'd introduced you. Just some guy. He wasn't important." The words stung as they left my mouth, but there was a cruel honesty in them.

"Whew, ok. I can't start forgetting now..." Her voice faded but burst loudly, "While I have you... there's an event." The long pause meant that she knew she would ask for too much. "A masquerade thing. It's a play on the circumstances. All of the approvals and permits are in place for it."

Her sentences became more fragmented the further she descended into her request. "It's going to be one of the first big ones since everyone's meandering back to being around each other again."

"And?" I said, waiting for her to deliver the punchline.

"They want you there. It's not an award, just a swanky event for writers who had successful books released in 2020. Nothing big, it is a black-tie event though, so you'll need to go shopping. I don't think you've bought anything new since *Glass Heels* was relevant." Her rambling took a dark turn.

"Wow," I said, teasing.

"Yeah, I didn't mean it... you know what I meant, right?" The concern that she'd offended me took over.

"It's fine, you're not wrong. I need to get out anyway. I'll go this weekend after Emma leaves."

"Oh, Emma, *again*, is that getting serious?" Cass asked with a devilish curiosity.

"Actually, no. Emma's made it clear I am *not* to fall in love with her." I was honest. I didn't think it was fair to protect Emma's reputation with my best friend.

"Ew, she did not." Cass's disgust for people who set stipulations on relationships showed through.

"I hope the sex is good because that's ugly." She added.

Cass being overly protective of me wasn't new. I might have even intentionally cast Emma in this negative way so that Cass would side with me on pushing her out of my life.

"It's fine. I'm telling her we can't see each other anymore, anyway. It is a problem, and I don't think I should keep pretending it isn't." I admitted.

"Who are you, and what have you done with my best friend because... that's insanely mature, and I love that you are learning to love yourself," Her pride swelling in her tone.

"Oh, honey, I gotta run. New client calling. We can video chat later. Love you!" Before I could say goodbye, the call had already ended.

It was growth, wasn't it? Or was I acting out of fear of what the Walls would take from me next? A pierced jolted me in my gut, *Cass*.

No, they would... *Never.*

✶✶✶

Emma arrived Friday night, and we hadn't come up for air by Sunday morning. We'd locked ourselves in the Estate and made love on every surface I could find. The kitchen. In front of a raging fire in the sitting room. The grand staircase... that one was her favorite.

It hadn't been my plan, but there was something different about her. About how she was looking at me. The intent in her eyes shifted, and she pulled me in deeper. I think, *no*, I knew... she was falling for me the same way I'd fallen for her.

The way sparks lit under her fingers when she touched me and the way she quivered under my mouth as I kissed her body. This was love, of it I was sure.

I'd fallen, and this is what the novels tell you about.

The inescapable dread of having to live one more moment without someone. The pang of regret for having gone too long without knowing them and the curiosity that made you wonder how you'd ever lived without them.

The fear that now that you'd fallen, how much time would fate allow you to have before death, the true end, would rip you apart violently?

It was a dark thought for a mind burdened by the knowledge that other forces were in play besides luck and chance. A mind tainted by the understanding of a power that could make you non-existent in a moment. I shuttered.

It was in my very best interest to let Emma go, and it was best that I did it once I convinced her to put on her clothes and leave when all my heart wanted to do was tell her never to go and to stay.

I'd give her a room where she could paint, maybe the library, where she could set up her easel on the terrace and see the entire Halethorpe Estate. Miriam would make her all her favorite dinners, and we'd live a simple life making art for one another until we perished.

But the Walls would ask for her. I knew they would.

So I had to let her go.

CHAPTER 21

MASQUERADE
2021

I flew to California for the first time since I'd left in 2014. I stepped away from baggage claim, and Cass stood there wildly smiling with her arms out in an embarrassing show of excitement.

"I am so happy to see you." She said with a smile that lit up the world.

"Me too," I said as I yawned. My flight had been canceled, and then Cass got me on another, but it was delayed. I spent twelve hours at BWI waiting to depart for a flight I wasn't sure would happen.

Being away from the Estate was supposed to feel like a vacation, but I felt vulnerable, without the protective layer I'd grown accustomed to having. I was out in the world without my hidden superpower, even if my superpower had a bad attitude and an appetite for devouring anything that made me happy.

"You look good, Tay… like that's not me saying it ironically. You have a glow," Cass said as she pulled me into another hug.

"Let me take you to your hotel. You probably want a nap." She glanced down at her watch. And then we'll head out for dinner with Everbound and after… do some *shopping*." Her eyes lit up at the latter, and I almost thought she'd begun to drool at the thought of spending Everbound's money.

California, to me, looked the same, as if nothing had changed. Some things were dressed in more modern clothing, but they still had the same superficial air about them. I'm sure it was just how I perceived it now that I'd spent so many years in a crumbling Estate in a town that was barely a dot on a map.

I winced when a familiar storefront triggered a memory of Dante. Sometime at the start of our relationship, we walked down this street looking at the shops and restaurants, planning our future, and it felt like a whole new adventure.

The start of the life that never happened, I thought.

I rolled my eyes and went back to tapping on the screen of my phone. I wanted to call Miriam as soon as I'd landed to check in to ensure she was okay and that the Estate was okay. But I'd stopped myself.

"Is everything ok?" Cass asked while we drove in the back seat of the town car.

"Hmm? Ah-Yeah. I just haven't left home in a while. I forgot about the natural exhaustion of travel."

"You'll get used to it again, Tay," Cass said with a lowered tone. She hadn't realized that I didn't *want* to get used to it. I wanted to be in my Estate, my chest pressed against the edges of my old writer's desk and with the Walls whispering stories of love and bravery.

We pulled up to the hotel, a vision of expensive luxury.

"Everbound spared no cost, only the best for their most treasured asset," Cass said, her tone laced with layers of seedy sarcasm.

"I expect to have the best nap I've had in this lifetime," I teased, squaring shoulders, pretending to be a vision of class.

"I'll be back around seven to pick you up. Same car. Here's your key. You're already checked in." Cass remained seated while the driver pulled my luggage from the trunk.

"It's a date," I smiled and walked toward the lobby with my key in hand.

***

Dinner with Everbound went exactly as I expected. They fell over themselves about *All Good Years*. We talked about the concept and how it came to be. They mentioned seeing the first chapters of *The Clockmaker's Wife* and that I'd outdone myself again with it.

We clinked glasses, and the 'tink' reminded me of the last time I'd celebrated with them. A sound I'd said always reminded me of success, and here it was, reminding me that I'd done it again.

Cass and I scurried away with an Everbound credit card and no budget. I bought a few outfits and a leather bag, Cass said I needed for my laptop. But the shining moment of the night was when we walked into a designer dress store, and the perfect gown for tomorrow night's event hung delicately on a mannequin.

Cass gasped when she saw the delicate beadwork and intricate lacy patterns. It was timeless and elegant. It was Taylor Halethorpe, not Taylor from Halethorpe. She brought back the boutique owner and forced him to pull the dress off the display. His eyes widened. "This is an original, are you... Sure?" Cass nodded intently, frustrated at his uncertainty.

She sent me back to the fitting area, plopped herself down in one of the luxurious sitting chairs, and waited for me to emerge like a monarch butterfly from a cocoon.

The way the dress clung to my skin in the right places, the darkness of the deep violet fabric against my smooth, pale skin. I'd be lying if I said I didn't feel like royalty with this dress on.

"We'll take it," Cass told the owner as she handed him the Everbound card.

"Miss... do you want to know how much?" He was pale, a layer of sweat glistening on his skin.

Cass stood and walked over to him. He was shorter than her, as most people were. She smiled and looked at me, admiring myself in the trifold of mirrors. And then she looked back at him, "Do you know who that is?" She raised her eyebrow and crossed her arms. "That's Taylor Halethorpe, the greatest writer of our time." Cass said with a certainty that made chills flutter up my back, "So we'll take the dress. And that one over there, too." She pointed to a simpler, more contoured dress on a form about her size.

✱✱✱

Cass had told me that the masquerade event wasn't a *big deal*, but judging by the crowd forming outside the event space, I'd determined she'd undersold me to ensure I'd come. If I'd known it was as large or as flashy as it was, there's a good chance I would have politely declined the invitation.

And then, when we bought a ten-thousand-dollar dress, it raised my suspicions more, which have been confirmed here—*now*.

I wasn't mad, I understood. Part of her job was corralling cats. Authors, being the cats. I was an inside cat who enjoyed lounging in the direct beams of sun coming from the tall, open windows of my magical Estate.

But I'd decided I'd play a different part tonight. She handed me a mask that elegantly fastened to my hair with gems and beads but covered my face in a majestic draping. Her light-colored short fairy dress and my modern, dark, late Victorian gown, two women standing on opposite ends, couldn't be more different but shared a bond stronger than ever.

She pinned her mask on, and together, we exited the limo and walked toward the hall's entrance.

We toured the guests, shaking hands and nodding in acceptance before dinner was served. The champagne was actively flowing, and the entire event reminded me of the end of the *Glass Heels* tour. Funny enough, no one even mentioned *Glass Heels*. It was as if that whole chapter of my life had been erased, and all the world could see me for was *All Good Years*.

Just like all of the swanky parties before, the only thing missing from this party was—

Dante.

I saw him from across the room. My eyes caught just a glance, but I kept them moving. I couldn't imagine he'd recognize me with the mask and the gown. I braced myself against a chair, and heat seared my face. The mask covered my flushed embarrassment, and my makeup did the rest.

Cass put her hand on my shoulder. "Is everything okay? " she asked, concerned, as she handed me a small glass of water. "Here," she said covertly, still smiling and waving to those passing by.

"Dante's here." I breathed out from behind the cup.

"No..." Cass opened her phone and began scrolling a guest list that she'd personally had a hand in preparing.

"He... must be someone's plus one. His name is *not* here. I would have *never*." Cass was scrambling, preparing to do damage control.

"Want me to have him removed? We can do that. You're the guest everyone's here to meet. If—"

"It's fine. Removing him would cause a scene, and I'm not ready for the fallout." I replied, catching my breath and staring at a single spot on the wall to center my mind.

"It's not like that. We can be discreet." Cass was still trying to convince me to use my power and pull to have him removed.

"I'll avoid him. He'll never know it's me." I paused. "It will be fine." I smiled at her and nodded, trying to fool myself into believing it too.

"This is very Shakespearean of you," Cass chuckled, never passing the opportunity for a book joke.

"Jokes aside, if you change your mind, just give me the word."

I nodded, matching her sly grin with my own.

As we finished our drinks, the coast felt clear, and I desperately needed fresh air. I walked toward the glass doors that exited to the grand outdoor terrace. I smiled and tilted my head in acknowledgment as I passed by the other partygoers, their faces a mere blur while I made my grand escape.

The cool air pressed against my skin as soon as the doors opened. I took a breath in and let it sink deep into my chest. It had become suffocatingly warm inside, perhaps due to the combined heat from all of the bodies. But here, the air and cool moisture of the evening were calming.

The moon's soft glow cast dappled shadows on the terrace's patterned stone railings. Twinkling strands of lights webbed overhead, lighting the terrace ever so slightly. Just enough to catch the glitter of the eyes of the next person.

It was a sight to be seen, the hundreds of lights like lightning bugs along a midnight landscape by the forest. It was picturesque. Perhaps this *was* like the Capulet Ball, except for all the electricity and the rival—

"I thought that was you," the familiar voice pierced the peace I'd found for so few moments. "Taylor?" He pressed again when I didn't turn around.

"You're right to ignore me. I don't deserve your time." Dante said, his tone somber and remorseful. I didn't turn around. I stayed facing away, pretending I didn't hear the man who broke my heart all those years ago trying to half-ass an apology.

Suddenly, Cass stepped onto the terrace, her disgust made instantly apparent. "Excuse me?" she spoke sternly but softly. "Mr. Graves, don't you have somewhere *else* to be?" She gestured for

Dante to take his leave, and he disappeared quickly without a sound.

"I am so sorry," Cass said, resting her hand on my shoulder. "I knew we should have kicked him out," She said regretfully.

"It's fine." I smiled. "Let's go back in and eat. I'm starving." I put my arm over her shoulder, and we walked back in together. "I think a steak in there owes me royalties." I laughed as we left the moon to its own devices.

After dinner, I found myself at an interesting crossroads. I could let Dante's presence overshadow celebrating my return to my craft, or I could reclaim my lost confidence—which he'd so easily shattered without a second thought.

I chose the latter, a comeback story for the ages. I would not let Dante or anyone else take what I sacrificed so much for. Isobel wouldn't cower at the sight of Dante, nor would I.

I spent the rest of the evening playing my role, being the focus of everyone's attention. I casually glanced up, and Dante's withering shadow crossed my peripheral vision, but it did not matter. I'd turn my attention quickly to another artist, producer, writer, or supporter and pretend he didn't exist.

If only the Walls had asked for him.

Cass and I sipped from the rose-tinted glasses of Dom Pérignon in the back seat on our way back to the hotel. I sighed and slowly removed my mask, the cool air tickling the damp skin that had been under it for the night.

Cass reached over and moved a stray hair from my face.

"You deserve this, Tay," something she'd always said but hadn't tonight. "The parties, the celebrations... your writing is spectacular, *you* are a wonderful artist." She paused again, taking a sip from her flute. "And Dante, Everbound, *no one* should ever make you feel like less." She held her glass out and clinked mine with hers.

"The sound of success," I smiled and said as I took a matching sip.

The driver opened the door for me, and I stepped out carefully.

"Goodnight, Cass," I said, smiling. "Thank you for everything, always," I said, hoping she understood that I meant *everything.* Cass believed in me when no one else did, not once but repeatedly.

I gently lifted the bottom skirt of my dress, hiking it up so as not to trip as I ascended the stairs to the main entrance. The dim golden lights of the most exclusive hotel in town looked like a scene from a movie. The empty lobby, the silence, and the smell of freshly cut lilies permeated the air. The sleek, modern furniture, usually filled with people, was empty, the shine of the leather reflecting the dainty glow of the baubles above them.

My heels lightly tapped against the marble floors, like a princess scurrying away from a ball after midnight. I quietly walked through the hotel lobby toward the private VIP elevators. I stepped in, pulling the deep violet lace train and fabric in. As the doors began to close, a hand jutted through and made them change their minds.

I'd never missed the Estate more than at this moment.

Dante.

I'd made a promise to myself, and I would keep it. As the man I recognized waltzed into the elevator with a smug smile, I rolled my eyes, returning the sentiment.

"You looked stunning tonight." Dante's first words to me echoed out and almost made the champagne I'd just drank sizzle back up my throat. I said nothing as I watched the door close, trapping me inside a box far too small for the size of his ballooning ego.

"I just—"

I interrupted him, "There is no world where I speak to you in this elevator. Mind your business, get off on your floor, and leave me alone." I'd said it exactly the way I'd wanted to in my head. That rarely happens. Usually, I squander the chance for a perfect tell-off or compile a quality list of things I *should* have said after the moment has passed.

His floor arrived, and he stared deeply into my eyes. Waiting for me to change my mind. A sigh exited his mouth as he shook his head. "Well—I'm sorry for everything." He held the door to the elevator as he stood in his suite's hall. "There's nothing I can say that will make what I did *better*, but I need you to know that I wish I'd done so many things differently. I wish I hadn't been scared of you, your success… all of it."

I smiled at him and nodded complacently. He removed his hand from the door and stood, waiting for me to relieve him of the harm he'd caused. Waiting for something that would *never* arrive.

"Take care," I said as I slammed the door close button.

The doors clamped shut faster than expected, a blessing I'd thank someone for later. I made it to my floor and entered my suite, my heart racing as if something other than my toxic past was chasing me.

I unlaced the back of my dress and left bits and pieces of clothing in a trail leading toward the massive bed made from the clouds themselves.

I held my phone tightly in my hand, slowly building the courage to do what needed to be done. I pressed the call button over Emma's name. A quiet, sleepy voice answered on the other end. A detail I forgot to consider was that it was after midnight here, meaning it was probably 3 am there.

"Emma..." I said, the champagne taking the next words from my mouth haphazardly, "I am madly and entirely in love with you, and I can't pretend anymore."

A silence sat between the ends of the call, and then... it disconnected. I let out a sigh. It had been worth a shot. Either she would feel the same, or this was all I needed to do for her to run as far away from me as possible.

The Walls couldn't take anything else from me that mattered.

***

I'd decided to stay in California one more day, delaying my flight. Something told me that I was ready to head back to Maryland. I surprised Cass at the Everbound Press corporate office. When I entered, the receptionist looked surprised at my guest appearance. I didn't come to these offices often, if ever.

I sauntered in, giving small tokens of appreciation to everyone there for putting up with me as long as they did. I walked through the halls of the modernized office. The breakroom had a shuffleboard and a foosball table, with a snack bar and every flavor of seltzer water you could think of.

A millennial's dream office.

The meeting rooms were all glass walls. You could see directly into them, so I casually walked past where Cass was sitting, not once but twice. The second time, I caught her eye and flicked up my middle finger as I walked by with a devilish grin.

I watched her almost choke in surprise and slyly excuse herself from the important meeting.

"What are you doing here?" A smile widened across her face, her arms out for a hug. I could tell that my visit was unexpected.

"I extended my stay for a day, thought I'd come by and see what it looked like on this side of my novel." I smiled, "Where the magic happens..." fluttering my eyebrows seductively at Cass.

"Novels... plural," She said. I could see the excitement building behind her eyes. She gestured for me to walk with her.

"That meeting was about *The Clockmaker's Wife*. Editing was sent back, the design is done with *multiple* cover options, and they're considering releasing it in no less than 90 days." She could barely contain herself. Her face lit up as she told me the good news.

"Pete's saying he thinks you could have movie deals on this one. The market for historical heroine women is booming right now. This couldn't have come at a better time."

I smiled at Cass, "That's all really exciting," I said with a certain melancholy I couldn't strip from my voice no matter how hard I tried. We entered her office, and I tossed my sweater onto her guest chair.

"What's wrong? Is everything ok?" Cass immediately sat in her office chair and set her hands delicately in front of her, giving me her undivided attention.

"Eh, I broke things off with Emma last night," I said, revealing the source of my sorrow.

"Oh—" Cass started, but she saw the tear trickle down my cheek. "Oh, honey..." she rushed over to me and threw her arms around me. "Everything is going to be okay. I promise." She laid her head on my shoulder, and, for a moment, everything did feel okay.

"Oh, and Dante..." I hesitated. "Was at the same hotel last night," I said slyly. "Ask me how I know," I added, waiting to see how flabbergasted she would become.

Her head shot up off my shoulder. "He was what?" She was shocked. Her expression curled her mouth into a frown. "Tay, this is borderline *stalking* at this point. Do you want me to file something? We have a legal team here."

"Don't worry, it wasn't too bad. He said some things in the elevator and left me alone." I paused, "But I am sure he was waiting for me." I went to rub a missing bracelet. "So he knew I was there." I added, "It was too coincidental the whole thing." I stopped.

"Okay, so maybe it's borderline stalking."

"What did he say? *'Sorry, I'm a small man with a big ego and no brains?'*" Cass asked sarcastically.

"Am I stalkable now?" I let her question go unanswered while my focus wandered.

"Oh, uh—he said 'Sorry' in more words." I looked at her and shrugged, "The way he ended it sucked, but we were both at fault for what didn't work." I admitted.

"The way he did it was unnecessarily cruel, Tay. It sent you into a seven-year spiral," Cass added.

"Was it a spiral? I can hardly recall." I smiled. "Thanks for the reminder." I widened my eyes and let out an uneasy chuckle. "I think more of that was my *mom*—you know... dying." It was a confession that didn't need to be said, but I felt comfortable saying it out loud now.

"I miss her so much sometimes." I looked out the window of Cass's high-rise office. Everything seemed so small from way up here. I reached for my wrist again, a habit I wouldn't soon stop. It's void, my only reminder of the deal I'd made for the fame that was returning with every day. A little reassurance that my deal with the Wall was still beneficial.

"I know you do. It's in your writing. It's got a different tone than *Glass Heels*."

"It's *better* though, right?"

"You are a phenomenal writer. You always have been. You don't need *anyone* to tell you that." She took a breath, "But your writing now… it has a depth you didn't have before, and maybe that's experience, or wisdom, or some shit…" She smiled.

"Yeah… some shit alright…" I repeated, gazing off into the distance.

"The world is eating it up, and Taylor…" She used my full name, "There is no limit to how far you take yourself."

Her words were the reassurance I didn't know I needed. I took a deep breath and let it out in relief. "Well, this was fun. *Not.*" I stood, wiping a small tear from the corner of my eye.

"Tay, what are we doing with Dante?" She asked seriously.

"I haven't decided yet." I sniffled. I pulled my sweater off the back of her guest chair, swung it over my shoulder, and walked out of her office.

I nodded at the receptionist, who panicked every time I made eye contact with her.

Did I believe in second chances?

***

I was determined to find the pupusas from my favorite food truck while I had one more night to wander. My driver stopped all over the city trying to find where they were parked, and it was a miracle we found them at all.

Back in the hotel lobby, I held my tray and fumbled with my bag to get out my badge to scan up to my floor when Dante brushed past me and into the open doors of the elevator. I set my to-go container down and began rummaging through it until I found my badge stuck at the bottom.

"Figures," I mumbled with napkins and other papers in my mouth.

The elevator door opened, and as I stepped forward, Dante was still inside. I rolled my eyes and entered anyway. I didn't want to wait any longer to be in the comfort of my room. Moments like this made me grateful for the Estate's embrace. I didn't have to interact with hotel *strangers* there.

He looked at me, standing in silence, paying no attention to him or his doe-eyed stare.

"Is that... *Sabores?*" he asked inquisitively.

"Leave me alone," I replied.

"Wow, they don't come this way often. Where did you find them?"

"I put in a little effort, and I called them," I said, digging deep into a wound I knew was sore for him.

"I deserve that." His words triggered me.

"Deserve? I've heard you say that twice now, which is far too many times for it to be natural in my extremely short visit to this vast state." My anger bubbled from deep in my chest.

"You don't get to talk about what you deserve because you're foul, and how you treated me... was not only cruel, but it was cowardly." I snarled at him, barely managing my volume as my rage seethed.

We rode the next ten floors silently, and he exited without looking back. I'd realized when the doors shut that perhaps I'd wanted him to look. I wanted him to feel what I'd felt. A tear, a sob... a cry out for forgiveness?

The doors opened again, and the arrival sound rang out like the start of a harmonic symphony... music to my ears. I entered my suite, where I immediately devoured the finest-tasting pupusas California had to offer me.

✳✳✳

I left Dante and the memories of savory pupusas in California and flew home first class the following day, courtesy of Everbound

Press, for my friendly and *uplifting* appearance at the office. I'd always looked at publishers as little soul-sucking, money-hungry monsters who wanted to strip writers of control, but Everbound had been very generous and supportive *lately*. I especially thought so when the flight attendant handed me a cooling face mask before takeoff.

I tilted my head back and laid the gel mask on my face. I let out a small, relaxing sigh. I was heading back to the Estate, *finally*. I'd arrived here feeling unprotected and vulnerable, but I warmed up to the California air on my skin quicker than I thought.

Proof that I didn't *need* the Estate.

Perhaps the Estate needed me.

CHAPTER 22

SECOND CHANCES
2022

The Halethorpe Estate during springtime was a sight to behold. The property was dotted with magnolia and dogwood trees, and the sweet fragrance of a world awakening tickled your nose.

Miriam opened many of the giant windows, seemingly made to embrace the newly shifted beams of sunlight, highlighting the new bright tones of everything inside the Estate. The lightness of the warm spring breeze forced out the heavy, dusty winter air.

After the official release of *The Clockmaker's Wife*, and what I had to give up to take the story from the Walls... I'd decided to wait before I asked for another. I wasn't ready to struggle with the turmoil of what they might require for the next one. If they kept taking the *people* closest to me, it would be a cost I wasn't ready to pay.

I put more money and time into the Estate, slowly restoring it to its former glory. Upon my return from California, I noticed how run-down it looked from a distance. It was in my best interest to ensure the Estate would live on long after I was dust.

I had restoration companies specializing in historical buildings begin slowly replacing and rebuilding, starting with the exterior.

Additional security was also necessary, as fans of the novels had been found trespassing on the property more than once since *The Clockmaker's Wife* was announced as a full-length feature film.

I glanced down at my phone and searched for Emma on social media. Her photos hadn't changed since I'd looked at her profile last. She looked happy, and that's all I could have ever asked for. I knew how I felt, and that was all I needed.

As I was preparing to slide my phone into my pocket, a California number I'd never seen before called. I hesitated but stepped away from the contractors ripping cedar shake siding from the second story and answered.

"Hello?"

"Hey, it's me. Before you hang up—"

"Who is me?" I interrupted the anonymous caller.

"Dante." The response wasn't at all surprising

"What do you want?" I asked, not understanding why I hadn't hung up. It was as if I wanted Dante to beg, to grovel at my feet. It was an odd feeling to be the top in a power struggle, but I had to admit, it felt good.

Better than good, it was exhilarating. I see now why some people play the villain and why some people even *love* the villain.

Or perhaps I was not a villain at all but the hero who finally found her footing. It was strange how it really could go either way.

This was the inciting incident, the catalyst—and the following chapters were going to be me...*kicking ass.*

"I'm in Baltimore and wanted to see if you'd get dinner with me."

"This is stalking, Dante," I said sarcastically as I walked further away from the calamity of the construction.

"Or I can come see you... at the Estate?"

"It's under construction, sorry." It wasn't a complete lie.

"Taylor, I can't fix my mistakes if you don't let me." He said, pressuring me.

"I don't need to let you fix your mistakes. That's not my responsibility."

"I'm trying, Taylor. I hoped you'd see that." Despite my refusal to engage, he confessed that his attempts at contacting me were valiant.

"Dante, there's nothing left," I admitted, knowing I had no more love for him. It might sting to hear it, but I have nothing for you." I dropped the bomb, expecting it to explode and handle the remainder of the conversation, except...

"Then have dinner with me anyway, as friends."

I sighed. "The Estate, at six. If you're late, the security will be told to refuse you, and I will have my legal team file a protective order *tomorrow*."

✷✷✷

Dante arrived promptly at 6 pm at the gates of the Halethorpe Estate, and Miriam had prepared a delicious meal for us. She set the table and scampered off to her quarters as he arrived.

I opened the doors and invited him in. His face lit up with wonder as he admired the grand staircase. "The Halethorpe Estate," I announced jokingly as I hung his coat by the door.

"This place—Taylor," He sounded breathless, "It's incredible."

"What were you expecting?" I asked, a curious grin growing on my face.

"Something... *smellier*, honestly." He chuckled as he answered, still enamored by the delicate engraving in the banister or the gold embroidered pattern on the wallpaper. He ran his fingers over everything.

It was safe to say that almost anyone who stepped into the Estate had the same reaction—it was instantaneous. It was surprising how many people felt the need to reach out and touch it like it wasn't real. It was as if the Estate was a piece of art they were observing from a distance that didn't become a reality until it was tangible to their fingers.

"It's real," I said, my eyebrow arched at Dante, who was letting himself get a little too lost in the details. He shook himself from the distraction and looked back and smiled, my arms folded over one another, waiting for the excitement of the Estate to wear off.

"This place must be worth a fortune..." He breathed, still admiring the layers of historical brilliance. "You'll take me for the grand tour after dinner?" He asked, leaning toward me for a hug.

"It doesn't matter what it's worth. It's not for sale," I said as I twisted at his advancement, but he caught me mid-panic, and I succumbed to his warm embrace. The smell of leather and cardamom with that slight floral finish hit my nose, and memories of the good times came flooding back.

I forced the thoughts from my head, and I patted his back spastically to trigger his release, "Great, yeah. Umm, Miriam has dinner served." I quickly diverted his attention toward the dining room with an awkward swooping gesture.

"Miriam?" He looked at me strangely.

"Miriam," I said definitively. I didn't feel like going into the intricacies of my inheritance, so I left it at that.

Dante nodded as we took our place in the dining room. I'd made Miriam blow out the massive candlesticks before Dante arrived, I had said, as friends and a candlelit dinner gave the wrong message.

"Taylor, I have to confess something," Dante started the conversation as he lifted the cloche from over his plate. His eyes stayed focused on me as I mirrored him.

"I had a feeling you might," I said as I sipped Miriam's perfectly paired wine.

"I've never stopped thinking about you—us. I know that what I did was not *okay*. I've probably beat myself up more over it than you'd ever know..." He paused as he took a bite from the steaming plate, and I saw him pause how perfectly tender the filet was, savoring it. He patted his mouth gently with the cloth napkin. "If there were anything I could do to make it up to you, I would do it, you know that?"

"What I find strange, Dante..." My eyebrow raised. "Is that you've never stopped thinking but have only just now acted."

I set down my cutlery.

"It seems you've waited until... what?" I paused.

"My fame started to return. I started making a comeback?"

"No—Tay, that's not it at all." His voice sounded desperate.

Desperate for a moment of clarification.

"I didn't feel my regret so intensely until I saw you—you've been reclusive, *out of sight.*"

I scoffed. "Reclusive?" I repeated.

"Are you going to make me beg?" He asked, his tone subtly darker. I'd almost missed it. The playful edge, the *yearning.*

"Perhaps I enjoy having you beg?"

I knew exactly what I was doing. I was lowering my voice into a sultry song, and I was *teasing* a man who was begging me for my attention.

The scrape of cutlery against the delicate porcelain plates echoed in the room, but his stare was louder than any of the ambient noises, including the screaming inside my head begging me to stop.

I pushed it away. I didn't listen. I couldn't have Emma. She didn't want *love.* But Dante was begging for mine.

Perhaps I did believe in second chances after all.

CHAPTER 23

ALMOST PERFECT
2022

We picked up right where we'd left off. Once he'd begged back into my good graces, it was like no time had passed. I'd never admit it, but there was still a part of my heart that didn't trust him entirely, but I'd imagined that just like the rest of it, with time, it would fade.

But *why*? Why had I let this man who'd nearly ruined my life back in? After the hell I'd healed from the wreckage he'd left. After he ripped out my heart without a second thought.

But the truth was there was an easier answer. Dante was expendable. He was a love that I knew I could live without. I'd done it after it was abruptly ripped from my grasp.

I'd lived without him and could do so again should the Walls decide they want to continue to take everything I've ever cared for from me.

Dante would appear to be just that, and if they decided to disintegrate him into nothing, the world would experience no significant loss. Perhaps his untimely exit would leave this place a little less in the red.

I could only hope I'd moved the pawns around enough to keep the Walls away from Emma. I periodically checked her social media to tease myself or burden myself with what I might miss out on. While primarily private, she appeared to be living the life she always wanted, carefree and filled with purpose and deeper meaning.

When I felt nostalgic, I'd sit in the Study and look longingly at the delicately hung painting on the wall. Her technique and style were unmistakable, but the woman she'd painted felt distant and gone. She'd caught the minor details about my smile, my hair... and even a tiny gold bracelet wrapped around my wrist, symbolizing the peace before the chaos I'd invited into my life.

I recalled our conversation from that night about whether we'd been in love and how simple letting go of the past truly is. Ironically, to take her advice now would be to let *her* go. But there was an ache in my heart that told me I didn't want to lose her, not entirely.

Dante attended every event by my side, *publicly* as my boyfriend. He outwardly showed his affection and spoke about me in a way that would make other women swoon. Of course, he still hadn't left California, and much of our relationship was long-distance. I hadn't the heart to tell him I had no intention of moving back to LA or even California.

The Estate was too important, and *The Clockmaker's Wife* was a story I could only ride for so long before another one would need to be written. I certainly couldn't just come here to write, as the Walls would be offended by the audacity, and I wouldn't dare test them. No... it was abundantly clear that I was to be a permanent resident of this Estate. Much like my mother, I'd live and die walking these halls and singing the stories of these Walls—of this, I was most certain.

Construction on the exterior had been completed, and the interior was slowly restored. I left explicit instructions that the Study was not to be touched. While I knew *all* of the Walls were collectively speaking to me, I considered the Study a vital organ, perhaps the only organ... I couldn't risk what restorative construction might do to whatever keeps the Estate haunted.

I looked up at the darkness of the painting, the flutter of my heart and a pain clattered through my chest. What *would* the Walls want next? What would they ask me to give up for the next story that would make me millions of dollars and solidify Taylor Halethorpe as a world-renowned storyteller?

What if I didn't need the Walls anymore? What if I could find a story within myself? The truth was that I hadn't even tried to write on my own since I'd discovered them. I leaned back in the leather chair and opened my laptop. I clicked open a blank screen and looked deeply into the plaster across from me.

I started typing out an outline:

A Revenge Story
1. *Two wives married to the same man.*
2. *They find each other and begin to plot his demise.*
3. *They meet to plan his death, but not before taking out massive insurance policies.*

"What is a mystery without a plot?" As if the chattering of my keys awakened the Walls from a dormant slumber. It knew I was writing.

"I haven't yet asked for your input," I replied matter-of-factly.

"Not yet, but you will," The Walls responded with as much confidence as I had.

"Why create a mystery when there is one to tell from the archives of my mind, Taylor?" The Wall sang, its voice drawing me in. I knew it was caressing me, pulling me toward it, and begging me to ask it for another story so that it could take another piece of me.

"The stories come at too high a cost for me to ask without trying first," I replied.

"Taylor," the Walls velvet purr, slipped into the room. "You are more than you've ever been without Nick."

"If you think it was getting rid of Nick that made me better, you underestimate me," I replied as I continued my outline.

4. *But before they can finish the task, one wife goes missing*
5. *The suspect is the other wife*
6. *But we find out that the husband had a third wife!*

The Walls cackled. It wasn't just a laugh. It manifested itself as vibrations that rattled the foundation, beneath the floorboards, flicking the lights.

My fingers hit against the keys.

"That is a terrible story." The Walls crooned, their insult smooth in its hammering honesty. "Predictable. *Tsk*, not your best work, Taylor." The Walls snapped their tongue with a click, but... where had it come from? This was an inanimate object—a house.

A horror.

And it was *mocking* me.

"We had a deal. You need me just as much as I need your stories. I could choose never to give you another." The threat squawked from the back of my throat.

A snapping of beams and the distant crumbling of something old rooms away crept in from the hallway.

"Who will you manipulate then, if not me?"

"You wouldn't dare." The Walls hissed in unrelenting anger.

"Will you make me disappear too?" I asked pointedly.

There was a pause but no answer. A damp silence filled the room and the space between the Walls and I.

"Write this little story, Taylor, and see how it fares in the hands of your loyal readers who have come to expect better from you."

The lights resumed a steady brightness, their wavered flickering faded, and the tension evaporated from the room.

The Walls' presence faded away, and I was left in silence. Alone.

I highlighted the entire page and deleted it. It wasn't a great idea, but not all of them are. I'll find one. I knew I would. I just needed a little *inspiration*. I looked at the painting again, and a thought lingered on the lobes of my creative mind for just long enough for me to catch it.

I needed something *good*.

Something the Walls couldn't fight.

✳✳✳

I had Cass send me a few art exhibitions in the area that she would attend if she were here. *For research purposes,* and well, it wasn't a lie. I needed something refreshing, something new. I needed a new way to think about how I created stories.

I would prove to the Walls that I was still a talented writer without them. All the Walls gave me were the ideas. It was still my prose. It was still the words I chose to connect to form imagery and thoughts. These stories were still *my* writing.

I quickly looked in the mirror, adjusted the bottom of my leather jacket, and tucked part of my shirt into the top of my jeans. There was motivation out there just waiting to find me. I felt it.

The blur of street signs flew past as my driver pulled up to the front of a small coffee house. An unassuming and relatively *small* venue for an exhibition, I thought as I made my way to the door.

Cass called and added me to the list, so I walked through—as a VIP.

This adventure was mine alone. Dante was back in California for a big case he'd been working on, and I'd told him I was asleep hours ago. It took so little to convince myself that I wasn't the problem.

The space was deceivingly large. Had I stepped into another dimension? The outside didn't match the elegant and modern interior. Soft glows of bright white LED lights along the ceilings, high-gloss black floors that showed not a single imperfection.

I stepped toward the bar, grabbed a glass of wine off the tray, and quickly walked toward the first piece. The lights were strategically placed to highlight only portions of the canvas, leaving the rest dark and almost impossible to see.

I think that was the point, the *deeper meaning*, that there was an entire piece of art on this wall, but we could only see what was being shown *to* us.

I'm starting to get it. I thought to myself while I admired the creativity. I took the first sip from the free wine and immediately recognized the assault on my tongue. I dribbled the gulp back into the glass without being noticed while wiping my face with the napkin. I unassumingly looked for a place to leave it *accidentally*.

"It's *the worst*, isn't it?" A familiar voice said from behind me. One that I'd never forget.

Emma.

She handed me a new glass. "It's banana. One of the artists here made it in her garage."

My eyes widened. "Banana wine?" I snorted. "Just saying it sounds wrong."

"Tell me about it. She brought it to set up and lied to our faces when she'd said it was the best wine she'd ever tasted," Emma smiled.

"Maybe that's the art. She knows it's fucking awful, but we're all pretending and committing to her lie... willingly." I said, raising an eyebrow while I sipped the new glass Emma had given me.

"Look at you, Tay, all introspective and shit," Emma said, slurring her words slightly.

She was drunk.

"Ah, but how many glasses did you have?" I teased her as I walked toward the next piece. We both stared at it silently for an exceptionally long time before she turned to me, "Listen, Tay, I'm so sorry." She confessed, the wine getting the best of her no matter which flavor it has been.

"Emma, it's fine. You don't have to apologize." I reassured her, "But it's good to see you." I added.

There it was.

The adventure.

Emma leaned in, the wine's hint of fruit on her breath, but the light scent of daisies was still strong on her skin.

I loved that smell.

"I loved you, too." She whispered, barely getting the words out. "But you scared me, you scare me. Big successful writer... I live paycheck to paycheck and drive a twenty-year-old Volkswagen."

I'd never thought of Emma as someone who worried about what kind of vehicle anyone drove or that my success was any contributing factor to how we felt about each other. Emma had put on a good show, being a carefree artist who couldn't be caged, but I think she wanted something *more.*

But perhaps all artists were doomed to tussle with and battle against their own devaluation, forever unable to see their worth.

But, the Walls, they'd take her... like they'll take *everything.*

"Emma, we should get you home. What do you say?"

"I thought you'd never ask." She looped her arm in mine and leaned hard into me as a crutch.

I had my driver take Emma back to her apartment. We climbed four flights of stairs that seemed to never end. Arriving at the top, panting and entirely out of breath, she leaned her back against her door, her loud laugh certain to wake up all her neighbors.

"Shhhh!" I teased her as we stood back against her apartment.

She leaned out, grabbed my leather jacket, and pulled me in. She kissed me exactly how she had that first night she came to the Estate, that first tantalizing kiss that snatched my heart from my chest. She'd taken it like a thief in the night and never returned it. But I hadn't asked her to. I loved that she had my heart in her hands.

I melted into the kiss, and when it became an almost violent urge to be more than a kiss, I pulled away. I brushed a curly hair from her face and tucked it behind her ear.

"All I ever want is for you to be *happy*," I said calmly, holding her face in my hands while she bit her lip, smiling. I closed my eyes, imagining what our life could have been like while her warmth washed over me. She didn't see it coming. I watched hope deflate from her eyes. The gold flecks that made them so intricate and beautiful turned dull under the single glowing light flickering above us.

"But I have to go," I said, taking the moment away from us.

The car ride home felt less hopeful than I imagined, but I knew I'd done the right thing.

✳✳✳

"What about a romantasy? They're blowing up right now on social media." I said as Cass's video went blank.

"Really? You're going to make up advanced magic systems and entire worlds like... Nefarlandia?" Her face popped back into the frame, covered in a green face masque.

"Oooh! They could be *green?*" I chimed with a slight giggle.

"Next idea," She demanded.

"Two star-crossed lovers who can't be together because their families are mortal enemies?" I said while thumbing through a catalog of office supplies that mysteriously appeared on my desk.

"Ok, *Shakespeare*," Cass said, annoyed.

"What did you do to get the ideas for *All Good Years* and *The Clockmaker's Wife?* Just do that again.

"Those came to me in a dream, and I can't just *dream* good ideas on purpose." I lied. And it sounded real enough. Artists and writers could say off-the-wall things, and most just considered it to be artistic genius.

"I think you need to go back to the drawing board. Like all the way back, to when they invented the drawing board and start there because wherever these ideas came from... Not it." She was harsh, but I knew it came from a place of love.

"Ok... This time next week?" I questioned.

"I'll put it on the calendar. I love you!" she shouted as she closed the call before I could reply.

"Rude," I whispered as I held my head.

I was rapidly running out of freedom without any ideas for a new novel. Everbound wanted to keep up this rapid release momentum because, as of right now, my name was *everywhere*. People were hyper-consuming Taylor Halethorpe's stories in either book or big-screen form. The soundtracks were killer. The marketing team was unmatched. Absolute all-star casts signed up for both media projects.

Even *Glass Heels* was being mentioned in mainstream media again. As expected, it was over-glorified as a *classic* masterpiece when it was the lazy musing of my angry teenage mind. It proved that you could *do no harm* once you were in society's good graces.

I debated asking the Walls for another story, but I wasn't that desperate—not yet. I still had time to create a story, build a plot, and write the pages that made the readers fall in love again.

On my own.

✳✳✳

The fire flickered and cast its larger-than-life shadows onto the walls of the sitting room. Its roaring heat was a comfort I'd appreciate as the halls of the Estate felt more frigid and damp than usual this evening. I'd been playing with plots and ideas, moving little bits and blocks around on the glaring white screen for hours.

A barely noticeable knock at the door thrust my heart into my throat, and my body convulsed into a panic. I had security at the gates for a *reason.* I thought to myself.

My reaction was entirely the result of my reckless reading about unsolved murders in Maryland, page by page, for hours on end. I had been hunting for a backdrop for a possible murder mystery.

And now, a knock at my door when I *had* a costly security detail to prevent this type of interruption from happening. I opened the heavy iron viewing panel, something I'd rarely done in all my living here, and looked carefully through.

Dante.

A surprise visit.

I closed the panel with a clank and unlocked each bolt quickly. I smiled as they opened, and he remained on one knee in the cool rain of the evening.

I think I did it to cover my expression.

I held my hand to my mouth, and a small gasp escaped. Panic rolled through my body, a familiar type of gut-wrenching pain, like my heart was breaking all over again at the idea of marrying Dante.

Fear.

But I went against everything it was trying to tell me.

And I said, "Yes."

CHAPTER 24

WILDFLOWER
2022

"Pete nixed all of your extraordinary ideas, Tay." I heard Cass hesitate to give me the bad news, but I was distracted by the enormous diamond on my left hand.

"Yeah, some were... really bad," I admitted.

"Is everything okay?" Cass asked. I felt her concern, knowing that a few years ago, I'd gone dark. I knew she felt the tension as we turned up empty-handed on the idea list.

"Yes, Cass, just a little writer's block is all. I'll get through it."

"We can't keep throwing noodles at the wall to see what sticks. Pete's getting antsy."

A vision flashed across my mind of tossing a bowl of spaghetti at my Walls. A light chuckle forced its way out.

"*Pete...* can fuck off if I'm being honest." I sat up on the stool at the kitchen bar and focused on the conversation now that I'd flung spaghetti and an insult. "I get it, but pressure and I don't mix. I... am not a diamond." The sparkle couldn't keep me from staring at it. A silence lingered before she asked.

"So..." She playfully planned her question. "How big is it?" It was an artful change of subject that I appreciated.

"Five carats, so much bigger than the first one," I said, realizing it was a little grim to compare. "And everything's fine, we're all fine," I repeated, trying to convince Cass *and* myself.

"I just want you to be happy," Cass said, brushing off the fact that we both knew that deep down Dante couldn't be fully trusted, not *yet,* at least.

And it reminded me of those last words I'd said to Emma.

"I'm going back to the drawing board. I'll call you later," I said quickly and hung up.

I closed my eyes and let the memory of that night serenade me. If I tried hard enough, I could smell the faint tang of clementine that always danced along her neck, the lingering hint of daisy in her hair, and the way her smile felt like a glowing hearth in the dappled darkness of an empty room.

God, I needed a book idea. This longing for the artist who didn't want me was becoming unbearable, even for me.

I opened my eyes, and I was in the study. I hadn't walked here, had I? Last I remembered, I was in the sitting room, in front of the fire.... and now I was at my desk, the old typewriter I'd pushed into the closet in front of me.

Had the Walls done this?

Were they pushing me toward their call, begging me to be under their influence?

I had to admit that it was exhilarating when the Walls were singing their stories. It was the rush of an idea, and the way the words tumbled out of me thoughtlessly in such a poetic motion. I barely had to think. It came through my body so naturally. I missed that thrill. The high of my next best work dripped from my mind like honey from a comb.

But I fought the urge to ask the Walls for their help. At least for one more day. I sat before the typewriter, waiting for the first words to come to me. I closed my eyes and took a deep breath.

She smelled like clementine and daisy, and I was head over heels in love with her.

It wasn't a story and had no plot, but it was all I could think of, so I began writing about Emma.

The pages kept flowing, and as I reached the end of one page, the clang of reloading would be the only pause. I'd lay my thoughts face down next to me, and as the sun set, the stack grew taller, and my prose grew wild and vivid. I'd written over a hundred pages.

When I finally stopped, I grabbed the stack and reread over my musings, looking for a way to turn them into something tangible.

I spent another two weeks turning the scraps and ramblings into something worth sending to Cass. It's how I'd written *Glass Heels*, and that was good enough for an entire society. Stitching together the scraps of my existence had worked before. It captivated a whole world at one time. I could do it again—*without* the Walls and with my ideas.

Not a story of hate and madness but one of love and desire.

A story of love deferred or perhaps unrequited.

An adventure.

I emailed Cass a rough first draft of *The Adventures of Loving a Wildflower* on Friday, and she called on Sunday.

"Hey, Tay." I searched her voice for acceptance.

"Pete's ok with Wildflower. He said it's not your best work, but we do have something quality."

I let out a sigh of relief.

"Tay... is this about Emma?" The question was rather direct, but that was to be expected with Cass.

"Yes, actually, it is."

"What's Dante going to say about this? It's pretty heavy stuff..." Cass' concern for the health of my fresh engagement was endearing.

"I am a writer, Cass. A *fiction* writer." The agitation rose in my voice at the question.

"I know. But I think it's unwise not to consider him." She said, pausing to let out a sigh.

"He'll get over it."

"And what will *she* think?" Cass asked something I hadn't considered.

"The name is changed enough. She'll be fine." I leaned back in my chair and put my hands to my face in frustration. "No one knew we were dating." I hesitated. "You couldn't even call it that. We were nothing."

"This story says otherwise... I'm not trying to upset you. I want us to be realistic about what comes next once we send this out into the world." Cass's thinking about the consequences was new to me. Is this what it was like once the stakes were higher? I'd always known her as a charge-into-battle-and-worry-about-the-odds-only-when-we-were-outnumbered kind of person.

"I want this published."

Those were the only words she needed to hear.

"The Adventures of Loving a Wildflower - Taylor Halethorpe's artsy dedication to a love unrequited falls short, but is it just misunderstood?"

I read the headline as I attempted to sip my heavily sweetened coffee. "Story of my life," I grumbled when I realized the cup was empty.

The release was highly anticipated, and pre-order sales were up, but something happened, and the brightly colored bar charts showed sales taking a nosedive.

Everbound wasn't thrilled, but it wasn't a total loss. The book had a small dedicated following that was doing a new kind of street

185

marketing to target people who had never read a *"Taylor Halethorpe"* novel.

It was disheartening to know that a story I'd written myself, created from nothing but my love for Emma, was close to being considered a flop. The Walls cranked out stories of love and had the world eating out of the palm of my hand.

But *my* love? Not the same.

Not even close.

FROM THE ADVENTURES OF LOVING A WILDFLOWER

CHAPTER 17

Lucia sat stiffly on the edge of the chair, her wrists angled on the desk, hovering above the old typewriter. Her fingers were ready to press deeply down onto the keys and release a flood of beautiful words and poetry. But the room was silent, like the first night in a new house, only the clatters and clangs of strange mechanisms working faintly in the distance.

The only recognizable sound was the soft scratch of a brush moving across the textured canvas. Violet had warned her not to move—not an inch, not even speak—for sometimes the wrong words could ruin the right moment.

Lucia couldn't help herself. She shifted her position and darted her vision to the beautiful Violet, but she could only see her golden eyes peeking out from the top of the easel. Lucia smiled at her in awe of the mastery of her chosen art.

"Stop looking at me," Violet murmured playfully, her voice low, but Lucia could tell the smile was there.

"Then stop being distracting," Lucia shot back, though it was said with an endearment that couldn't be confused.

Watching Violet paint had become a favorite thing of hers. She was all focus and frenzy, unfazed by her surroundings. An unruly mess, her hair tangled and paint in places it shouldn't be. Even the paint found her skin a more worthy canvas.

"You're something else," Violet said, her brush keeping even strokes with a tattering of speckling or shading. She was telling a story of her own on that canvas. Lucia was certain Violet was chasing a fleeting feeling and spilling out in front of her with colors.

Being painted was a vulnerable feeling, like being unwrapped and unraveled by someone who looked beyond it all. But being painted by Violet in this darkened room left Lucia exposed entirely. It was a calculated risk whose reward had not yet been revealed.

Lucia's hands grew tired, positioned over the typewriter. She couldn't write, not like this. Not with Violet staring so intensely into parts of her she'd kept hidden for all these years. She saw her for all she was, including the pieces she even lied to herself about.

"This is ridiculous," Lucia said finally, breaking the silence and building the tension between them.

"Then write something, Lu," Violet replied without hesitation. "But... *don't* move."

Violet smiled as she said it.

Lucia's cheeks flushed, and she pressed keys delicately on the typewriter. Now, the heavy metal clanks pierced the moment, filling it with something other than tension.

"You look perfect," Violet confessed, admiring her momentary muse and work as she stood back. "How your face changes when you think about finding the right words... It's like you have to catch them before they flutter away like a butterfly."

"You're moving into poetry now? How bold?" Lucia teased Violet to deflect the intensity of the flattery.

"You make it sound like I'm—"

"Whatever you're about to say, don't," Violet demanded. "You are the universe." The moment hung between them, surrounded by the calm calamity, the sounds of their arts mingling.

"Just keep writing," Violet said softly, "And I'll keep painting."

"And maybe we can meet in the middle, somewhere between light and ink," Lucia said profoundly as she typed the exact words heavily on the typewriter's keys.

CHAPTER 25

THREAT
2022

"And then we can sell the Estate, and you can move back to California." The words danced off his lips slowly, like the graceful poses of a ballet dancer who'd mastered thirty-two perfectly timed Fouettés. His eyes met mine, and I'm certain he recognized the shock, the horror, and my disgust at his audacity.

"Oh… you weren't thinking we'd *stay* here?" He paused, lifting his mug to his lips, sucking in the black coffee with an egregious slurp that felt like nails down a chalkboard. For a moment, I was grateful that something was blocking his mouth to shut him up, but the repulsive sound was worse. "You can't have a writing career in… Maryland, Tay." He gave me almost no time to assert a response, to push back.

"I'm not selling the Estate." It was all I could muster. It was the only sense I could make. If I pushed any further, I'd say something regretful. "This Estate has been in my family since it was built. What a strange thought it was for you to think I'd be the one to offload it." I finally calmed enough to make sense of it.

I eyed him.

"We can't possibly afford the upkeep…" He trailed off, realizing that we were both highly successful in our careers and that excuse was obliterated by my royalty checks alone.

"I'm not having this conversation again. I'm not selling the Estate. Not today, not tomorrow, not in a week. Never." I said as I took my coffee cup from the counter and walked into the next room, away from him and his repulsive face.

He followed me.

"Do you plan to move back to California at least? To LA?" He was spiraling. I could hear the desperation in his voice.

"Honestly, Dante, *No*. I hadn't thought about it, and if you asked me right now, this Estate is where I want to live." I was honest for the first time in our relationship. That's all I could be. I took a deep breath.

"When you left—"

"When I left? How many times are you going to bring that up, Taylor? *It was a mistake.*" Dante's face was bright red. He was losing his calm demeanor, another first for our relationship.

I was finally seeing something *real*. I'd begun to believe he was only made up of superficial exchanges and trivial chatter, but his expression showed frustration and anger... But in the glowing light of the fireplace, he looked like a child throwing a temper tantrum, and the thought repulsed me, shrinking away any attraction I might have had for him.

"Right! A mistake that you'll have to spend some time making up for. Including living in Maryland for a while." I smiled half-heartedly, hoping he'd see the reason and back down. I stepped quickly toward the stairs as a sign that I wanted to be left alone.

✳✳✳

Wildflower had done so poorly in all avenues that the book tour was canceled. There just wasn't enough interest to sustain the costs. Everbound was adamant that the only way to get over the flop was to kick out another novel as quickly as possible.

"Good writing takes time." I was audibly frustrated.

"I know, Tay. I know... I'll do everything I can." Cass's voice was stretched thin, like she, too, was exhausted.

"They need to have more realistic expectations." It was the last thing I said before I hung up abruptly.

I stared at the empty space on my laptop screen.

I took a deep breath in and a slow breath out.

Repeat.

There was a knock at my office door. Miriam approached with folded papers and envelopes gently held in her hand. I reached out, took the mail from her, and sighed deeply.

"Another story? Already?" She questioned me, noticing the multiple empty mugs of coffee on my desk, which were just from today.

"Let me take these," she quickly said, pulling the dirty cups out of my way. "If you don't take a break, there might be nothing left of you to tell the beautiful stories," she said calmly as she made her way back out of the office, carrying away the evidence of my caffeine addiction. She stopped at the door. "Too many Halethorpe women have lost themselves chasing stories."

"Without stories, I am nothing." I groaned, but she was already down the hall.

"Without the stories, I am nothing," I repeated. I had never believed it more, except the part I wasn't admitting was, *without the stories the Walls gave me,* I was nothing. My own stories weren't enough.

I wasn't enough.

A soft shift in the air filled the room, a breeze but with no open window.

"Perhaps you've learned a valuable lesson?" The deep voice questioned with authority.

"Oh, I can't wait to hear this," I grumbled, my hands laced deeply into my hair at the roots, tugging ever so slightly in frustration.

"A story without my blessing will fail. It doesn't matter how beautiful the words, or how captivating the chapters."

"That can't be true," I replied, tearing my hands from my hair and slamming them down on the desk. "That wasn't in the bargain," I cried out.

"The bargain was that you would tell *my* stories, not your own, Taylor."

"I'll write whatever story my heart desires." My answer contained a grimness I knew the Walls sensed, but we had not agreed on exclusivity, and I wouldn't be bullied.

"I shouldn't need to warn you, Taylor, but there will be no more stories I haven't given you, no more *Wildflowers* or wildcards. My stories are the only ones that you will publish."

"And if I don't agree?"

"Then perhaps you will wither away, a no one. Irrelevant and without a purpose."

I wasn't ready to give up my life as an author to retire into obscurity. I still dreamed of writing my masterpiece, the story that would captivate every reader and enthrall every audience—a novel that would be talked about for years after I was gone.

I wasn't ready to give this dream up *yet*, and if the only way I could guarantee my spot among the great writers was to tell only the Walls stories, then... I suppose I would.

CHAPTER 26

TRUST

2023

Dante flew back to Maryland a week after our argument, and when he came through the doors of the Estate, I met him wearing one of Miriam's aprons. I had smeared sauces and ingredients all over me. It was stuck between the strands of my hair and adorably splattered across my cheeks.

"What is this?" he grinned at the sight of the growing catastrophe that was me, *cooking*. It's not something I ever did or had ever done. Even when I lived alone all those years in my crummy apartment, I'd survived on the luck of the food poisoning fates, Ramen, and gas station California rolls.

"Dinner." I smiled flirtatiously at him, hoping it was enough of a truce for him to relinquish his need to *talk* out whatever was going wrong between us again.

I knew it certainly wasn't the correct answer, but I didn't want the chaos of an argument. I didn't want something else to fall apart, as I'd deemed my career on a downward slope after *Wildflower* bombed.

With no new ideas in mind, the Walls are now threatening me, forcing me to stay within the boundaries of this Estate. I wasn't ready to pay the fee for another world-shattering story. Not yet.

"I've never seen you cook," Dante flashed a teasing smile. "If that's what you call this," his eyes darting across the kitchen that I'd all but destroyed.

"It's beef and barley soup, to start," I smiled, pointing to a pot with brown-colored ooze dripping down the sides. Followed by grilled salmon and roasted vegetables."

"Wow, what a meal," Dante said sarcastically as he slowly cut through the mess and pressed himself against me, wrapping his arms around my waist and pulling me close.

He *always* smelled so good.

He brushed a stray strand of hair that had slipped from my bun to the side and kissed me. A passion that he and I hadn't had in a long time came violently pulsing through my body. I'd felt like this with him before, connected... *love.*

Had I faked it so well that I'd tricked myself into genuinely falling for him again? I met him in the middle, a compromised kiss where I gave back the same energy that he was putting in, and as quickly as he'd made his way through the maze of the kitchen, he'd lifted me and carried me out.

We made it to the sitting room, where he met me and laid me down gently in a vigorous display of his strength and masculinity. I waited patiently for what came next.

A gasp rose to my lips, and for a moment, I'd let all my worries lift away with Dante's affection. I forgot about *Wildflower.* I'd forgotten about the Walls' control over me. I'd even forgotten about *dinner.*

Soup!

The slight scent of burnt food had already made its way to my nose, and I snapped from midway through a meteoric rise to pleasure, cutting us both off before it could materialize into anything more. I jumped from under him and ran for the Kitchen.

Miriam had made it to the pot first and corrected my mistakes, cleaning up the mass of dirty dishes and platters. I quickly rushed to the Dutch oven resting on the gas cooktop.

"I've already tended to it, Lady Halethorpe." Miriam interrupted my frantic dash to save my appetizer.

"It's not ruined." She smiled at me, tossing a towel over her shoulder like always.

"It's delicious. I tasted it." She raised an eyebrow and gave me a side-eyed smile. Her opinion on the matter was something I had very much valued. Miriam could cook and bake anything, and it always tasted like the Gods had made it from bits of heaven and angel dust.

"I will finish this, please, return to whatever it was you were," she paused and let a devilish grin rise on her lips, "*doing.*" She finished her sentence, and it made my skin crawl with embarrassment.

I poked my head out to the sitting room, and Dante was nowhere to be found. I looked around to see if he'd wandered down the lower-level hall, but there was no sign.

I walked through the rooms and glanced up the grand staircase banister. Little bits of his clothing lay out on a tantalizing path to our bedroom.

I let out a light sigh, refocused on the stairs, and led myself to a darkened room where I might rekindle parts of my engagement that had long lost their fire.

✳✳✳

Through the door into the darkened room, Dante stood before me. He ran his fingers down around my waist and slowly untied the apron. It fell to the floor, and a soft bristle of fabric pierced the radiating silence. He reached for the bottom of my shirt, and as he lifted it, I raised my hands delicately above my head. The cloth grazed the hot parts of my face as he tossed it to the side.

He lowered his mouth to my bare skin and planted soft, supple kisses in places he hadn't gone in *months*. My skin prickled underneath the warmth of him as he ran his hands down my body, loosening my pants and letting them fall gracefully to where we stood.

He dropped to his knees, kissing every inch of me. My chest, my stomach, my hips, and my thighs, and as he dove deeper, I laced my fingers into the softness of his hair at the euphoria his mouth was creating.

My knees weakened, and I descended to meet his face with mine. He smiled at the recognition of pleasure on my face, and he pulled me onto the floor gently, placing his hand behind my head as we crashed onto the plush rug.

He teased and caressed with the tips of his lips and the soft warmth of his fingers while I selfishly enjoyed all his incredible efforts. I let him take my worries away, his mouth begging my body to unleash what it held back.

As soon as I did, a rush of ecstasy roared from my lips as I called Dante's name out into the darkness of the room. The wild moment of his name's release was a beckoning for him to fuck me until I had nothing more in me.

He towered over me, his muscular arms holding his body above mine. He pushed forward, and as it happened, we both called out to a God neither of us believed in. The heat of our bodies pressed against one another was incredible, a tingling sensation that electrified and amplified every sensation.

The intensity of the moment was overwhelming my every sense. If my eyes were open, I couldn't see. If there was noise, I only heard the absence of all sound. A dull roar of silence intermingled with the panting of my fiancé.

He took his time, letting me feel every heartbeat, every slow movement, every forward, and every pull backward. My body squirmed under him, knowing that this pace was designed to make me beg, to make me crave the power I knew he had. He was waiting for me to ask for it, but I wanted him to want it. I wanted him to *crave* me.

His face buried in my chest, lightly teasing with a flutter of his tongue.

I whispered it—I know I did.

"I want you to *want* to."

As it registered, like a challenge he willingly accepted, Dante effortlessly turned me over, pulled me back onto him, and pressed my head down into the faux fur of the rug. I arched my back, and he pushed harder and deeper, demanding my pleasure, my hands gripping and clawing at anything to hold on while he ravaged me, pleading for *another*. He was relentless, and when he thought he might fail, when the noises and soft moans I'd let escape slowly began to fade, he pulled himself back and buried his mouth in the void and twirled me around with the warmth of his violent tongue.

I felt my entire body roll with pleasure, a vibrating, uncontrollable spasm that I *wouldn't* even try to stop. Together, we collapsed, out of breath, drenched in sweat, our bodies glistening in the faint moonlight from a distant window.

Dante and I enjoyed our two-course meal across from each other at the large dining hall table. The scrape of the metal against the ceramic plates was the only sound while we both refueled all that was lost in the hours before. There was barely a glance shared between us during the entire event.

But when we finally did, I started to remember why I'd chosen him in the first place. There was something about him that I loved. I saw it in his smile and his confidence. The way our conversations were elevated and intellectual, he challenged parts of me that neither Nick nor Emma ever had.

The Dante that left wanted a relationship but also wanted to force his future wife to offload her priceless family legacy... He liked the *idea* of a relationship, not the complexities of being in one.

That wasn't the Dante positioned across from me, gazing handsomely into my eyes with a stare that claimed me forever.

This Dante whispered sweet nothings about reinvesting in the Estate, bringing it back to life, raising a family, and expanding.

This Dante sang whispers of our permanence, rebranding, and reviving the Halethorpe name. *And even about giving Miriam a raise.*

It was like he'd come back from California with a different agenda. It was as if he'd had a goal, and it was to *make* me fall in love with him—every movement of his hands, every well-timed affectionate kiss, every perfectly placed statement.

I'd been entranced and enthralled with the after-love-making glow, but as the euphoria faded, I could see in his seedy eyes that there was something else brewing behind them.

I'd call it deceit, but I couldn't understand why. Why deceive me? I'd call it ambition, but his career was as successful as mine. What would prompt someone to infiltrate my heart and play games with such cruel intentions?

It seemed that Dante might be finding more than one way to fuck me.

CHAPTER 27

LOST LOVE
2023

"In 1927, The Halethorpe's hosted a grand ball, which began with the sparkling of a rare diamond necklace and ended in a murder."

The murder mystery I'd been searching for was right here, in the ballroom of the Halethorpe Estate. I'd never read anything in my research that pointed here. It must be a hidden story, one untold. Another secret was buried behind the wisps of wallpaper that covered the devilish Walls of the Halethorpe Estate.

I may be the only one able even to tell it.

The Walls' abrupt, unruly voice was filled with the certainty that I'd say yes. "But I need something for my words, Taylor."

"I know, but what this time?" I halted, afraid to ask the question, knowing—deep down—that the price would be too much for me no matter what it wanted.

"I've given you everything I have," I whispered, my voice cracking in an emotional pain I couldn't begin to describe.

There was silence accompanied by a dense stillness. The echoes that normally filled the room became dampened as if the room were soundproof.

"Memories."

My breath caught, and my eyes darted to the portrait hanging delicately against the body of the voice I knew was prepared to ask me to sacrifice the memory of one of the most real loves I had ever felt.

"What do you mean, *memories?*" A moment fluttered across my mind... What if I pretended she was of no importance, of no matter? Perhaps the Walls would make another choice.

"Your memories of Emma," The Wall now mumbled instead of clearly pronouncing its desires—like it knew it was asking for too much.

"I want the nights you spent tangled together, the smell of clementine and daisy, and how her laughter broke you open. All of it."

There was a long pause while the pain of the cost danced in the heavy air of the room. I wasn't breathing. I'd stopped. The pain in my chest was pressing me down, suffocating me. I let out a gasp.

"It's not for nothing, Taylor Halethorpe. I will give you a story that makes you immortal."

A well of tears formed behind my eyes, and I wrestled with the thoughts. Images of Emma flashed through my mind: her wild hair, the way she painted chaotic swirls of color that made no sense, her touch, her voice, how she made me feel alive when I was a ghost walking through a haunted life.

I clenched my jaw as the anger took over. My heart was pounding inside my chest, clanging against my bones and ricocheting up into my ears.

"Why her?" I begged.

"Why does it have to be her? Take Dante." I'd said it so fast that I didn't even feel guilty. I'd give my fiancé up to keep just memories of an abandoned, unrequired love. What life was I truly living?

"Dante, as you will soon see, is worthless in your story." The Walls clamored back, this time with authority. I'd attempted to bargain something useless, and they'd taken offense. They rippled with a new anger, a relentless force.

"Emma is the part of you that's free, that fights against me. She takes up too much space inside of you." The Walls knew she was what kept me tied to reality. She *did* take up so much of my heart. I mean... she *was* my heart.

"My last novel was a flop. How can you guarantee anything?"

"You wrote your last novel without my assistance, against my wishes, without my voice. You wonder why it failed?"

"It didn't *fail*. It was truth, and it was beautiful."

"But what did it lack, Taylor? What was missing?" The Walls asked, already knowing the answer.

"*You*—it lacked you."

A long silence hung between the Walls and me.

"Will it hurt?" I whispered, my voice cracking, *afraid* of the answer.

"No, you will simply go to sleep, and she will be like a dream you had once and nothing more."

The idea of losing Emma this way should have felt like an arrow to my heart, a critical wound that would take me toward the light. But, as I came to think of it, she'd already been fading so quickly. I'd written her down. I'd have the *Adventures of Loving a Wildflower* forever, and when I wanted to remember, I'd read it. I'd remember. I would fight against the Walls' power, and I'd know that I was loved.

I believed in a world where love could persevere, even through the absurd magic of talking walls. In exchange, I'd be more than *Glass Heels*. I'd be better than *All Good Years*. *The Clockmaker's Wife* was a beautiful novel, but only another chapter in my story. With this *last* one, I'd solidify my place in history as one of our generation's greatest writers.

I'd have nothing left to prove.

It would be the last. It had to be. Nothing would be left for the Walls to take after I couldn't remember Emma.

"Will she remember me?" I asked quietly.

"Yes." The Walls thundered.

"Take her," I whispered in a breathy surrender.

The dense air dissipated from the room, and the subtle echoes of the fireplace and radiator crackled. A calm wind swept across, fluttering the long velvet drapes.

"Now, unlike Emma, I shall tell you a story you will never forget."

✷✷✷

The Walls had said I'd hold onto Emma until I fell asleep, so as they chatted away with the details of this next novel, I took a detour through every moment I'd had with her. The nights spent in each other's arms, the promises we left unsaid, the feeling of being *seen* for who I was and not who I was supposed to be.

When the Walls had slowly melted away, I'd felt their presence in the room fade to nothing while I looked around, feeling empty and broken. Again, shattered by the demands of the consuming debts that kept growing larger and larger.

The Aurora sat, sparkling, and everything else surrounding it was dimmed with a light layer of dust. It glared back at me, untouched by debris, as if it wanted to be the brightest thing in the room.

I snarled at it like it was mocking me with its pristine condition on top of the mantle. Without thinking, I approached it. I let my fingers run down the rainbows trapped inside the fractured, cut glass. It was a stunning award for a story I'd worked hard on writing but now disgusted me.

It was heavy when I picked it up—far more so now than the night I'd won it. Perhaps this was a metaphor for how it had come to haunt me, weighing down my career with its compounding expectations.

I tossed it into the fire, and as the flames shattered and charred it into nothing, I revisited all that Emma had ever given me and tried to hold onto every moment, breath, and scent.

I begged my eyes to stay open, even long after the Wall had abandoned me. I jerked myself awake, sitting in my deteriorating leather chair. I smacked the sides of my face, opened the window as wide as possible, and let the cool air sting against my cheeks.

I'd ask for just a minute longer with her.

Just one more....

CHAPTER 28

SHADOWS IN THE BALLROOM
2023

The words were already written, and the prose was placed in perfect pecking order. The soliloquies were spoken, and the pentameters preached. Each letter was carefully placed, one before the other, the beginning before the end.

Only then, once the last T had been crossed and the last I had been dotted, did I realize that the mystery I'd written was about *Florence Caldwell.*

Miriam's mother.

The words tumbled from the plaster walls into my ears and then out through my fingers, attacking the keyboard with fervor—tears formed in the corner of my eyes, carving paths down my cheeks. I was connected in a way I'd never been before, writing the story as the walls confessed it, from the perspective of someone scared and lost...

I was retelling the true story of a gradual unraveling. When I met the unreliable narrator and heard her final words, I felt her final thoughts on that dreadful night of a sparkling grand ball— the invisible housekeeper whose jewels had been snatched from her grasp, stolen without cause. An heirloom passed down from generation to generation, only for this treacherous Estate to swallow it whole and end such a legacy here.

I had to talk to Miriam.

I'd given The Walls *something* I knew I had but couldn't quite remember what, and this story… It had to be told, for I knew I had paid a cost too great.

But Miriam…

Was this even my story to tell? The Walls had given it to me, yes. That was true. Is it fair for me, Taylor Halethorpe, to tell Florence Caldwell's tragic legacy?

This Estate had already taken so much from Miriam, including her mother's sanity and their family heirloom. Now, it threatened her right to privacy by giving me *this* story—of all the stories.

The Walls tricked me into sacrificing some part of my life that I could not, for the life of me, remember… for a story I may not even be able to tell.

Could I?

The Walls had beguiled me. I'd bargained with the devil. I received a story that would solidify me as one of the great writers of my time but for twice the cost.

Would I lose Miriam if these words were published?

I *had* to talk to Miriam.

FROM SHADOWS IN THE BALLROOM

CHAPTER 65

"It was me." I stared into the mirrored wall, the cold reflection showing me an empty room. A room I had cleaned, time after time, party after party. I had tidied the misplaced flatware, shined silver platters, and polished glass until it was invisible.

But never, in my darkest thoughts, had I imagined I'd be cleaning up my own mess. Mopping blood from the glossy parquet floors.

I never imagined dragging this man—this thief who weighed twice what I did—across the ballroom. I never imagined pulling him to the boiler room, where the air seared my lungs and soot clung to my cheeks. Without a second thought, I heaved him forward, let his weight fall, and watched the flames catch him in their welcoming arms.

This is my legacy now. Once there was a priceless diamond necklace, now a curse, a stain on my soul and my family's name. "Florence Caldwell," I panted, pulling the dead weight along. "The housekeeper..." I grunted again, teeth clenched, "...who became something evil."

I pushed the lifeless body over the edge. He fell into the bottomless, fiery pit, and I watched as the fire nibbled him and then consumed him all at once, searing him into the nothing he was.

It was a cleansing for both him and me. Of course, this fire would leave no trace of him, no evidence of his demise. The only memory of his demise was what I now carried in my heart. The guilt and the crushing disappointment of not having reclaimed the necklace despite the blood that was on not just my hands but my entire being.

I tore my clothing from my sweat-drenched body, the dampened soot smearing across my face, leaving stripes where my fingers touched my bare skin.

I hesitated momentarily and then tossed the balled-up apron and housedress into the last gasps of a hungry flame.

I slowly sank to the floor. The dull glow of embers filled my eyes with an amber sorrow I would never cure. I would learn to live with the dull ache that manifested deep within my chest, but I may never be free of it—not entirely.

When I finally emerged from the tomb, I speared my body out into the frigid cold of the night. The moon's pale light reflected off my bare skin, and the chill sent my body into an uncontrollable shiver. I pulled my arms around me to hold some heat while returning to my quarters quickly.

I passed the ballroom—dim, silent, pristine. There was no sign that a life had ended here. Everything was back in its rightful place. The chandeliers hung, their candles almost spent, slowly went out like the fading stars in the night sky. The music, the laughter, and the clinking of glasses vanished. Only silence remained, broken by the pounding of my heart.

I scurried across the darkened room on the tips of my bare toes, trying not to leave a single smudge or to make a single sound. I paused at the doorway and looked back one last time, as this was an *ironic* ending.

Freedom from a life in prison but forever trapped in this house of secrets and lies. A created prison, an inescapable one.

The Halethorpe Estate would never let me go.

Not now.

***

I was in the office for what felt like a single night, but when I checked the calendar, it had been weeks. I had been on autopilot in between writing sessions. Dante was back in California for a high-profile case, and I hadn't heard from him.

Or I had, and I'd ignored him.

It was still unclear.

Emerging from the *Shadows in the Ballroom* was surreal. I looked at the vast empty room, the star of the story I'd just written, and it was now just dust and canvas covers over ornate furniture. I had seen it alive in my writing, in the imagery. When The Walls chanted their story, I could close my eyes and *time travel* as if I had just landed directly in the heart of 1929, during prohibition.

I could smell the depth of the party, of the spills of secret wine and bootlegged fine spirits. I could feel the dense air damp with the sweat of partygoers and their frenzied dancing. My feet clung to the floor, covered in the sweet sugar of sprayed celebratory champagne.

I'd been to parties that were supposed to have felt like this but had *never* felt like this. There was magic that didn't exist in the world anymore, but in 1929, it was still wildly present. Here, everything was coated in a lighted gold glaze of allure, something most knew nothing about except for me and only when the Walls allowed it.

How lucky I was to be their voice. What a spectacular gift? It wasn't enough to be a Halethorpe but also the voice of this Estate.

But sometimes...

Miriam.

I broke myself from the daydream and ran for the kitchen. If Miriam was here, that was where she would be. I flung the swinging doors open, expecting to see her sipping tea or gently scouring a pan or dish, but she wasn't.

The longer I stood in the silent grand kitchen, the more I realized that there was no evidence she'd been here this morning. There was no coffee brewed, no cups set out. The milk and cream were not pulled from their cooler...

"Miriam!" I called, my voice erupting through the silence and ricocheting off the kitchen tile. I stood pacing as residual visions of the *Shadows in the Ballroom* flashed when I blinked. I saw Florence, Miriam's mother, clawing her way away from the man who'd stolen her necklace. I saw the accidental death and the panic... I saw the secret that tore Miriam's legacy from her hands.

I was in a panic. Had Miriam been my sacrif—

"Lady Halethorpe?" Miriam came in from outside and removed her overcoat. Her finely pressed button-down shirt was left without a single wrinkle. She was still here.

Thank God.

"Miriam..." I said, practically out of breath, not from physical activity but from the racing of my heart.

"You know... this place..." I said I was barely able to get the words out.

"This place?" She added, her eyebrow raised, her lips pulling at the corner as they did when she was confused.

"This place... it's magic, you know that, right?" I'd said it. I'd finally said it. I haven't broken the rules yet. I didn't tell her that the Walls *spoke.*

"Yes." She hung her coat on the hook at the rear of the kitchen and walked toward the coffee maker without missing a beat.

"I've seen it... the magic."

"Of course you have. That's where you get your stories."

Miriam had known the entire time.

"It told me a story..." I waited to collect the right words. "An important one." I wiped a tear from my face. "It was about Florence."

I stood staring at her. Waiting for the realization to travel from her ears to her mind and then to her heart for it to *feel*.

"I..." It barely escaped her mouth before she began to weep.

Miriam, the unshaken, stoic, sturdy woman, finally faltered. She put both hands on the counter and leaned forward, taking a deep breath. Slowly, her shallow breaths became muffled cries, and I rushed over to comfort her.

"And you will write this story?" Miriam asked as she wiped away a tear.

"I have to. I gave something up, and I can't remember what... but I know it was important; without this story, my career...." I realized what I was asking her. It wasn't an easy or simple thing.

"What did these Walls tell you?" She fiddled with the carafe on its pedestal. "That my mother lost our priceless family heirloom? That she flaunted it carelessly, and it was snatched from her neck?"

I stared at her, unable to confirm. My eyes welled with more tears. They felt endless. Miriam was the closest thing I had to family. Telling this story felt like a betrayal. It felt *wrong*.

"Did they tell you that she destroyed an innocent man trying to find it?" Miriam's patience had run out, and she grabbed the coffee from the counter and poured a jet-black cup for herself before putting it back.

"I..." I couldn't get the words out fast enough.

"My mother's story has been a heavy burden to carry." Miriam smiled faintly, but it wasn't a happy smile. It was sorrow-filled.

"Maybe you feel the weight of it now, too?" Miriam added, taking a slow sip from her cup.

I exhaled slowly. "Maybe I—can you just read it?" I asked. "No, I *need* you to read it. Because I am not sure this is my story to tell." I said it. That's what was bothering me. This wasn't *mine*.

Miriam put the cup on the counter and looked deep into my eyes, "Tell the story."

"Please read it first," I begged.

"I'll read it," she said quietly, "But you need to know what this might mean—for both of us."

My face softened, and I sighed, "I don't even know what anything means anymore."

Miriam's expression softened again. "Sometimes, the house takes more than we realize, Lady Halethorpe. This is just its way of reminding us. Your mother knew this, too."

A revelation that wasn't at all surprising. I'd figured it out. This *is* why my father hated writing and storytelling. He did everything he could to steer me in another direction, to prevent me from the bargain that might ruin my life.

My father had been trying to protect me, and I'd made him a villain.

My gaze was stuck on the large window at the sink. A faint laugh and the smell of clementine tickled my nose. I couldn't place where it was from.

"Maybe it does, but look at what it's given me, too," I said drearily. "A career, a home, and... you," I said as I looked delicately into Miriam's eyes. I hoped she knew what she meant to me.

I slowly returned to the study, arriving at a crossroads between my selfish desires and what was morally right. I didn't *want* to tell this story. But it was the only story I had to tell.

I sat down at the desk, ran my fingers gently over the ornate carvings that decorated the drawers, looked around the room, and stared at the curious painting on the opposite wall.

It was me, writing in this office.

I *wondered* who painted it.

CHAPTER 29

HISTORY
2023

Shadows in the Ballroom was my best-selling novel—there wasn't a question. I repeatedly asked myself if I would have even released it if Miriam hadn't given her blessing.

I didn't know. I didn't want to know what kind of desperate person I might have become if she'd said no. But I was grateful that it was a choice I didn't have to make.

Miriam hadn't waited long. It only took her three days, and at that moment, when she stopped by my office to tell me that she had read her mother's story and took great pride in the words I'd written.

The Walls had given me yet another masterpiece I knew came with a sacrifice. I had undoubtedly relinquished something special for this idea, and I was left with a painless emptiness—a growing hole that felt familiar, but I couldn't quite put my finger on the feeling.

The uncertainty of what I'd bargained away disappeared within a few weeks. When the first promotional material was distributed, *Shadows* was poised to be quite possibly one of the most prominent novels of the year.

The readers were happy.

The publishing company was thrilled.

The production companies were elbowing each other to get in line for series and full-length movie rights.

Meeting after meeting, staring out into the bright blue California sky, I was dreaming of the dark dampness of my Estate in Maryland. I missed the chattering Walls, their stories of times grander than 45-second videos, likes, and swipes.

The human experience has been reduced to counting engagements and forgetting about genuine interactions. Even these meetings involve practically no eye contact and heads buried behind the faint blue glow of monitors.

This is why I preferred being alone with my novels.

I stood in the now empty conference room, where I had no place to hide from the staring eyes through the walls made of glass.

My Walls, the walls of the Estate, were made of intricate wallpaper handmade and painted meticulously by artists who'd mastered their craft, plaster hung onto perfectly placed slats, and the rest of the magic left in the world.

Not glass.

They weren't so telling.

They weren't so open.

They concealed the secrets of many. Even my own.

I opened the door to Cass's office, and her eyes darted toward me.

"I was just going to come look for you. Come in." She smiled as she stood and adjusted her pencil skirt and tailored blazer.

She held a manila envelope in her hand, her fingers padding lightly against the surface. It was a minor sound, but for some reason, it was amplified. I watched with unease. There was anticipation about the moment building, but I hadn't the slightest clue why. The thuds of her fingers against the paper were loud, unbearable.

"Say it," I said abruptly, breaking through the hammering and interrupting her finger beats. "Whatever it is, just out with it," I added, sighing hesitantly.

Cass smiled at my discomfort. "Someone's on edge," she fanned herself with the envelope. "It's time to switch to decaf."

She stalled the moment, but her excitement was nearly uncontainable. Granted, torturing me with the slow burn reveal was annoying, but it reassured me that this wasn't bad news.

It was good news. But what?

She took a breath. "Ugh, you're no fun." She handed me the envelope and returned to her chair. I fiddled with the brass clasp, holding my breath, waiting for whatever secret was hidden between the parchment papers to show itself.

I finally pulled out the delicate translucent vellum printed with the finest reflective golden ink. Cass gave me a moment to read through the excessive script text before she broke the silence.

"You've been nominated." She clicked away at her laptop, "The Lamplight Award... for *Shadows in the Ballroom.*"

Her words grew into the shape of a person, and they seated themselves next to me in the open chair. Their presence lingered with a density I wasn't entirely fond of.

I flashed back to the night I'd tossed the last award I'd won into the fire and watched it shatter and hiss in the flames, haunted by the aching hole of wondering *why* I had done such a thing. It wasn't until Miriam found the shattered bits and pieces and the molten glass melted to the bottom of the hearth that I realized I'd done it.

Probably a wine-fueled temper tantrum...

That tracked.

But... Lamplight.

"This is a huge deal, Taylor, you know because—"

"No one has ever won an Aurora and a Lamplight," I said slowly, still stuck gazing at the personified words that shaped a shadowy sitting figure beside me. I could have reached out and shaken the specter's hand if I had desired. Perhaps this was the ghost of the fallen Aurora that had come to haunt me from beyond.

"You could make history," Cass said matter-of-factly.

"You will make history," she corrected herself.

Her words felt muffled as I focused on the figure I knew wasn't *really* in the room but a figment of my wild imagination. It was how I was coping with what burdened me. I was giving life to the darkness that followed me around. Guilt. That's what was in the room with us.

My insufferable guilt. The guilt I couldn't escape.

Had I *killed* Nick? Was I a murderer if the magic of the Walls had made it so he'd never existed? Is it death if no one remembers the life?

Who else had I lost to get here?

"Tay?" Cass broke the trance I'd been stuck in.

The Lamplight Award was different. It honored another kind of story. The Aurora was for social impact, and the Lamplight was traditionally for stories that gnawed at the soul. It was for the gut-wrenching, harrowing tales of the human experience. The ones you read that forever creep into the back of your mind whenever you think you've forgotten them.

It's for the stories that become a permanent part of who you are.

"I don't know if I want to make history," I whispered as the figure finally dissipated into a mist and went away as I readjusted my focus on a grinning Cass.

"Why not?" Cass said curiously, "You've worked your whole life for this recognition, Taylor. You deserve it."

Those words. Cass's favorite words to say to me when I let self-doubt take over. "This isn't the one that should win an award."

This one left me empty, a void I couldn't understand. There was a reason I felt so disconnected from it. It hadn't been my story to win an award, and I'd given up something incredible to write it.

Whatever I'd sacrificed or given the Wall in exchange must have been a foundational part of who I was because I felt... *less*. Winning the Lamplight Award would mean telling the universe that it was *all right* to take parts of me and sell them for credit and renown.

It would be crossing a line I wasn't ready to cross, trading parts of myself for stories that would never let me go.

And, yet, the idea of being the first to hold both an Aurora and a Lamplight was a temptation that whispered faintly in the ambitious part of my mind. The part that might have released this story without Miriam's consent. The part that easily traded Nick's life for a story that didn't win a Lamplight.

"What happens if I win?" I asked, picking at my nails, afraid of what Cass might say.

"Then you'll be the first to bridge two worlds. The first to prove that an author can shine in the light and thrive in the shadows."

It was so poetic... it sounded like I'd written it myself, but my throat clenched, and a frown burst onto my face.

"And if I lose?"

Cass shrugged, "Who cares? You're still making millions."

✳✳✳

I waited at BWI Airport for my car to take me back to Halethorpe. My luggage was late, stuck in the conveyor of chaos, also known as the *baggage claim*. My driver had to loop around, but I waited patiently as the airport anarchy unfolded around me. California trips were always a delight, but this one left me with a dread I hadn't yet buried.

"Taylor?" A soft voice from behind me, and as I turned, I saw a woman with beautiful golden eyes and wild ringlets of dark hair staring back at me. Her cheeks flushed, but her expression was as if she'd seen a ghost.

"Taylor, I... we haven't talked in a while. I read your book, the wildflower one... I had no idea that's how you felt." The woman was hesitant, but the light in her expression relayed her vulnerability in her words. It felt like a confession, something from her heart.

"I'm sorry," I said, shaking my head and offering a subtle, comforting smile. "I've just been traveling all day... Have we met before?" I was delicate and genuine. Wildflower was my favorite, and I adored readers who felt it was special, too.

"Tay, it's me? Emma." The woman's face drained of what little hope it had into a bit of shock. Her eyebrows furrowed in the middle, and her expression had a hint of familiarity... like I'd seen her somewhere before.

Or, like I had loved her.

"You don't... know me?" She said, confused.

"I'm so sorry. I meet a lot of people. No, I can't recall—"

Her eyes locked mine, and I saw her crack. I saw the tiny arms of the fracture travel along her expression, severing her bright smile, forcing it into a frown, passing through down into her heart, where it ended, shattering her into pieces.

I'd never met a fan so *invested* before.

There was something more to this, but I could only offer a slight smile and a nod. As uncomfortable as it was to watch her break, my heart also hurt with a vast emptiness, and I wanted to hug her and console her.

Before I could fully react, she stormed off, dragging her rolling carry-on bag on its side. My driver pulled up in the standard black SUV and loaded my luggage into the vehicle as I watched her plow through the patrons standing in pick-up until she was just a tiny dark shape that blended into nothingness.

I stood frozen in thought for a moment before I realized he was patiently waiting for me to get in.

Wildflower? I thought to myself.

I dug through my bag and pulled out a folded and tattered copy of *The Adventures of Loving a Wildflower*, the one I'd always carried with me, and I started reading again from page one.

I called Cass as I skimmed the pages. "I landed. Just wanted to let you know."

"Good, um..." There was an uncomfortable pause. "Have you thought more about the nomination?"

"No, I really haven't. Do I have to accept?" I asked, knowing the answer. I asked the same question the last time.

"I've told you this before, and I'll tell you again... It would be career suicide not to," she paused, "but... you've done worse." Cass replied, "We can't make you accept a nomination or an award."

If Cass was even considering a refusal, it meant that I'd likely surpassed the stage of stardom where I no longer have to make cautious decisions. My wild behavior would be considered *artistic*, mysterious even.

I quickly changed the subject.

"Hey, when I wrote *Wildflower*, did I talk to you about anything? Like, inspiration or something?"

"You were seeing someone, I think. I can't... remember her name," Cass remembered *everyone*.

"I was seeing a woman?" I questioned, looking down at the ring on my finger that I knew was from Dante, who was very much a *man*.

"Are you alright, Taylor? How could you forget someone you *dated*?" The question was valid. "You don't remember? It was a whole thing. I guess you were experimenting. She was *uhm...* a bartender." Cass said confidently, "Yeah, that's it, she was *definitely* a bartender. " She sounded distracted.

"Ok, love you, gotta go." She hung up before I could ask what she looked like. Perhaps *she* was what the Walls had taken from me. If they could make it so that Nick would never exist, could they have made me forget her, too? Maybe I'd written Wildflower for a reason. Perhaps I'd written it to remember my own *Violet*.

***

After about a day, I agreed to let go of the woman at the airport. If I *had* made such a trade, I needed to leave whoever she was in the past. I couldn't risk breaking the bargain I had with the Walls. They'd been eerily quiet since Miriam had acknowledged that she knew of their power. Who knew what kind of wrath they had if you'd upset them? Not something I wanted to find out.

I was getting married to Dante. And there wasn't anything or anyone that would change that.

No, we hadn't set a date.

No, we hadn't discussed any details an engaged couple would typically discuss. I didn't look too deeply into what was *expected* with Dante. We were a unique combination, and I felt like social norms only half applied.

When I walked through the Estate's doors, it was dark. The only light was the soft glow from the fireplace, casting still vast shapes onto the patterned wallpaper.

"Hello?" I called out.

It went unanswered.

Suddenly, I turned the corner to see the grand staircase lined with pillar candles, illuminating the path forward. At the top of the stairs, Dante is holding a bouquet of red roses.

"Oh, wow...." I was speechless.

"Congratulations, Taylor," He announced as I stepped up the glowing steps toward him.

"Congratulations?" I was confused.

"A Lamplight is a *huge* accomplishment." He replied, smiling.

"Oh, Dante, I... I am not sure I will accept the nomination." I hated letting him down, but I hadn't fully settled on the idea yet.

"You'd be a fool not to, Tay." He scowled at me, and his response took a small bite out of my heart. The ache made me retaliate with a defensive vengeance.

"Well, when you write *your* novel, you can accept whatever nomination they give you," I said, pushing past him with my arms full of luggage.

"Taylor, I'm sorry. This was supposed to be a romantic gesture." I saw the hurt in his eyes. I wanted to put it behind me, but a fire rose in my chest, and I couldn't let the tantrum subside.

"Words can only be said once, Dante," I scoffed. "So *romantic*," I snapped, muffled by my aggressive escape. I closed the door to our room before he could follow me.

I looked around at the dark shapes, the moon shining through the sheer curtains and reflecting off the ornate furniture. I began to unpack slowly before realizing I didn't care about anything. Midway through, I tossed everything to the floor and crawled under the soft protection of the dense comforter, using its weight as a makeshift hug.

Eventually, when I'd sulked long enough, I let Dante make it up to me, not once... but twice.

And I decided that I would accept the nomination.

CHAPTER 30

A LAMPLIGHT AWARD
2023

I didn't prepare a speech because the chances of my winning this award were an impossibility.

"Improbability," Cass corrected me, "Impossibility implies there is zero chance, and a nomination alone means it is *possible*." Cass dug into her bag, looking for something obscure, while she rambled into it.

"Improbable," I repeated while staring at the stage and the vast audience seated at their dinner tables. I'd spoken in front of this many people ten years ago when I won the Aurora Prize for *Glass Heels* and periodically at events after.

I wasn't ready to do it again.

"It's not the Oscars, Tay." She paused. "*Gotcha!*" She pulled a beautiful pink lipgloss from her bag and awkwardly applied it without a mirror, using the camera on her phone.

I stared down at the champagne glass. I focused on the tiny bubbles popping to the surface and disappearing forever. *Disappearing...* A thought I'd had at least twice since sitting down and just walking out through the back, calling a car, and rushing as fast as possible back to the Estate.

I held firm with a bit of *help*. I grabbed the glass and knocked back whatever was inside. A cold, tingling sensation radiated down my throat.

"That's not what that's for." Cass smiled at me as she picked hers up and kicked it back, signaling the wait staff to bring another round.

"Relax a little. This is supposed to be *fun*. Remember that." She smiled. Dante glanced over at me and squeezed my hand, resting in his as if he agreed with what Cass was saying.

"Taylor Halethorpe, for *Shadows in the Ballroom*."

My name rang through the massive banquet hall. The applause erupted in the silence, and I glared back at the faces now focused on me. My face felt hot, flush with embarrassment. Why was everyone suddenly staring at me?

"Tay, *go*," Cass whispered, nudging me lightly on the shoulder to pull me back into reality.

"What?" I replied, confused.

"You won," Dante whispered into my ear. Go get your award."

I stood, smoothing the crinkles of my blazer. I flashed a humble smile as I approached the stage and stepped up to the mic.

I nervously cleared my throat, and the roar of the applause and congratulations faded to a silence—one that meant I was supposed to *thank* those who'd made this possible.

I couldn't thank Nick for letting me give him away. I couldn't thank the strange woman at the airport for forgetting her. And, well, I certainly couldn't stand here and thank my haunted Walls for talking and giving me the stories that had me standing in front of a room full of people I'd *fooled.*

I'd fooled them into thinking that I deserved to be here, that I was a writer who earned such acknowledgment.

"*I hadn't prepared a speech because I thought this was an improbability.*" I smiled, and the room chuckled. "*If the walls could talk, what story would they give us?*" I paused, looking for a face to anchor my stare onto. "*That was what I asked myself, sitting in the*

Halethorpe Estate just before I wrote Shadows in the Ballroom." I flashed another smile and took a deeper breath. *"They answered back with the delicate but dark story of Florence Caldwell, allowing her to confess and be relieved of the harrowing secret she'd carried for too many years."* I let an unsteady pause linger for too long. *"May you never know such pain. Thank you."*

I quickly walked away from the microphone and returned to my seat, holding the glass statuette with my name deeply engraved. I couldn't thank anyone, so I didn't.

I sat and took a deep breath.

"It's not your best work, but that wasn't bad," Cass said as she handed me another full glass. "The world loves a mysterious woman," she added, nodding. I could see the wheels turning on how she could spin my speech, which failed to captivate an audience.

"Writers are writers for a reason. The speeches... well, they're not always stunning," she smiled as she swallowed a giant gulp of champagne, too.

I won.

Again.

A wave of anxiety washed over me. The last time I won an award like this, my career almost came to an uncertain end shortly after. A part of me couldn't help but make the connection. Would this statue haunt me, curse me, and follow me around like a thunderous cloud over my head?

***

If there is one thing that award ceremonies never fail to deliver, it's the celebrations *after* them. We were served a delectable meal that I knew was delicious, but I could hardly remember the details. The colors were grayed out, and the sauces and seasonings were tasteless. I rushed through the small talk and left the party early, sneaking out through the back exit.

I didn't want to appear ungrateful, but an uneasy feeling set in. I let the idea that this wasn't my story overwhelm me. I felt like a fraud. I felt undeserving of this attention, standing among some of this country's best authors and writers. I didn't even compare.

So I made a quiet escape, leaving Dante, Cass, and the rest of Everbound Publishing & Media to fend for themselves. I watched the hotel entrance fade away and then disappear in the night's calamity of lights, all of the yellow and red blurring into a mass of oranges.

The driver of my car was only slightly suspicious of my lonely exit, but when he saw the concern on my face, I think he understood.

"Big night for you, huh?" he asked, carefully concerned.

I squeezed the glass statue a little firmer. "A little too big," I replied, wrapping my scarf around my neck. Something in his eyes felt familiar, making me relax enough to carry on the conversation.

"You ever wonder how you got somewhere?" I asked, open-ended and mostly rhetorically.

"Don't drag me into your existential crisis, lady. I've got my own." The man chuckled. Even the laugh was something I was sure I'd heard before.

"Existential crisis," I mumbled, recalling when Nick had said those exact words to me in one of our frequent arguments about my success or lack thereof. The driver made a few more turns, and suddenly, I looked at the identification placard in the car's rear.

"Andrew Foster."

Foster.

This was Nick's father, or... the man who *was* Nick's father before I erased him from this world. He'd told me he drove for a private company that transported A-list celebrities, and that was how he got a few of his acting gigs.

"You have kids, Andrew?" I asked, knowing what he'd say.

"Nah, never happened for me. I always imagined I'd have a son... with a hell of a baseball arm," he smiled. I saw the dimple on the side of his cheek through the rear-view mirror. Nick had the same one.

"Yeah, me neither," I added softly as I gazed out the window.

"You got time, young lady." He smiled, and although I knew he meant well, something in his smile ripped through my heart.

He looked so much like Nick.

But even the face I once knew so well was fading rapidly from my mind. As vivid and detailed as my memory always was, those of Nick had started to crumble as the walls of Halethorpe Estate had. I had a mind that clung to the finest details, a mind that remembered the subtle indent of his dimples and his messy hair, eyes that tore down my walls with just a soft glance.

A curse to remember the details, but diabolical to begin to forget them.

The car came to a slow stop at the Halethorpe Estate, and as we passed by the security gates, I thought about telling Andrew that, in my world, he had a son. He was flawed but beautiful. He was tragic and broken by the world but loved up until I had him erased from it.

I sat lost in thought as Andrew stared at me in silence. I realized the space he was giving me to lament in what was most definitely an existential *crisis.*

What if he believed me? What if he knew it, too?

If I had a friend in my solitude, could we share stories about him to revive the fading memory? Could I wish Nick back into existence if I just sat here in the silence of this car with his *father*?

"Miss, I..." Andrew's voice interrupted me.

"Oh, right, I'm sorry..." I dug for cash in my bag, pulled a crumpled bill from it, and handed it to him.

I walked toward the Estate, holding my bag and statuette. As I stood in the doorway, my knees buckled below me. I fell to them and let out a wail that I had been pushing back, swallowing down... pretending it didn't want to break free from my chest. It finally tore through me as if it had come exploding from the broken heart that seeing Andrew had created.

Miriam ran to the foyer. I felt her gentle touch try to console me, but the sorrow was too vast, my cries too connected to the shattered parts of me that I was carrying around.

I collapsed on top of my bag and melted onto the floor.

Everything went dark.

CHAPTER 31

A DREAM IN A NIGHTMARE
2023

I was restless on the leather seats of the sedan. The name placard was glaring at me *again.* Although I knew I had escaped this moment, I was in the back of Andrew Foster's car *again.*

I looked out the window and saw the Walls of the Estate, not the city we'd been driving through, but the delicately papered Walls that had been ruining my life since I'd met them.

Suddenly, I looked back and saw that the driver wasn't Nick's father. It was a beautiful girl with wild hair. I recognized her, but from where?

"He's not gone, you know." Her voice was smooth as honey, unafraid of the insanity ensuing in this vehicle. "He's just in the Walls, waiting for his story to be told," She added as she turned the wheel, and we shifted direction.

Another glance out the window, and I saw the Estate from the far street. Our pace slowed to barely a forward movement as if we were stopping to admire it like visitors or tourists.

"Who are you?" I asked, staring at the honey-gold eyes fixed on me from the rearview mirror. "I've seen you before."

"Don't be silly, Taylor. It's me, Emma Delacroix, *your wildflower.*" Her response was coy and her smile devilish.

Suddenly, the sticky, dense leather of the vehicle disappeared from under me. I was no longer in the back of the car heading home from the awards ceremony. Andrew Foster wasn't driving me through the security gates and waiting for me to snap out of my daydream.

No—I was in the study, moonlight washing over the gentle curves of my naked body. I could feel the dead stare of The Walls, watching me with their rippling floral irises.

The small fireplace flashed violently against the gold embroidery as if it were a warning. The Walls quickly became irritated and tortured by the ghastly vision of what was unraveling in the room closest to its beating heart.

I lay delicately, my skin brightly lit across the antique desk, sprawled messily on top of the stack of stories I hadn't yet been told. Emma and I pressed into each other, my entire body tingling from a volcanic sensation thrumming inside me.

The unsteady sound of delicious panting ricocheted from the empty corners of the room. My back arched over the stacks of the Walls' precious words, and I gripped down onto the desk, ripping and tearing into the gifted parchments under me, casting them aside and relinquishing myself from their hold.

The curse can take whatever it wants *tomorrow.*

The desperate noise of being tangled in each other's euphoric touch rippled the wallpaper, causing it to retreat, tatter, and fray. Our worlds collided with a force that made the Wall's cursed magic recoil in fear.

Our mouths and teeth scraped gently against each other's skin, and a tightening tension released as we came together, forcing the Walls to react to the climax. We were everywhere and nowhere simultaneously—an inescapable madness that the Walls were made to endure. For they had no reach here, we were *untouchable.*

A slight burn appeared on the Wall's edges as our desire ignited the entire room, bursting it into flames around us as we freely shared our love for one another.

There was no indication that this moment would end. It felt infinite. It was as if seconds were hours, and we could continue like this forever. The taste of Emma lingering on my lips, the sweet, breathy sounds of her calling out my name, reminding me of everything I have ever loved. It was poetry. It was prose. It was everything in between. We were light and lust, intertwined in the most beautiful moment I'd ever fully experienced.

My stare fixated on the Walls with a beguiling intent, a knowing glare that pierced into them as I watched them crumble and burn. It was what I imagined *hell* to look like. Our world—but forever on fire, with nowhere to escape.

But perhaps... not hell, but instead... love?

The Walls grew more barren and scorched with each deep breath I let loose while Emma teased my body with the bending of her wild tongue and the tickle of the faint brush of her fingertips trailing the curvature of my hips.

The faint scent of smoke and coal lingered around us while wisps of charred paper landed on our glistening, sweat-drenched skin, marring us with smears of ashen battle paint. The only way the Walls could touch us is when their decaying bits fluttered through the air, hoping to land close.

Despite the desolate appearance, this moment was flawless. This unadulterated perfection was most certainly divine, and if there were a Heaven, I had found it—Here, with Emma, watching the Estate fall around us as if it had never existed.

The Walls in the study cracked and hissed as they turned to dust and ash in the wreckage of what we created. Their power—useless, and their curse—powerless. The stories intended for me to tell were burned to nothing.

And then my eyes darted open.

CHAPTER 32

AN END
2023

The room glittered with Cristal and candlelight, but my skin felt cold and my stomach uneasy. Hundreds of people had arrived at the Estate, flowing out from the never-ending loop of black vehicles with tinted windows. I couldn't remember when this Estate had been so full—at least it hadn't during my time here, outside of reliving the Walls stories and seeing the ghosts of past celebrations.

The music from the small string quartet wafted through all of the halls, and for a moment, if you didn't know what year it was, you'd have thought it was 1919 and the Estate was in its prime. The golden glow drenched every surface, and the night *glittered.*

As the folks in their black-tie attire strolled in through the entrance, they congratulated me. After the first hundred guests, faces started to blur together. Who were these *people*, and who had invited them?

I certainly didn't remember a guest list this excessive. The people I genuinely would expect to be a part of celebrating our engagement were countable on a single hand.

Hand.

Dante's hand slowly brushed down my back until it paused casually at my waist. He leaned in and whispered, "An engagement for the ages. Can you believe any of this?" His words scratched at me, though they should have been comforting.

I looked deeply into his eyes, begging to see something more profound and praying to see something other than his perfect smile and pristine complexion.

But the only thing I recognized in his expression anymore was ambition, and I questioned everything I'd ever done to land me in this over-the-top ball gown in my grand Estate, staring into the desperately beautiful eyes of a man whose heart I barely knew.

"I need some air," I whispered as I pulled away from him. I walked along the quiet hallway toward the grand terrace. We'd closed it to the attendants as the library was still in the midst of its renovation. A clatter echoed through the empty shelves as I pressed open the brass door that led to one of my favorite places.

You could see the entire property from here, every inch of the farmland that once provided resources to this town, the small buildings that processed what was farmed and kept the livestock safe, and the faint, busy lights of the city that had grown up around this preserved historic landmark.

The cool air let relief wash over me, and I stood for only a few minutes. Before I knew it, I'd been here for half an hour. I collected myself, pulling together all the wherewithal I'd need to mingle and engage in small talk about dividends, Dante's investments, cases, and what I'm working on next.

I hated *small talk*.

I heard the words amplified as if the Estate had made them louder than they audibly should have been. They were nearly a roar.

"...Once we're married, and the Estate is secure. I'll convince her to sell. I'll leave her no choice. She hasn't even mentioned a prenup."

The floor felt like it had tilted under my designer heels, and my breath lodged in my throat. Without hesitation, I rushed forward and stepped into the doorway. While I had intended to yell, my voice only let out a trembling whisper.

"Is that why you're marrying me? The Estate?"

He turned, and the surprise on his expression slowly turned to annoyance.

"Taylor, you misheard—"

"No," I cut him off. "I didn't."

The walls pressed in, the silence louder than his excuses. His eyes reflected the truth, and I'd seen it the entire time.

I'd repeatedly questioned our lack of genuine connection and the uncertainty of our love. I'd asked myself why I would have given him to the Walls without even a second thought or an ounce of guilt.

The loss of Nick destroyed me, but Dante... I'd willingly sacrifice ten times over. And now, here he was, trying to scam and sell the only thing I had left.

Get rid of...

The thing that *made* me who I was.

The only thing that made me *real.*

I had ignored all the red flags while chasing after the life I was *supposed* to have. I'd known Dante wasn't the one from the start, but I kept trying to shove him into my life because he merely looked nice there. The blonde hair, the blue eyes—the smile that stopped your heart.

I took off the ring. The metal was cold against my palm. "You can keep the lies, Dante. I'm done."

I heard the Walls' subtle foreshadowing of Dante's worth tickle down my spine.

"As you will soon see, he is worthless in your story."

I dropped the diamond at his feet and walked away quickly. I made it to the top of the staircase when I saw Cass. She immediately recognized the horror and humiliation that had grown into tears and smeared mascara down my face like a clown's face paint.

"Let's go," she whispered as she handed a stranger the two glasses of champagne she had in her hands. She grabbed two random coats from the back of a chair, and we darted for the first running vehicle.

We crawled into *someone's* limo. The rear heated seats felt like a warm, embracing hug. My face was smeared with tears, and I sobbed uncontrollably while Cass held me in her arms.

We didn't say a word. We didn't need to. She saw the missing ring and understood without the noise of an explanation. That's what soul mates did. They knew without the words, without the long-winded explanations. They took the pressure off the retellings and sat with you in the sorrow, making it their own. Sharing it so you wouldn't have to bear it alone.

"There was always something off about him," she said, trying to reassure me that no matter what I felt now, it would feel better, eventually.

"No, I *know*," I sniffled out.

"You *know?*" She delicately popped the cork on a chilled bottle in the ice bucket. This was someone else's after-party that she was helping herself to.

"Everything in my soul fought back against him, but I—" I choked up, "I wasn't listening," I admitted. Cass's eyes met mine but she let the silence linger.

"I'm actually relieved." I'd finally said it out loud for someone else to hear. I'd finally said what had haunted me since that ring had encircled my finger.

I trusted Cass. I knew she wouldn't hold it against me, or judge me. The fact that I was *playing* engaged with a man I'd felt nothing for.

Had I wanted this to happen? Had I asked for it? Or had the Walls cast their magic onto Dante, tantalizing him with the things he desired also? *Money and renown.*

Fame.

The Walls presented him with an irresistible offer, and he couldn't turn it down.

Dante considered me expendable, too.

"Oh, thank god," Cass breathed a deep sigh of relief and broke me from the spiral of thoughts I was declining into just before I was sucked into the morass of darkness.

"I did not like him, Tay," Cass said as she sipped champagne from the only thing she could find in the limousine, a plastic color-changing cup with the event company's name on the side.

"Classy." I sniffled and let out a wide grin.

"So? What do you want to do?" Cass asked me as she handed me the cup to take a sip.

PRESENT DAY

THE VICTORY ERA
2024-2025

CHAPTER 33

GOODBYE
2024

Weeks passed, and I didn't feel like writing. I hadn't a story to tell, as a large part of my life had crumbled apart after the embarrassing party where my *engagement* had both been announced and rescinded.

And my, what a spectacle it had been.

Cass and I consumed a limo's worth of champagne and ran chaotically through the Estate, shooing all the folks back to their cars. The looks on their faces when Miriam announced for them to *'Please set down their hors-d'oeuvres and exit the Estate calmly.'*

A snack, interrupted by the demise of an engagement.

Dante had fled the Estate that night, and by the following day, I had all traces of him shipped to his flat in LA. While I felt no sadness for the loss of Dante, I felt ashamed.

Humiliated.

By now, a few news articles had been published about our *sudden* falling out, but since we were both declining to comment, they wrote a story of their own.

In one version, I was sleeping with Cass, my *long-time agent*. In the other, Dante is now *rebound* engaged to a volatile little redhead, and they're expecting a baby. I saved the articles in case I felt inclined to use them as writing inspiration in the future.

Today, though... Words were coming to me easier. My thoughts weren't clouded by a relenting discomfort that had settled in my heart. No, in fact, this morning, I felt *free*.

At least, I was until I entered the Study. The dust had settled over everything in a thin layer. It smelled of old paper and slightly burnt coffee. I had walked in hopeful, but then I sat staring mercilessly at the blank screen that was now mocking me. The hope drained from me, and I grew bitter.

This room was no longer a place where I could write freely. No, it felt like a prison. I felt trapped as if I was stuck here in the Study with my insanity enveloping me like a suffocating cloud of smog.

I'd never known the lack of a plot to hurt. I'd never felt the ache of not finding words. But today, these things *stung*. I felt assaulted by every affront. The tears stuck behind my eyes began to swell and *ache*.

A sharp pain in my temples as I previewed potential, each story on a carousel that wouldn't stop. Idea after idea, they encircled my head before the dizziness made me sick.

I vomited my lunch in the steel trash bin beside my desk.

My body was holding the weight of being unable to think of anything original. Instead, I grasped at remnants of ideas I'd already thought and had to wade through the rising sea of ideas someone else had already written before me.

What if there were simply no more stories to tell in the world? What if they had all already been told? Is that why Glass Heels was a *retelling*? Because I hadn't an original thought in the entire core of my body or mind? I shattered the pressure of the silence, breaking it with a wavered scream.

"You used to *help* me!" I shouted—the raspy scream, tattered by the release of my welled-up tears. I wasn't sure if I was talking

to myself or the Walls. But I knew they were listening, watching...
They were always listening, always watching.

The wallpaper's floral pattern seemed to ripple at the
harshness of my words.

"You used to give me *stories*." I groaned lowly. My voice had
reduced itself to an ache. The tears poured down my face and
landed shamelessly on the desk's dusty surface.

"You've taken everything and left me..." I wiped my face.
"Hollow—I'm empty."

I repeated it, barely a mumble now.

"Empty."

My hands slammed down. "Say something!" I shouted again,
the words ripping out of me. "You were so chatty before, weren't
you? Whispering your stories, giving me just enough to keep you
alive." I gasped. "Where are you now, huh?"

Only silence answered me.

"You knew this would happen, didn't you?" I spat the
accusation.

"Without memories, *love*... what else is there?"

I was asking, but I knew. There would be nothing if there
weren't any love or memories of my life. There would be nothing
left, and that was why I was *hollow.*

"You knew what Dante was doing. And you just let it happen.
You let me make a fool of myself." My face grimaced as a final, slow
tear dripped from my eye. "And is this what you wanted? To watch
me fall apart. To disintegrate into nothing?"

The Walls groaned faintly, or perhaps I'd just imagined it.
The bright pastels I'd been staring at seemed to dim ever so
slightly, as if losing the colors they'd luminesced into over these
years. The Walls were pulling themselves away—retreating...

I stood and pushed myself from behind the antique desk. "You
know what?" I scoffed with a ferocious attitude.

"I don't need you." The sting in my tone surprised even me. "Do you hear me? I don't need you *anymore!* You'll see. I'll find my own stories!" I was out of breath, exhausted from arguing with myself, with Walls that wouldn't fight back.

"I don't care if I never hear you speak again."

A draft that came from nowhere chilled me to the bone. For a moment, I thought I'd heard a sigh or a deep breath, but the room was still—the air dead. The wallpaper faded even more, almost completely restored to its dull and lifeless tones on the day I discovered it.

I stood silently, my chest heaving, my hands clenched tightly into fists I wished I could throw at the hardened plaster. But the unnatural silence of the Estate swallowed me whole.

I waited for them to fight back, to beg, to threaten. But nothing came.

This time, they weren't trying to stop me. They were letting me go. I hated how that made my stomach twist.

"You're not real," I cried, tears streaming down my face. "You never were."

A breath of air curled against my ear.

"And yet—"

The whisper was soft, almost amused.

"—here you are. Talking to us."

My chest clenched. I refused to turn around. A slow, almost mocking buzz rippled through the stillness. Not a voice, not a word, but a presence.

"You'll need us again."

It was barely there, faint but undeniable.

I clenched my jaw. "I won't."

Silence. And then—laughter.

A gust of wind shot through the room, rustling the loose pages on my desk, sending them scattering like dead leaves. The candle flames snapped, nearly snuffing out—then righting themselves again.

The Walls had left me. Or maybe... Maybe I had finally left them.

I swallowed, turned toward the door, and forced my feet forward. My body was shaking—from adrenaline, exhaustion, and the weight of it all.

"We'll see you soon, Taylor."

The whisper slid through the room, featherlight, barely there.

I froze.

Not because I believed them. Not because I was afraid. But because, for a single, terrifying second—

I wasn't sure if it was them that had whispered it.

Or me.

CHAPTER 34

FALLOUT

2024

It was three nights later when I saw him.

I'd retired for the night. Printed sheets of prose and half-finished poems littered the floor of the Study. They blew down the hall like paper tumbleweeds, the ghosts of thoughts that never bloomed into realities. They were now just desolate words that I'd deemed *not good enough* and pushed far away from my mind. The Estate was a graveyard of draft scraps that taunted me with their *almost* perfection.

But none of them were right.

I poured myself another glass of wine, but the Study had already turned its cold shoulder to me, and I'd wandered down to the inviting flames of the living room. I'd spent so little time here recently that I'd forgotten how mesmerizing it was when the fire cast its dancing shadows along the paper, how the amber glow blended so beautifully with the embossed gold accents embroidered into the wall.

"Taylor."

I froze.

The voice was soft and familiar. It was like a call home that I'd been waiting for. I hadn't heard it in... *God,* so long. I thought I was imagining it, my subconscious yearning to hear Nick's soulful, scrappy voice in this room. But I suddenly felt the pushing presence of not being alone.

My heart hammered in my chest as I turned slowly. My eyes closed at first, afraid of what I might see, but I craved to answer the call of my name. It sent a seductive chill down my spine, instantly taking my breath away.

And there he was.

Nick stood in the doorway, hands in his pockets, a crooked half-smile on his lips. He looked exactly as I remembered him. The details that had all but faded from my mind came rushing back at the sight of him—here, in my living room, like *before.*

"Nick," I whispered, my voice hesitating over how strange it felt to say it out loud. I hadn't been able to say his name, not like that, not with *feeling.* The syllables were no longer hollow as they rolled off my tongue with a yearning.

His smile widened. "Tay, this place... you can fix it up all you want, but... it will always give me the creeps." His casual coolness was so desperately different than the heated confusion I was experiencing. It felt out of place, strange.

I set the wine glass down with shaking hands. "How—where did you come from?" The question sounded ridiculous as it left my mouth, but I couldn't think of another way to ask. He stepped into the room, and it stopped me in my thoughts, my head buzzing in a panic as if it had been filled with static.

"I just wanted to see how you were doing." He grabbed the glass I'd set down and sipped it. He had always stolen my drinks.

I had to be imagining this. This had to be a dream. I'd wake from this and find myself buried in the dead words I'd written with an empty bottle of Cabernet lying on the floor.

"*Where* did you come from?" I reached out and put my hand on his arm, and the warmth shot electricity down my entire body.

He was real.

I blinked hard to see if it would reset the mirage before me. "I thought..." I stopped myself from finishing the sentence.

I thought you were gone. I thought you didn't exist anymore.

How would you ask someone such a thing? It would sound ridiculous. I would sound *silly*. Right now, he was as real as the flames dancing in the fireplace.

"You've been busy," he said, gesturing vaguely toward the Study. "I heard about the Pulitzer. Big deal, huh?"

I let out a laugh—nervous. "Lamplight." I rolled my eyes carelessly.

He moved closer, his dark eyes fixed on me. "You look tired, Tay."

"Thanks?" I said, the sharp edge of sarcasm slipping into my tone. I couldn't help it. The sight of him, the sound of his voice, the pressure I felt radiating off his closeness. This was all too much, too impossible.

"You alright?" he asked softly, as he always had when *trying* to love me.

I nodded. "Yeah, I think so. It's just..." I was struggling to put it into words. Dante's second betrayal, the Wall's silence, the ache in my chest, the sense that something was *still* missing from my memories, but I hadn't known what. Nick reached out and brushed his fingers against my cheek.

Real.

Tangible.

For the first time in weeks, the tension in my chest eased just a little.

"I'm here," he said, and I wanted to believe it. I wanted it so badly that it hurt. A small tear fell from the corner of my eye, and Nick's thumb brushed it away.

"No, don't do that," he whispered into the corner of my neck. His warm breath and the insinuation of his mouth sent static down my spine, and I shivered slightly in his arms.

He lifted my face toward him and captured my mouth in a kiss. If this were a dream, this would be where I would wake up. This would be the moment that my mind would pull me away from perfection, to keep me humble, to tease me into giving up, giving in. Resigning.

But I didn't wake, and Nick's hands brushed down my body, and I felt him lift me into the air, my legs tangling around him, wrapping him with the thought of *never* letting go again.

He carried us toward the grand staircase. Midway up, he paused and gently set me down. He stared down at me, propped under him on the royal pattern of the runner. He slowly lifted his shirt off and then crawled over me and delicately unbuttoned each of the bright blue buttons on the front of mine.

He slowly kissed the bare skin on my chest, and I ran my hands down his back, feeling his muscles ripple while he hovered over me with precision.

He brought his mouth to the points of my hips, and it sent a sensual tickle through my entire body. He pushed down further and unbuckled the clasp of my pants, exposing more skin for him to press his warm mouth against.

I tipped my head back onto a stair, letting it hold me in place, and I released the air that had been trapped deeply in my chest, waiting to wake from this dream. I succumbed to the idea that this was real just as Nick pressed his lips on the exact places that made me shatter into a million pieces.

He carried me to the darkness of the bedroom and tore through me with everything he had, just like he used to, and when we finally came down from the euphoric high that we lingered on together, he placed his head gently on my chest and fell into a deep sleep next to me.

✳✳✳

I awoke the next morning, nestled under the density of my comforter, completely *naked*. I immediately remembered my dream. It was so vivid and... real. *Nick*.

I reached clumsily for my phone, and there was an unread text from Nick Foster.

"I had a great time last night. See you soon?"

It was real.

Had I escaped the Wall's magic? Was I free from its pull? Was everything back to normal? I quickly opened the browser on my phone, but my eyes still had difficulty focusing on the bright screen.

I typed my name into the search engine and sighed with relief that I was still Taylor Halethorpe, dual award winner and critically acclaimed novelist.

The Walls hadn't rescinded all that they'd given me...

"Still me," I groaned as I tossed my phone onto the empty side of my bed and pulled the blanket back over my eyes.

Nick was *back*.

CHAPTER 35

EXISTENTIAL

2024

The Walls had stopped speaking to me. Nick had returned. It was as if all the damage this Estate had done was erased. I hadn't much thought about writing—well, *anything.*

Did I miss the endless nights clattering away at my keyboard? Did I yearn to chase the story with poetic prose and scintillating adjectives?

No. I was enjoying the weight that had seemingly lifted from my shoulders. The gray cloud that had often found its place hovering above me had dissipated, and only clear skies and sunny afternoons remained.

Nick and I spent our days lingering around the grounds of the Estate. We spent more time outside, lounging in the fields, reading, and hiking the acres that had my name but I'd never fully acquainted myself with. Having him back and seeing his face… was something I was so grateful for. The guilt I'd felt knowing that, for that time, I was the one who decided for him not to be a part of this world.

We lay sprawled across a blanket under a tree. The Estate was a mere dot in the background. I lowered the book I was reading onto my lap and looked adoringly at Nick, enthralled by the historical fiction he'd picked from the library.

"Nick," I paused, "You ever wonder how you got somewhere?"

He chuckled, "Taylor, are ever not in the middle of an existential crisis?" He dropped his book to his lap and crawled toward me. He hovered his strong body over mine, leaned in, and kissed me. His affection was a grounding experience—something I'd fought so hard for before, and now he gave so freely. Nick's second existence with me was easy—easier than it had ever been.

"I don't *wonder* so much," Nick answered as he pulled away from our embrace. "It's strange... I felt like I'd just disappeared for a moment there. That I hadn't existed, that I was watching my life in an out-of-body experience." His expression turned pensive, and I found it incredibly attractive.

Nick was already physically beautiful, but when he flexed the power of his mind, he became an unstoppable force.

I shuddered at his recollection of the time he'd spent *gone*. I didn't dare ruin this by telling him I was the reason he'd faded away. It was I who bargained him away so freely. It was me who gave him up for fame and recognition.

It was a secret that I'd need to take to the grave with me, along with the secret that the Walls had given me all of the stories that had ever amounted to anything—that every story that the world loved wasn't mine. I was a fraud. I couldn't risk losing Nick, too, if I'd already lost writing.

"And what about now?" I asked him, pushing my hair behind my ear and sitting up.

"I feel *alive*. Taylor." His excitement was uncontainable.

"Weeks ago, I couldn't taste or even see colors." He paused, looking around at the beautiful landscape while the faint sound of bird songs chimed around us. The shade from the giant Oak we sat under mottled his face with dark shadows that offset his piercing eyes.

Aly Anders

"Now, here... with you?" He sighed deeply. "It's everything I've ever wanted." A slight smile that had a sadness behind it. "I've waited so many years for you."

I accepted his answer with a smile and a nod, leaned back onto him, picked up my book, and resumed the captivating story I'd started. He did the same. We read in peace until the sun set on the horizon, when the fireflies lit our path home, back to the Estate.

CHAPTER 36

THE LAST STORY
2025

Cass ended the call abruptly, but not before telling me that Everbound needed chapters sooner rather than later.

"Publisher Pete with his undying thirst for my blood, sweat, and tears." I poetically whispered to myself as I gathered everything from the kitchen where I'd enjoyed my third cup of coffee just this morning.

Since my falling out with the Walls, if you could call it that, I've been trying to avoid writing in the Study. I understood that the entire Estate was speaking to me when I heard the voices. I'd always visualized the Estate's *face* as the blank wall my desk sat across from. That wallpaper I'd watch slowly morph from a dull and lifeless spattering of *'grandma'* florals to a vibrant scene from a beautiful spring day. The coral of the petals was silky enough that if you ran your finger gently over its texture, you'd believe it was *real.*

I couldn't help but compare myself. It felt like an odd metaphor for what I'd become. I'd arrived at this Estate in disarray, torn apart by the passing of my mother and ripped to shreds by the guilt of having not taken care of her in those last days.

Through the Walls' influence and my writing, through the telling of the stories, through the eyes of this gift she had left me... I'd blossomed. I was healed from the trauma, knowing that the guilt was what blocked me from being my best self.

And now... I had it all.

A career that could rise no higher, and a found family in Cass and Miriam. Nick returned to me in better condition than when he'd been taken.

Like me, the Estate came to life in recent years. But now, they'd felt empty... vacant. They hadn't so much as sent a delicate breeze over me since that night I'd refused them. Now that the Walls had rescinded their offer, everything was as before... They were desolate, empty. The paper faded, the glory gone.

But my writer's block was perpetual. The stories I tried to pen, the wisps of thoughts I tried to catch in words, alluded me completely. Just out of my grasp but dangling on the horizon of my mind.

I'd regretted what I'd said. I beat myself up over how it ended but was drenched in relief. Relief that I'd stopped the descent into madness before it had gone too far.

Before my story became *someone else's* to write.

I had been angry—angry that for all their power, they could have warned me about Dante. They stayed idle and watched him infiltrate and dig his way back into my heart, knowing that his intentions might separate me from them. They could have taken less... If they had left me whole, perhaps I might not have let Dante infiltrate our lives in the first place.

But the Walls just wanted a *story* to tell the next person. They let him and all of it... *happen* to me, and I refused to believe they couldn't have stopped it all. They could have changed everything.

I was angry that instead of protecting me, protecting the Halethorpe that kept them alive, they took the things that made me who I was—devouring them whole. Slowly, they replaced my identity with stories that belonged to others. Their loss had shattered me into nothing but a pawn. The Walls were chaos incarnate. If they should ever return, it would be under my terms.

CHAPTER 37

THE WRITING IN THE WALLS
2025

"You're overthinking again," Nick said from the armchair by the window, his long legs stretched out casually. "You always get stuck when you do that."

I glanced at him, irritation flickering beneath my exhaustion. "It's not *that* simple."

He raised an eyebrow. "Exactly what an overthinker would say."

I sighed, running a hand through my hair. "You don't get it. Everyone's waiting for the next *Shadows in the Ballroom*. Something just as big but *new*. I can't just—" I gestured at the screen, where the cursor blinked on a still empty page. "—pull it out of thin air."

Nick leaned forward, resting his elbows on his knees. "Who says it has to be something new?"

I frowned, turning to face him. "What do you mean?"

"You've got this whole house," he said, looking around the room. "This history. Secrets. You pulled *Shadows in the Ballroom* out of it, didn't you? What's stopping you from doing it again?"

I shook my head. "The Walls—" I stopped. I couldn't tell him that the Estate whispered stories that I turned into my own. I couldn't confess to him, not entirely.

"There aren't any more murder mysteries hiding in this Estate, Nick," I said with a deep sigh. "There no stories here, at least not that I want to write."

"If these walls could talk, I bet they'd tell you otherwise," he joked. "This place... " he mumbled as he popped a candy into his mouth. "It's like it's alive."

He was coming too close to a truth I couldn't admit. I needed to change the subject. I *had* to change the subject.

"I don't need the Walls to talk, Nick. I need to think about what's important and write about *that.*"

I'd said the answer. Write about what's important.

"And what's important, Tay?" he grinned and flashed an accomplished glance that made me believe he thought he was helping.

"Figuring out who I am, *now.*" It fell out of my mouth before I could stop it. Was that what I felt was important? It was the first time I'd ever said that. I hadn't heard him move, but he stood beside me, his hand resting lightly on my chair.

"I think you're too scared." His voice had a slightly sinister tone as if he was purposefully being ominous and vague.

"I'm not scared." I was confused. "Scared of what, even?" I was genuinely curious about where Nick thought he could take this.

"Scared to figure out who you are." He plucked a dusty book from a shelf. I hadn't even looked over these books. I'd sat in this room twice since moving into the Estate. It was all woefully unfamiliar. What was he digging around for?

"Why would I be scared to figure out who I am?" It was a good question. Why would I?

"Maybe you won't like what you find?" He stopped, frozen. "Or... Maybe you'll find that you're out of stories?" His words hit me like a stone in my chest. My jaw clenched, and my fist balled up.

He wasn't wrong.

I'd never said it out loud, and I'd never heard anyone say it to me. Nick is the one to point out that perhaps I've never found my voice because I *didn't* know who I was. I've never known. I let the Walls take even the few parts of me that I'd discovered.

And then I let those holes be filled with stories that weren't my own. I've regurgitated everything I've ever been fed and merely repurposed it, and for what? Fame?

It was surprising. Nick wasn't usually this profound, but I'd never let him write with me... either.

"I don't even know where to start," I admitted. "I'm almost forty years old, and I can't honestly tell you who I am." The revelation sank me into the firm leather chair. "This Estate, I'd made it my entire identity."

"Write it." Nick urged me with an excited whisper. He delicately slid a leatherbound book toward me. Pushing it across the desk and presenting it to me like a gift.

I'd seen it before.

It was the blank book from my desk.

"Write it." He repeated, a command this time.

I pushed aside the typewriter, and I grabbed a pen. The first sentence scrolled out, perfectly printed in a straight line. The words felt true—better than true. They felt *right*. Nick leaned against the wall, arms crossed, his smile slow and knowing. "There it is," he said softly, almost reverently. "That's the one."

✳✳✳

"It's perfect," I whispered, more to myself than to him.

Nick stepped closer, his hand resting on my shoulder. "It is."

The words on the paper blurred as my eyes filled with tears. A weight lifted from my aching shoulders. The doubt that haunted

Aly Anders

the hollow parts of my mind had been erased. The fear, that gnawing fear that I'd run out of stories, had been erased.

I'd done it.

I've finally written something *real*. Something *true*.

Nick's hand lingered for a moment before he stepped back, rounded the desk, and admired the leather tome in my hands.

"You did, Tay," he said. "You really did."

I glanced at him, his figure half-lit by the rising sunlight streaming through the window. His face was perfect in this light, shrouded in half-darkness but illuminated by the sun's birth on the distant horizon. As I studied him, I saw a flicker of something different.

Something I hadn't seen before.

I turned back and held the book tightly between my fingers. The slight scent of leather battled with the dust of the barely used room. The first sentence was almost glowing in its perfection.

My masterpiece. My redemption. My legacy.

Without the influence of the Walls, on my own—a story that rocked my entire world. I carefully set the book down and pressed the cover shut, as if without the dark cognac colored leather pressing down on them, the words might run off the page and be lost forever, scattered around the Estate, leaving me with nothing but blank pages and a dream, shattered.

I stood and stretched, feeling my body come to life after having been crumbled and crouched over the desk. My hands were cramped and my fingers numb from weaving the waiting words with ink for endless hours.

Days—we'd been here days. Maybe weeks?

"I think I'll go for a walk," I said, half smiling at Nick as I took a sip of water. "Clear my head." I rubbed my hands together, pressing into the muscles to relieve the ache.

Nick nodded, his smile unwavering. "You deserve it."

254

I paused as I walked toward the door, looking back at him. "Are you coming?"

He shook his head, his hand sliding into his pockets. "Not this time."

I hesitated to walk away. Something still felt off. He'd been talkative and engaged until I typed that last sentence, but now his presence felt different. Finite. Like he was ready to say "goodbye."

I forced a slight, calm smile, urging myself not to worry about whatever was churning inside of him.

✳✳✳

As I left the room, a breeze that seemed to come from nowhere lifted the cover protecting the manuscript. The first words shone brightly on the page, untouched and eternal.

FROM THE WRITING IN THE WALLS

CHAPTER 1

I'm unsure if I wrote the story or if the story wrote me. But here we were in an exclusive ballroom at *The Royale* in Baltimore. The champagne flowed from bottles like a raging, bubbling river whose current had no intention of slowing despite the wafting drunkenness in the air.

The subtle *'tink'* of the glass flutes sprinkled in my ears, a sound I would forever associate with *success.*

ACKNOWLEDGMENTS

My Husband, **William**... Without you, my world would be woefully incomplete. Without you, Aly Anders wouldn't exist. You give me the space to write and create and the safety to do it in our beautiful home.

Rylan, while you are not allowed to read my books—yet.
Or Ever.
I want you to know that every book I write is to leave you a legacy worthy of who you are becoming. I hope that someday I have a book on a Target shelf so that you finally think I am cool.

Taylor Halethorpe, for teaching me that it's okay to fall into the madness, so long as we come out on the other side.

A special shout-out to Maddie P. and Jess P. for always hanging in there while I melted down or disassociated and disappeared.

Anyone who decides to read this story and finishes it. **Thank you.** Thank you for your time, commitment, and support of an independent author who writes, edits, designs, draws, and publishes their own books.

A special thank you to Ana at @sparkseditorial for seeing the heart of this story, even when I didn't.

THE HALETHORPE CHRONICLES

A Literary Gothic Series of Obsession, Haunting, and Fate.

Some places never let go.
Some souls refuse to be forgotten.
And some stories are meant to be told twice.

Welcome to **Halethorpe**, a town where the past lingers in the shadows, the dead leave their mark on the living, and the walls whisper secrets to those who dare to listen. Beneath its fading grandeur, Halethorpe pulses with something darker—a thread of magic, madness, and memory that entangles those who seek truth in its ruins.

Each novel in *The Halethorpe Chronicles* is a standalone gothic tale, weaving together cursed legacies, supernatural forces, and the aching pull of love lost and found again.

Aly Anders dives into the heart of humanity, telling stories deeply connected to facing the things that hurt you, refusing to be controlled by them, and learning that even if you lose pieces of yourself along the way, the things that matter—love, resilience, and the parts of who you once were—can never be truly erased.